The
White Witch

Book One of

The Serpent and The Sorcerer Trilogy

J. J. Morrison

Map artwork by J. J. Morrison

ISBN 978-1-9999589-0-9

First Edition

Instagram: @jjmorrison_author

For mum

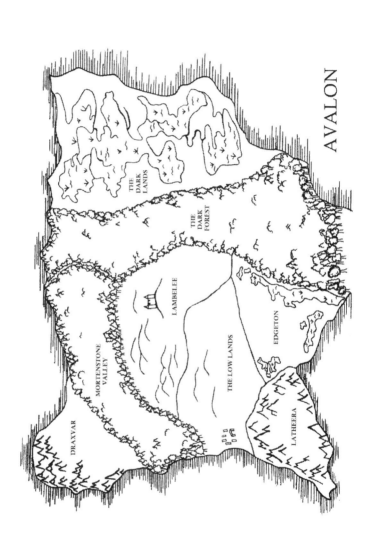

AVALON

THE DARK LANDS

THE DARK FOREST

DRAXVAR

MORTENSTONE VALLEY

LAMBELEE

THE LOW LANDS

EDGETON

LATHEERA

When young milkmaid Bessy came out of the shed,

She saw a great snake and lopped off its head,

But her cheers turned to screams as she noticed with dread,

A man in its place, headless and dead.

But do not fret, dear Bessy, the villagers said,

You have taken this life and spared ours instead.

For surely you see, said Butcher Hogsled,

That he came from the place where we fear to tread,

And would, had he lived, tear our people to shreds,

Even Mortenstones wouldn't be safe in their beds.

So, maid Bessy, we thank you, said Baker Wortstead,

You shall have, for all days, free meat and free bread.

PROLOGUE

The man picked his way carefully through the forest, treading lightly to avoid making a sound. It was cold, far colder than he had anticipated, and he wished he had brought his cloak with him.

When he came to a tree stump, he stopped and sat down, pulling a round, leather bottle from his bag. He took a long swig. The sweet wine warmed him nicely. As he sat there, he stared at a warped tree on the other side of the path. The trunk was thick and twisted, and its branches stretched out like broken fingers. It was a monstrous thing, so tall he had to lean all the way back to follow its ascent to the heavens. Often, when he looked at the forest from Stone Lane, he couldn't see the treetops at all, for they disappeared into the clouds.

He took a final sip of wine and pushed the cork back into the bottle. Then he paused, frowning. *Peculiar…* He stood and approached the tree. He ran his hand over the rough bark, inspecting it, and peeled a piece away from the trunk. It was grey. When he rubbed it between his fingers, it crumbled into dust. *Interesting.* He slipped his hand into the pocket of his waistcoat and pulled out a crumpled piece of parchment and a stick of charcoal. He made a note of his observation and picked another piece of bark from the tree, folding it into the parchment and tucking it back in his pocket.

A crow cawed high above. He froze, listening, breathing slowly, quietly. Nothing stirred.

Soon it would be nightfall and he did not wish to find himself alone in the Dark Forest then. He looked around in the gloom, trying to remember his way home.

A branch groaned mournfully. He turned towards the sound, his heartbeat quickening, and noticed a thin mist drifting through the forest, coiling around the trees and creeping over the ground towards him. The skin on the back of his neck prickled as an unnatural silence settled over the forest. He was suddenly aware of how moist the palms of his hands felt.

Somewhere behind him, a twig snapped. He whirled around. A hand came down over his mouth, muffling his scream. His eyes bulged as he felt the cold steel of a blade pressing against his throat.

PART I

1. THE BANISHED

'Thomas, can you tell me why the Dark Forest is so dangerous?' asked Master Hagworth, staring eagerly over the spectacles on his hooked nose.

Thomas Mortenstone shifted uncomfortably in his seat. 'Because it's the border between us and the Dark Families?' he said, as if asking a question himself.

The schoolmaster's face lit up. 'Exactly! And…?'

Thomas's brow furrowed. 'Err…'

Master Hagworth's smile withered and he rolled his eyes. 'Lucian?' he said, turning away from Thomas to the dark-haired boy at the next desk along.

'The Dark Families are vicious, traitorous filth. And no magic – defensive or otherwise – can be used in the Dark Forest. That makes all who enter vulnerable.'

'Well done, Lucian! And who are the most *despicable* of them all?'

'The Mordarks. They are evil, cold-blooded snakes.'

'Very good. My top student!' Master Hagworth exclaimed, with a pointed look at Thomas. Then he walked back to his desk at the front of the schoolroom. While he busied himself rearranging sheets of parchment, Lucian turned to Thomas and smiled smugly. Thomas's cheeks reddened with embarrassment.

Iris watched this exchange from her desk. Besting their younger brother seemed to bring Lucian immense pleasure; his eyes were glinting - he looked happier now than he had on his thirteenth birthday, when their father had given him a dragon's tooth. Well, she would soon wipe that smile off his face. She stared at the ink pot on Lucian's desk, focused all her attention on it, imagined it toppling. The wooden pot started to shudder. She narrowed her eyes, pushed the pot with her mind. Push, push, push. Suddenly, there was a loud pop and the contents of the pot exploded all over Lucian's neat work, splattering his hands and face. He jumped up and gasped. The pot toppled over, rolled across the desk, dribbling the last of the ink across his papers, and went over the edge, landing on the floor with a clunk.

'You!' Lucian shouted, lunging for her.

Before Iris had a chance to stand, he grabbed her by the hair and dragged her from her chair. She screamed and kicked as he hauled her across the floor and slammed her down onto the cold flagstones. Face purple with anger, he put his foot on her throat and pressed down with all his weight.

'Enough!' bellowed Master Hagworth, banging his fist on his desk. Lucian was snatched off his feet in an instant; he flew backwards across the room, crashing into a bookcase, which shook violently and spat out two large volumes. Iris choked and spluttered, clutching at her throat as she sat up. 'Never again in my presence!' Master Hagworth's hands trembled with fury.

They got to their feet. Iris did not look the schoolmaster in the eye, but Lucian stared back at him vengefully.

Eve, their younger sister, began to whimper at her desk in the corner of the schoolroom.

'You are dismissed,' said Master Hagworth, crossing his hands over his bony chest and vanishing.

Eve continued to snivel in the corner. Her limp hair clung to her arms and back in dark strands, outlining her fragile frame. Lucian glanced at her irritably.

'Why are you crying?' he said as he approached, pushing past Iris and Thomas. Eve wiped her eyes and sniffed. 'I said, why are you crying?' He kicked the leg of her desk and she shrank into herself, letting her hair fall across her face.

'Lucian, don't,' said Thomas, gripping his arm.

Lucian flung it away. 'What are you going to do?' he challenged. Thomas said nothing. Lucian turned back to Eve with a look of contempt. 'She's weak. Blubbering like a little baby. Mortenstones aren't weak. If I were father, I'd have her whipped.'

'But you're not father,' said Iris.

Lucian's blue eyes flashed. 'One day, I'll be head of this family, Lord of all Lands, and you'll wish you'd been a little bit nicer to me,' he said. Then he crossed his hands over his chest like the schoolmaster and, in the blink of an eye, he was gone.

Iris bent down beside Eve. 'Don't cry, Evie. Do you want to see father?' she said. Eve nodded and buried her face in Iris's neck.

They left the schoolroom and climbed the steps from the castle basement in silence. Eve gripped Iris's hand tightly; she was frightened of the dark, and almost everything else. At the top of the steps, they emerged into a darkened corridor and turned left, towards the Great Hall, where their father held important meetings. Iris knew that one must be taking place because all was quiet, as curious ears strained to hear what was happening within.

When they came to a tapestry depicting the great battle between their ancestor Merlin the Good and Lysander Mordark, the Serpentine Wizard, they stopped. The scene was set in a field of red, to symbolise blood, and Merlin's long beard stood out, a brilliant white, to symbolise his goodness and purity. Master Hagworth had dedicated a whole week's worth of lessons to the wall-hanging, which wafted now in the dimness, roused by a draft that whistled down the corridor. Iris looked around to make sure no one else was there and then snapped her fingers. The tapestry disappeared and, in its place, set into the vast stone wall, was a door.

Suddenly, footsteps echoed along the corridor. Thomas's eyes widened. He looked at the door and flicked his wrist; it burst open violently and crashed against the wall, sending pieces of stone crumbling to the ground.

'Thomas!' Iris hissed.

The footsteps quickened and a voice called out, 'Who's there?'

There was a sudden whooshing sound as wall torches began to ignite themselves along the corridor. The footsteps drew nearer. Iris pushed Eve through the doorway. Thomas followed, pulling the door shut with a bang as the torch next to it lit up.

A breathless servant rounded the corner then and looked around suspiciously. No one was there. Everything was as it should be. The torches burned brightly, the flames flailing in the cold breeze, which picked up sharply and made the great tapestry ripple dreamily in the empty corridor.

Iris, Thomas and Eve crept along a narrow passage until they reached a small door at the end, on the other side of which came the sound of voices. Thomas stuck out his palm to open the door but Iris batted it away, lifted her hand and gently swept it sideways through the air. The door opened noiselessly under the spell and a weak sliver of light leaked into the passage. Iris pressed her face to the gap and stared out at the Great Hall.

A dull light seeped through the high, arched windows and hundreds of candles burned in candelabras scattered about the hall. A fire roared ferociously in the great hearth and, beside it, three large dogs were snoozing.

From the shadows in the upper corner of the hall, Iris pushed the door open wider to let her brother and sister see.

Their father, Matthew Mortenstone, sat at a round table in between five middle-aged men and one older, leaner man with pointed ears and large eyes that seemed much too big for his head; Saskian the elf, Matthew's most trusted advisor. Together they sat, crowded around one half of the table, facing a gaunt-looking man, who stared about the room anxiously. The man's clothes were covered in muck and his greying beard was patchy and unkempt.

Iris held her sister back when she tried to pass through the doorway and approach their father. She shook her head at Eve and pressed a finger to her lips.

*

Matthew dragged his fingers through his beard as he stared at the man. This was not the way he had hoped his day would begin.

'Why did you try to break into my home?' he said in a low, even voice.

The man looked down. 'I'm sorry,' he said, nervously picking at the skin around his thumbnail.

Matthew watched him carefully. 'You didn't answer my question.'

The man's face crumpled and his skin folded into a thousand tired creases. 'We are starving. I have two children to feed, a wife. You have everything. I just wanted some food!' he cried shrilly, his hands trembling as he held them out in appeal.

Matthew drew a deep breath. There was nothing he could do to save this pitiful man. He sighed and shook his head slowly, his dark hair grazing his shoulders.

'My sympathies, sir, but crime is crime. You know the consequences,' he said, a dreadful feeling settling in the pit of his stomach. The man went rigid in his chair at these words. Matthew glanced at Saskian, who gave a sombre nod. He had almost hoped the elf would not concur, that there was another way. After all, it was a petty crime, the foolish blunder of a desperate man. But these were the Old Laws. They followed the Old Laws. There were no exceptions.

Matthew cleared his throat. 'I hereby banish you—'

'No! Please!' the man shrieked, rocking forwards onto the table and clutching it tightly. His knuckles turned white.

'I hereby banish you from The Light and sentence you to a lifetime without magic. You, and your family.'

'No! I didn't take anything! No, you can't do that! Please! Please!'

The great doors at the end of the hall swung open with a deep groan and six guards in purple cloaks entered. They strode towards the man, their black boots thudding against the stone, their silver breastplates glinting in the light.

When the man saw them, he got up and tried to run. But, as he staggered past the fire, the dogs sprang up and began to bark. The sound echoed, deafeningly, around the vast room. The man froze as the dogs closed in, snapping and jumping at him. His legs shook violently and he looked around helplessly. The guards seized him and hauled him, roughly, by the arms, back towards Matthew, who stood and waited until the man was in front of him.

'How old are your children?' he said.

'My eldest is f-f-five. My youngest is still a babe,' the man said, his lips glistening with mucus, which streamed from his nose. 'Please!' he begged, struggling against the guards, trying to break free. 'Please!'

Matthew felt sick. He could make it quick, but never painless. He hoped the children would forget, one day. He held up his hand reluctantly. His palm felt hot and his arm began to tingle. The sick feeling in his stomach drowned under a burning wave that surged upwards through him.

The man stopped struggling. He stared at Matthew's hand as if he were in a trance. The guards let him go and stepped back. The dogs whined softly, sinking to the ground again beside the fire.

Matthew's palm grew hotter and hotter. He held his arm steady against the power pulsing through it. The man began to convulse, his eyes swelling in their sockets, as his magic was drawn up through his body. Then, Matthew flicked his wrist and the man dropped to the ground, sucking in an endless, rasping breath, his mouth stretching open grotesquely. He made a half-hearted attempt to support himself on all fours but collapsed, wheezing.

Matthew watched, his jaw set, as the last of the man's magic drained out of him, white tendrils curling up into the air from his mouth. His arm stopped tingling. His palm turned cold. The feeling in his belly receded. It was done. He looked at the guards.

'Round up his family. Bring them to the square.'

*

Thomas pulled Eve away from the door as the guards began to file out, dragging the limp man behind them. Iris resisted when he tugged her arm, transfixed by the scene. She was older than Thomas, but he was stronger and he used his strength to force her back into the passage. He closed the door and they were plunged into darkness again.

Iris couldn't make sense of what she had witnessed. She loved her father; he was the greatest man she knew. She never dreamed that he could be cruel.

'Master Hagworth said he's going to test us on the history of the Dark Families. Perhaps we should go up to the library, or…' Thomas's words died in the grave silence.

They stood there for a time, saying nothing, listening to the distant thrum of voices, to the sound of pots banging and ovens roaring in the kitchens deep beneath the castle.

Thomas sighed. 'Come on,' he said, guiding Eve by the shoulders back down the passage.

Iris followed. When she came to the end of the passage, Thomas had already snapped his fingers and cast the spell. But, as he opened the door, it struggled against the weight of the thick tapestry hanging in front of it. She was too preoccupied to scold him or to correct the spell herself. She watched him shove the door open wide enough to let Eve slip through and went after her, pushing against the musty material as Thomas shut the door and the tapestry fell back against the wall, enveloping them all. Iris elbowed her way through, pushing Eve with her other hand. When she stumbled out from behind it, back into the cold, drafty corridor, a passing servant stopped in his tracks. The ear covers on his purple cap flapped as he looked from Eve to Iris to Thomas, who staggered out after them and froze.

'We were playing a game,' Iris said. The servant was young, perhaps only a year or two older than she was. He looked down at the silver tray in his hands; it began to tremor slightly. 'Don't tell father,' Iris warned him. His head snapped up. 'We'll know if you do,' she said. His eyes widened. He shook his head vehemently. Then he bowed and hurried away.

They walked on, emerging from the corridor into the bright, airy entrance hall. Daylight flooded in through the open doors. As Thomas and Eve made for the staircase, Iris hesitated. She glanced at the courtyard beyond the doors; it stood quiet and empty but for one dog padding around searching for scraps.

Thomas and Eve began to climb the stairs. Iris looked at them and then at the courtyard again. And she made up her mind. She would see what her father planned to do with that man and his family. Lifting her skirts, she turned and marched out of the castle.

In the courtyard, she summoned her cloak with the wave of her hands and felt an oppressive weight on her shoulders as it appeared, the wool dark and coarse. She fastened the ties and hastened across the courtyard.

Beyond the courtyard was the public square, where a large, boisterous crowd had gathered. A barrage of ferocious shouting emanated from the centre of the crowd, spreading outwards until even those on the outskirts were making impassioned threats, their faces red with excitement.

The gates were open; two guards were stationed in front of them. Iris drew up her hood, mustered her courage and darted past with her head down. She heard one of them shout something as she ran towards the crowd.

She weaved through the people, pushing her way deeper into the throng. She could hear a man's voice over the shouting. A clear, steady voice. Her father's voice. And then the crowd roared. Suddenly, the people behind began to push and jostle her. She fell against a person in front, who, too, began to fall forwards. And, before she knew it, she was being swept along, one foot tripping over the other, as the crowd moved with urgent haste out of the square and along Stone Lane, towards the Dark Forest.

The air was hot and rancid. People were jeering and gesticulating as they pushed forwards. Iris couldn't see over their shoulders but she was certain of whom they were jeering at. People leant out of the first-floor windows on Stone Lane and joined in with the mob, spitting down at the family as they were escorted to the edge of the realm.

Stone Lane sloped down to the Grassland, a flat expanse of land half cast in shadow for, flanking its other side, was the Dark Forest. The trees were still in the breeze, stretching on for miles to the north, east and south.

A hush came over the crowd as they filtered out from the lane and regarded the unmanned border. Iris had heard it said that, if you stared too long at the dark spaces between the trees, figures would form out of the blackness, figures with monstrous faces and dead eyes, and once you had seen one of these forest ghosts, they would haunt you forever. She never let her gaze linger on the forest and she noticed how other people, too, averted their eyes and fidgeted uncomfortably.

She saw her father in the distance, standing with the men from the Great Hall, facing the crowd. And, next to them, quaking and afraid, was the gaunt man and his weeping wife, who had a screeching bundle in her arms and a small boy clinging to her leg in terror.

Matthew turned and gestured the forest with the sweep of his arm.

'Go,' he said.

The man took his wife's hand and walked towards the trees. He looked back once. Iris could see the whites of his eyes from where she stood across the Grassland.

The baby's cries came in short bursts, but that did not seem to weaken Matthew's resolve. His arms were folded, his jaw set, his mind made up.

When the family entered the forest, the crying stopped.

As the people made their way back along Stone Lane, Iris heard an elderly man speaking to a woman behind her.

'They haven't a chance. The Mordark filth will hunt 'em for sport.'

'They might make it across to the Dark Lands. They could disguise themselves as one of them,' the woman said.

'What, with no magic?' the man said, incredulously. 'The Mordarks will sniff 'em out straight away.'

'Maybe they'll find the Land of the Banished...'

'No, it's too far. Mordarks will find 'em before nightfall. They haven't a chance.'

At supper, Iris seated herself far away from her father. He seemed to be in high spirits, smiling and laughing as though nothing out of the ordinary had happened that day. He had already devoured an entire roast chicken and washed it down with a goblet of wine. Now, he was tucking into a fruit cake.

Thomas and Eve were subdued; they sat quietly with their heads bowed, speaking only when spoken to, mumbling their responses.

Lucian took this opportunity to occupy his parents' undivided attention. He leant across Thomas to get closer to their father at the head of the table. Their mother, Josephine Mortenstone, beamed at him as he told them about his progress in lessons and his desire to attend meetings in the Great Hall.

Iris looked at her father bitterly as he clapped a hand on Lucian's shoulder and shook it encouragingly. When, suddenly, he turned his head and caught her eye, she looked down at her plate and pushed her cabbage around with her fork. She had no appetite. She wanted nothing more than to leave the table.

'Father, when can we go to Draxvar? I want to go on a dragon hunt. I want to be the youngest person to slay one without magic,' Lucian said.

'Is that so? Perhaps in a few years, when you're stronger,' said Matthew.

'No, I want to be the youngest man to do it. It should be soon or I'll miss my opportunity. Mother?'

'You are more than capable, Lucian,' said Josephine. 'Your father must see that,' she said, turning her cold eyes on Matthew, who smiled tightly.

'Merlin was seventeen when he slayed the dragon. You have years yet, and more important things to focus on for the time being,' he said to Lucian.

'What if someone my age does it tomorrow?'

'It's been more than a thousand years, Lucian, and no one has managed it. I'm sure we can afford to wait a few more years for your turn.'

'I'd skin it afterwards and use its scales for armour,' Lucian said, his eyes flashing excitedly.

'Of course you would,' Matthew said as he wiped crumbs from his clothes.

When the servants came forward and snapped their fingers and the plates and silverware vanished from the table, the bell began to ring for the children's bedtime. Iris backed out her chair and left quickly without kissing her father goodnight. She hurried down the corridor to get away. When she heard him call out behind her, she pressed on, faster.

'Iris!' His voice boomed down the corridor. She could hear his footsteps quickening. 'Iris!' he said again, closer now. She kept going until she felt his hand on her arm. She stopped. Matthew pulled her around to face him. 'Why are you running away from me, Iris? What's the matter?'

'Nothing,' she muttered, looking down at her shoes. Matthew cupped her chin gently and brought it up so he could look at her. 'We are on the good side, aren't we, father?' she asked. Her question seemed to puzzle him.

'Of course we are,' he said. 'We are descendants of Merlin the Good.' He looked across at a large portrait of the white-haired wizard on the wall. 'Goodness is in our blood.' He kissed her on the forehead. 'Now, let's say your bedtime prayer.'

Iris protested but he sat her down on a bench and knelt in front of her, closing his eyes and taking her hands in his.

'We pray to the White Witch,' he began. 'We pray that she may one day come to us and rid us of our troubles, our pain, our enemies, and bring light and life to the realm.'

Iris muttered the prayer with her eyes open, looking at her father. She realised then that goodness was a matter of perspective and that her family was not wholly good.

Five years later

2. THE FAILED REBELLION

The square was transformed into a giant stage with tiered seating all around on the anniversary of the Failed Rebellion. People had travelled far and wide, from the mountains of Latheera to the caves of Draxvar, to celebrate the event. The stalls were filled to bursting and the crowds spilled into Stone Lane and Brim Street and Merlin's Way. Many came dressed in purple robes with billowing bell sleeves; some had strapped on white beards in imitation of the Great Wizard. Street vendors on each corner of the square were selling fizzing candies and sweet bread and, for the children, Merlin dolls on wooden sticks and toy snakes with removable heads. Purple banners bearing a Silver Tree, the Mortenstone crest, hung from the windows of every house lining the streets, as well as the gates of Mortenstone Castle, where spectators turned their eager eyes as they waited in anticipation for the show to begin.

When the gates opened, a hush crept over the crowds. Guards began to file out into the square. They took their positions around the stall nearest the castle, which was occupied along its upper tiers by castle maids and servants, who grinned ecstatically, thrilled to be the focus of so many watchful eyes. As the last of the guards passed through the gates to stand beside the stall, the city of Lambelee stood in complete silence.

And then, finally, Matthew and Josephine Mortenstone emerged with their children, in gowns of purple and silver. The square erupted. Cheers turned to screams of elation. People stretched out their hands, straining to touch them. Matthew paused to wave. Lucian waited behind him, looking sullen. He despised the anniversary of the Failed Rebellion and often told his mother that, one day, when he ruled, he would cancel the celebration until the enemy had been destroyed once and for all.

As they moved on through the square, several girls in the stalls giggled and tried to catch Lucian's eye. He ignored them all.

Iris walked behind Lucian. Her maids had braided threads of silver into her golden hair. As she came out of the courtyard into the sunlight, the silver threads glinted and sparkled. People began to point at her excitedly.

'There she is! Lady Iris!'

'…the beauty of the realm…'

'Look, look at her! Behind Lord Lucian!'

She smiled at them, and at Lucian when he looked over his shoulder at her with disdain.

When they arrived at their seats, a man dressed in black came onto the stage and bowed before them. Then he raised his arms and the audience quietened.

'Welcome, all, on this joyous day. The day darkness battled light, and met its demise! The day Merlin the Good proved his worth - and that of his kin - for all eternity! Behold! The Failed Rebellion!'

The crowds cheered and stomped their feet. As the man left the stage, the sound grew louder and more impassioned, like a thousand war drums beating up a frenzy.

After the cheers died down, people began to fidget and look at one another expectantly.

Lucian leaned in to talk to his father. 'Why is nothing happen—' But, before he could finish his sentence, a ball of emerald-green light appeared, hovering five feet above the centre of the stage. It seemed to give off a low buzzing sound as it flared like a fire igniting itself again and again. The buzzing grew louder and then the sound began to transform into a snake-like hiss. Suddenly, the ball imploded with a thunderous clap. There was a brief silence as the audience watched the empty space in confusion. Then, a wizard materialised in the middle of the stage. He wore an emerald-green cloak. His hair and beard were grey and tangled. He circled around, regarding the audience, and his thin lips curled into a snarl.

'I, the Serpentine Wizard, shall take Avalon for my own. I will poison others against Merlin, and I will defeat him!' he declared.

The wizard began to shrink, his arms disappearing up the sleeves of his cloak. His face contorted grotesquely and a long, reptilian tongue flicked out of his mouth, before his head, too, disappeared into his robes. The garment fell to the floor and a snake emerged from beneath it.

A group of wizards came onto the stage then, deep in discussion. They took no notice of the snake as it began to circle them, hissing loudly. A green cloud of fog rose from the ground, drifting into their mouths and ears. Suddenly, one of the men lifted his head.

'We must rise up against Merlin,' he said. 'The Serpentine Wizard is our true leader.' The men all nodded in agreement.

'We must slaughter every man, woman, and child who does not follow him,' said another, to further nods.

They exited the stage and the snake vanished.

During the interval, as refreshments were handed out and children ran to the street vendors with coins they had begged from their parents, Iris sat back in her seat, bored. Every year, it was the same. She looked over her shoulder and noticed Master Hagworth sitting behind her.

'How did he die?' she asked, turning in her chair.

'The Serpentine Wizard?' said Master Hagworth.

'No, not him. Merlin,' she said.

Master Hagworth looked surprised. 'Dear girl, why would we concentrate on his death? Let us focus on his extraordinary life!'

Iris turned back around and folded her arms. The performance always began and ended the same way, at the same two points in time, with the same words. It seemed that all anyone really knew about Merlin was the rebellion he quashed. And there his story ended. Iris sighed. Master Hagworth looked at her pitifully and leaned forward to whisper into her ear.

'I rather like to think he died peacefully in his sleep in this very castle,' he said. 'But, in truth, Iris, all we have left are fables. Whatever became of your great ancestor is lost to history. I—'

A trumpet blasted, silencing Master Hagworth, and the man in black appeared again on stage to announce the second half of the performance. Eve clamped her hands over her ears and groaned at the noise. Her Companion hushed her and presented a Merlin doll for her to play with. Eve took the toy, placed it in her lap and then began to pinch the skin on the back of her wrist anxiously. Matthew looked down the line at her with concern but Josephine squeezed his hand tightly and told him to keep his eyes on the stage.

After a great deal of plotting, the final scene saw the Serpentine Wizard locked in battle against Merlin the Good. Bolts of light flew from their hands and clashed with one another. The other men on stage aimed smaller, feebler bolts at each other. Many were hit and fell down, while the rest continued to fight around the two great wizards, who stared at each other menacingly. Eventually, the Serpentine Wizard's bolt faded. Weary and pained, he dropped to his knees.

'You deserve death!' bellowed Merlin. 'But I will show you mercy. I banish you to a land of darkness, where you shall thrive.' He drew his arms back and then pushed them towards the wizard forcefully. A bright light shot forth from his hands and engulfed the Serpentine Wizard and all his followers. 'Light conquers darkness!' Merlin said.

The audience jumped to its feet and roared as the performers took their bow. When Matthew stood, they cheered louder - some even wept. Lucian watched them all from his seat. Suddenly, his eyes stopped on a bald man in the opposite stall, who had stopped clapping. When the man saw Lucian staring, he resumed his applause with vigour.

The actors came forward and lined up before Matthew.

'And where are you from?' Matthew asked, smiling at the man in black who had opened the performance.

'Edgeton, my Lord Mortenstone,' the man said, bowing. Master Hagworth let out a sharp laugh. Matthew glanced at him over his shoulder and then clapped a hand on the man's arm.

'Well, today you have made Edgeton proud!' he said.

When the man moved away, Matthew looked at Master Hagworth again and suppressed a smile.

Iris might, too, have found this amusing. But, as she watched Lucian, she felt a growing sense of unease. He was staring at someone on the other side of the stage and a dark look had settled over his face. It was a look she was familiar with, a look he had when he was thinking terrible things.

3. THE LORD OF THE DARK LANDS

Fabian Mordark sat in his seat of Blackstone at the end of a gloomy hall drinking wine. The sky outside was grey and offered little light to the room through its narrow windows. He tapped his fingers along to the drip, drip, drip of rainwater as it leaked through the cracks in the ceiling and splashed onto the floor.

His eldest son, Vrax, stood at his side, looking serious as usual, while his youngest, Tobias, was slumped in a chair three steps below with his legs dangling over the arm.

'The Swamp Creatures have drowned two of Belfor's boys,' Fabian said, taking another sip of wine. 'I would avoid him at all costs if I were you,' he said, recalling his own encounter with his distraught cousin that very morning. 'He's on the warpath. Wants to hunt them all down and burn them.' It was a humorous notion, he thought; the only thing Belfor could hunt down was a hot meal, usually from Fabian's own kitchens in the basement of Castle Mordark.

'I would gladly help him, father' said Vrax.

Fabian had to crane his neck to look up at him. Vrax had hollow cheeks that aged his face beyond his years, but the boy was still green. And with his youth came a readiness that, today, irritated Fabian.

'No. No one touches them. For all their faults, they keep the rats at bay. Belfor can have more children - I cannot live with rats.'

He turned then to the small man kneeling on the floor in the middle of the hall. 'And who is this anguished soul?' He set down his goblet and looked towards the back of the hall, where his second son, Alexander, was picking dirt from his nails with a knife. Alexander looked up, dusting the blade. The jewelled eye of the serpent on the front of his black, leather tunic flashed as he moved out of the shadows into the dying light of the fire, which spluttered and choked in its own ash.

'We've been clearing out the dungeons. This man here,' Alexander said, grasping the man by both shoulders, 'is our last living prisoner. He's been here for five years.'

'Five *years*?' Fabian said, surprised. 'Perhaps it is you I should be thanking, for keeping the rats at bay.' He laughed, his lips curling back over grey teeth as he made a munching noise and rubbed his belly. The man flinched and turned his face away.

'He's been teaching our carpenters how to build more effective bows and carts and other contraptions. But he's run out of ideas now. We no longer have use for him.'

'So why have you brought him to me?'

'He has asked that we allow him to return home, as thanks for his service.'

Fabian sat forward, gripping the Blackstone spikes on the arms of his chair.

'And where is home, sir?' he said, taking note of the tattered waistcoat the man was wearing, woven from finer wool than he had ever seen. The man looked over his shoulder at Alexander, who leant in closer and kissed him on the forehead.

Tobias began to snigger.

'Tell him,' Alexander whispered, running his fingers through the man's hair.

'The city of Lambelee, Lord Fabian. In The Light,' the man said. Several of his teeth were missing; the words whistled past his lips as he stared dejectedly at his feet.

Fabian sucked in his breath and spat at the floor. Then he wiped his mouth with the back of his hand and smiled.

'Get up. I grant you your freedom,' he said. The man stared at him warily, his watery-blue eyes trying to discern the trick at hand. 'Get up!' he shouted.

Alexander stepped out of the way.

The man looked around at them all. Finally, he tried to stand.

Fabian waved his hand as if swatting a fly. The man's feet flew out from under him; he landed on his shoulder with a bone-shattering crack and screamed.

'Whoops! The floor is a tad wet. We have a leak,' Fabian said, pointing at the ceiling. His sons laughed. 'Get up,' he said again.

The man got to his knees, clutching his shoulder. He made no attempt to stand. Fabian rose from his chair and came down the steps towards him.

'Please, no! No more! I have suffered. I can take no more. Please!' the man begged, holding up his good arm.

Fabian walked on past him to the doors at the end of the hall.

'Bring him,' he called. Vrax began to descend the steps. 'Not you,' Fabian said, pausing. Vrax stopped.

Alexander looked between them, pocketing his knife. Then he seized the man by the back of his waistcoat and hauled him to his feet. The man yelped like a dog as Alexander forced him out of the hall after his father.

Fabian strode along the parapet, his blood boiling. The rain fell hard, pelting his head, chasing the grease from his long, black hair. He stopped suddenly, turning on the man and grabbing him by the neck.

'Look!' he snapped, slamming him against the wall.

He stared out over the swamplands below. A low mist hung over the bog. On the hills that rose from the murky, fetid water stood crumbling stone huts, black with damp. Skeletal livestock wandered along the submerged paths between the hills; the light from the lanterns illuminated their sores and festering wounds. Horses stood tied to posts, their eyes closed against the rain, drenched hides twitching in the cold. The people tending to them were pale and sickly-looking, their bodies hunched and fragile.

'*You* have suffered?' Fabian hissed. 'Hand him to me,' he said, pushing Alexander's hand away and snatching a fistful of the man's waistcoat. 'We are off to the West Tower!'

'The West Tower?' Alexander said, looking uneasy.

'Is that not what I said?'

Alexander patted the man on the back sympathetically and walked away.

Fabian smiled into the rain. He could smell the man's fear. He stooped low to speak into his ear again.

'Shall we?'

The man shook his head hopelessly as Fabian pushed him across the parapet towards the tower, which loomed in the distance, a black shard of stone rising up to meet the heavens.

When they came to the iron door, Fabian kicked it open, shoved the man through the doorway and stopped him suddenly with a tug. A fierce wind rushed through the windows high at the top of the tower.

Fabian lifted his head and breathed in the cold air, while the man stared, transfixed, at the large, barred hole in the ground. He trembled on the thin shelf of stone that ran the perimeter of the tower as, down in the hole, something began to move.

'Do you see them down there?' Fabian whispered, tightening his grip on the man's waistcoat. 'I imagine you've heard the tales.' He kicked the man's feet out from under him, suspending him over the cage. 'I can assure you, they are all true,' he said.

The man screamed as he looked down at the beasts. Black poison oozed from their beaks and pooled around their scaled talons. Their dark wings flapped excitedly and a gurgling noise rattled in their throats as they looked up at him dangling over the iron bars; eyes, black as night, devouring him from the depths of the pit. Worgrims.

The man screwed his eyes shut. 'I pray to the White Witch. May she protect me and end my suffering. May she save me from this dark, evil place and deliver me back to the light,' he muttered feverishly.

In one quick motion, Fabian flicked his wrist, the cage opened, and the man plummeted into the hole.

Fabian left the tower to a frenzy of screaming and tearing, stopping to look out over his lands again. He pulled his black, feathered cloak about himself as the winds buffeted him. Somewhere in the distance, a dying lamb bleated. He crossed over to the other side of the parapet and stared at the Dark Forest; its shadow crept all the way up the hill, falling over half of the castle. No fire could warm the parts it touched, nor could any man tolerate the unnatural coldness for too long. Fabian dug his nails into the stone until he felt a biting pain and looked down to see blood trickling from his fingertips.

He returned to the hall and slammed the door shut. Tobias took his legs down from the arm of his chair.

Vrax and Alexander watched him cautiously from the steps. He strode towards them, coming nose to nose with Vrax, and breathed heavily for a time before he could muster his words.

'What is this?' he murmured. Vrax said nothing. 'WHAT IS THIS?!' He sprayed the words in Vrax's face but, still, he said nothing. Fabian stepped back and looked at the others. 'Their people talk of troubles when they know nothing of real suffering. Look at us, too weak to dream of hope! I will not live out my days here. This is no life.'

He approached Alexander and pointed a finger at him. 'I want what is mine. Their lands belong to me and to you. I will take them back from those tyrants. If it's the last thing I do, I will take them. I'll break the spell, I'll breach the border, I'll kill them all. I'll end their line. And you will help me. Find me a weakness!' he said. Alexander nodded. Fabian looked at Tobias. 'You and your brothers will do your duty,' he said. Then he turned back to Vrax and his eyes narrowed. 'Do not fail me.'

One by one, his sons crossed their arms over their chests and disappeared, until Fabian was the only man left in the room.

4. THE DARK FOREST

When Lucian awoke that morning, he went straight to the castle guards with an order. Find the bald man. He gave them permission to use force to extract information from the people of Lambelee. It wouldn't take long. Fear had a way of making people talk. He suggested they first pay a visit to the landlord of the Snake's Head Inn at the bottom of Stone Lane. He was most likely to know who the man was and where he lived; alehouse keepers knew everyone.

He decided to conduct proceedings in the entrance hall, for all to see. He perched on a step halfway up the staircase, waiting, while Matthew's advisors stood in a cluster at the bottom, looking at each other uncomfortably. When he heard a commotion just beyond the courtyard, he smiled.

'Here he is,' he said, as two guards carried the man through the castle gates, kicking and struggling in his long nightgown. They moved swiftly across the courtyard and into the entrance hall, where they put him down. He shook them off and stared up at Lucian, his face flushed with anger.

'This is outrageous!' he cried. 'I demand to know why I have been plucked from my bed by these brutes!'

Lucian tittered mockingly, amused by the spectacle.

'I was watching you yesterday,' he said, leaning forward to rest his elbows on his knees. 'You were not impressed with the performance. Why?'

'In what realm is it unacceptable for an old man to take pause to catch his breath? Answer me that, boy!'

'Be careful now,' said Lucian, his smile vanishing. 'I have people who tell me you are a Mordark sympathiser, that you conspire against my family. What am I to do with this information?'

The bald man balled his hands into fists and looked around the hall, exasperated. 'What people? Name them! I am a true supporter of your family. But I won't be treated this way by *you*. I will answer to your father and no one else!'

Lucian had not expected such impudence from the man. He glanced at a corridor branching off from the entrance hall; servants had begun to gather there, watching from the shadows. He felt his blood rising and smiled tightly.

'My father is not here,' he said, standing to descend the stairs. 'I have taken over his duties in his absence. So, you *will* answer to me.'

The bald man grasped the stair rail and put his foot on a step as he leaned forwards and sneered, 'You aren't fit to rule.'

The words struck Lucian like a cold slap to the face. He stared for a moment, stunned. Then an advisor below shouted, 'Treason!'

Lucian drew his hands to his chest and felt a cool wind, a lightness in his head, before the weight of the world fell upon him again. He opened his eyes. He was standing behind the bald man at the bottom of the stairs. The man turned around and his eyes widened with fear. Lucian filled his lungs and shrieked, pulling a knife from his sleeve and slashing the man's chest in a blind rage. The man cried out and fell back onto the steps.

'Banish him!' Lucian screamed. 'Banish him!'

The guards seized the bald man and dragged him out of the hall and down the steps into the courtyard. But Lucian was still furious; it did not feel like punishment enough.

The courtyard was packed with servants and workmen, who cleared a path as the guards hauled the man towards the gates. Lucian flew down the steps after them, his blade dripping with blood. People began to gasp as he came at the man again, slashing his back, tearing through the nightgown. The blacksmith's hammering stopped. A horseshoe fitter was knocked from his stool as a young filly kicked out in fright. Lucian cut and sliced relentlessly, until three pairs of hands prised him away. He turned on the three horror-struck advisors, panting for breath.

'Come back inside, Lord Lucian,' said the fat one, Alder Stonedge, stepping away from him as he spoke.

Lucian looked around the courtyard. Every face was turned towards him, frozen in shock. He walked back to the castle, scowling, as the bald man's ravaged body was carried away into the square.

He paced up and down the entrance hall. How could someone so lowly dare to speak to him that way? Did the Mortenstone name carry so little respect? Or was it him? Was he not fearsome? He paused when he glimpsed the servants in the corridor, still watching, like mice eager for a morsel to take back to the kitchens or gutters or wherever it was they came from. He gritted his teeth. They could have more than a morsel. He threw the bloodied dagger at them with all his strength. There was a gasp and a crash as the blade knocked the silver tray from one of their hands - he didn't see who, for they promptly vanished, leaving the upturned tray behind.

Lucian smiled to himself and flexed his hand, but his smile faded when he looked down at his clothes. They were ruined.

∗

The guards dragged the bald man across the cobbles of Stone Lane. He left a dark trail of blood in his wake. Iris watched from a herb stall further down the lane. As they passed her, her heart began to beat wildly. Others looked on in silence.

She had been nervous the previous night when her father announced he was leaving with Saskian at dawn for the Low Lands. Her mother had persuaded him to place Lucian in charge. Iris had given him a pleading look, which he ignored, though she was certain that he, too, knew it was wrong. Instead, he removed the silver ring from his left index finger and placed it in Lucian's hand.

'The Ring of Rulers,' he said. Lucian's eyes had sparkled.

Iris put down the herbs and followed the blood to the end of the lane. From there, she watched the guards cross the Grassland with the bald man, who stumbled, half-conscious, between them. Several people gathered around her to watch, muttering to one another in hushed voices. She heard one of them whisper Lucian's name.

When the guards reached the edge of the Dark Forest, they propped the man on his feet, struck him when he collapsed onto them, and pushed him into the shadows. Iris felt cold all over as the darkness swallowed him. She bit her lip, remembering the family who had gone the same way years before.

'Iris!' came a hoarse whisper from an alley next to the Snake's Head Inn across the lane. Thomas poked his head out and beckoned her over. She rushed to him.

'What's happening?' she said.

'That was Gerald Swampton, the animal healer. Lucian attacked him and banished him - but he's innocent!'

Iris had never seen her brother so outraged.

'Ride to father. Tell him to come home quickly,' she said.

Thomas nodded, crossed his arms over his chest and disappeared as an icy wind swept down the alleyway.

Iris waited there in the gloom until the guards passed back along the lane. The one nearest to her wiped his bloodied hands on his cloak and muttered something that made the other laugh. When they had gone, she came out of the alley.

There was a commotion outside the tavern. One man was gesticulating and pointing after the guards; his eye was swollen and turning a deep shade of purple. Most of the people who had stood to watch the guards banish the bald man surrounded him now, shaking their heads. Iris slipped past them all and returned to the edge of the lane, where she stared out at the Grassland. There was no sign of Gerald Swampton. She bit her lip. It would be hours, perhaps even a whole day, before Thomas returned with their father. What would have become of Gerald by then? With a quick glance over her shoulder, she made up her mind. And she bolted.

She felt exhilarated, alive, as she charged across the Grassland, eyes streaming, the wind roaring in her ears.

As she passed into the forest's shadow, she slowed. This was the closest she had ever come to the Dark Forest. She walked the rest of the way, feeling a sudden loss of conviction. The trees were as wide as the houses on Stone Lane and taller than Mortenstone Castle itself. Everything beyond was dark and quiet. She stopped, pressing her hand against the scaly bark of a tree, and peered in.

'Hello?' she said, stepping forwards onto a twig. It snapped and she moved back in fright. Her call went unanswered but she had an odd feeling that someone or something within was listening. 'Mr Swampton?' All was still. She looked over her shoulder one last time before she walked into the forest.

The silence was heavy and strange. It seemed to have a presence of its own, as if the forest was holding its breath. There was a wrongness to it all; the trees were twisted and deformed and there was a grey, deadened tinge to the bark, which appeared to be rotting. The ground was infested with black nettles and dead branches. Iris trod cautiously over them, looking back at the Grassland often, to make sure it was still there and, as she wandered deeper into the forest, to work out how quickly she could make it back. Five strides became ten, and ten became twenty, until the Grassland disappeared completely from view. Her heart was thudding in her chest. She felt small. The tree limbs over which she climbed were bigger than she was.

Suddenly, an ear-piercing screech sliced through the air. She stopped dead. The sound echoed through the dark woods, growing more and more distant. It was just a crow. Just a crow. She was shaking now. She wanted to go home.

'Mr Swampton?' she whispered, her voice quivering. But no one was there. Her words shrank into the dark quiet.

As she turned to go back, something grabbed her foot. She screamed as it pulled her down. She fell to the ground hard and rolled onto her back, fighting to get her arms free from the tangles of her cloak. She looked down at her foot in terror, as a black, gnarled tree root began to wrap itself around her ankle. She kicked and kicked. The root squeezed her foot tighter, winding its way up towards her knee like a snake. She leant forwards and struck it with her fists and then dug her fingers underneath it and prised it from her leg. As it writhed in her hands, she pulled her leg free and let go, crawling away frantically. Then, she pushed herself to her feet and began to run, back through the forest, leaping over unearthed roots until her lungs burned. Sweat trickled down her forehead, but she felt cold.

When her legs grew stiff and tired, she staggered on, pushing through the pain, hugging her arms to her chest. Her foot was throbbing. Pieces of skin from her leg were lodged under her fingernails.

Suddenly, she stopped. She had come to the edge of a clearing. She stared at the trees on the other side; the bark seemed darker, almost black, in the dull light that filtered down through the thinning canopy above. As she looked around from tree to tree, her heart began to pound faster and faster. She had come the wrong way. The Light was far behind her. The knots in her stomach tightened. She would have to go back the way she had come, face all the horrors again. She looked over her shoulder, scanning the forest. She couldn't run; her feet had already begun to swell. She was exhausted. She turned her back on the clearing, staring into the darkness. Which path had she taken? She couldn't remember.

'Is that it?' a voice behind her said. She froze. Every muscle in her body clenched tight. She turned around.

A boy with brown hair and bright eyes was leaning against a tree at the edge of the clearing. He smiled wryly at her and stood up straight, unfolding his arms. He was tall, far taller than she was. He looked strong.

'I don't bite,' he said, raising both hands in a gesture of peace. 'I'm walking, just like you.' He began to walk in a wide arc, moving closer to her. Her heart was pounding furiously as he circled her. 'What is a girl like you doing all by herself in the Dark Forest?' he said, stopping to kick at the dirt.

'I'm walking, just like you,' she said. He looked up sharply and stared at her, amused.

'And you're from…*over there*?' he asked, pointing to the space behind her. Iris nodded, thinking desperately of Mortenstone Castle in the vain hope that she could transport herself back there. But all the power in the world was useless in the Dark Forest. Even her father wouldn't have been able to. The boy smiled. 'What's it like? A lot better than where I'm from, I imagine.'

Iris shrugged.

The boy smiled again and began to advance. Iris's breath caught in her throat as he came right up to her, close enough to touch.

'I'm Alexander,' he said.

She looked into his eyes and the Song of the Realm drifted ominously to the front of her mind.

> … *Mordark eyes of emerald green*
> *The eyes of cunning, traitorous fiends…*

'Alexander Mordark,' she said, a heavy feeling settling over her.

'You've heard of me?' he said. 'Who are you?'

Iris hesitated before she answered. 'Geraldine… Swampton.'

The boy could not contain his laughter. 'Swampton!' he exclaimed.

'It's rude to laugh at a person's name,' she said sternly, though her hands were shaking.

Alexander's laugh died on his lips. He stared at her for a moment, then shook his head. 'Surely you were warned about the Dark Forest? The Mortenstones love to tell the story,' he said.

'Yes.'

'But you came anyway?'

'Yes.'

'Why?' he said, eyes narrowing as he scrutinised her. 'You don't look the adventurous sort.' He laughed again. 'Don't look so upset. Fine, I believe you. You're a thrill-seeker. You love danger!' he said. He was mocking her.

'I came here to look for someone, actually.'

'Oh?' he said, serious now. 'Who?'

Iris bit her tongue, wishing she hadn't said anything.

'My…father. But he must have returned home. So, I must go—'

'Wait!' he said, clutching her arm. She stiffened. 'I think I saw him pass by. He went that way,' he said, pointing eastwards, deeper into the forest. 'I'll look with you.'

Iris could not steady her nerves. She felt her legs trembling. It was a trap. The Mordarks hunted in the Dark Forest. And, as Alexander watched her with those wild green eyes, she knew she was his prey. She had no choice but to accept his offer, nodding politely with a tight smile that betrayed no hint of fear.

As they walked out of the clearing, darkness enveloped them once more. A chill crept through the air, raising the hairs on her skin. Alexander walked beside her and bashed the trees with a stick he had picked up.

'Do the Mortenstones live in your town?' he asked. Iris nodded, avoiding his eye. 'What do you think of them?' he said. 'Don't worry, I won't tell them. We aren't close.'

An idea came to her then. If she could keep him on side, he might let her go. If she told him everything he wanted to hear, that made them allies of some kind.

'They're cruel. They treat us terribly. I…hate them.'

Alexander's lips turned up at the corners. He seemed pleased with her, like she was a pup that had remembered a trick.

'You're not loyal,' he said, smiling to himself.

'You don't know what they're like.'

He stepped out in front of her and blocked her path. 'I know what they're like,' he said, his eyes flashing.

Iris held his gaze, feeling that to look away would reveal her identity. When he turned around and continued, she exhaled heavily with relief.

'You're quite brave. For a girl,' he said as he picked his way over a lattice of unearthed tree roots.

'For a girl?' Iris said, giving the roots a wide berth. She could see he was smiling. 'Clearly you don't have sisters.'

'No, thankfully!' he said. Iris nudged him. 'Oh my! A smile at last!' he said, opening his arms and throwing back his head.

Their pace slowed. Iris stole a glance at him and quickly looked away when she caught his eye.

'What is your family like?' she asked. Alexander seemed surprised by the question.

'You mean you don't believe the horror stories?' he said. 'I have two brothers, Vrax and Tobias, both less charming and handsome, of course.'

'And do you get on with them?'

'Yes,' he said. 'Don't you get on with yours?'

Iris shook her head and looked at the ground, thinking of Lucian.

'Why not?'

She paused for a moment, then said, 'Too adventurous for their liking.'

Alexander began to laugh and Iris found herself laughing, rather bashfully, as well. But their laughter came to an abrupt stop as a tortured scream punctured the air, lifting silent birds from their nests.

Alexander's head snapped up and his hand darted to the dagger in his belt. Iris could hear the blood pulsing in her ears. She opened her mouth to speak but he silenced her, drawing a finger to his lips. He walked towards the sound quietly and beckoned her before standing deathly still again. She followed, too frightened to turn and run. Alexander's brow furrowed in concentration. Then, he placed a hand on her shoulder.

'This way,' he said, tilting his head towards a path thick with brambles.

Iris planted her feet. 'No, I need to go back!' she hissed.

'Come on!' He took the path, moving swiftly through the thicket and out of sight.

Iris looked around warily. She could have run, but instead she went after Alexander.

He was far ahead of her, whipping past low branches that protruded from tree trunks like hands, trying to clutch at him. When he reached a small clearing, he stopped. Iris pursued with haste, but as she saw him kneel over a mound on the ground, she slowed, afraid of what she would find. The closer she came, the surer she grew. And, stepping reluctantly into the clearing at last, she looked down. Gerald Swampton's body lay on the damp, blood-soaked earth, a knife jutting out of his left eye socket. His right eye was wide open and terror-stricken.

Alexander looked up at her. 'Is this…?'

'No,' she said. 'He's not my father.'

Alexander stood and put his hands on his hips. He looked down at the corpse as if it was as dull and ordinary as a stone.

'Who did this?' Iris said faintly.

'Vrax,' he said, gesturing the dagger. 'He leaves his mark.' He bit down on his lower lip, looking amused.

'This isn't funny!' Iris said, shoving him in the chest.

'I'm not laughing!'

'A man has been killed – murdered – by your brother!'

'He's nobody. What does it matter?'

Iris's eyes stung with hot tears. 'He's a person, just like us.' She squeezed her eyes shut and wiped the tears that rushed down her cheeks.

Alexander looked disgusted. 'Mordarks are not like you, or him,' he said, raising his chin. 'You are Low Lives.'

'That doesn't make it right. His children won't have a father. You're evil, you and your family!'

'I didn't kill him!'

'You might as well have. You wanted to laugh, I saw you!'

Alexander rolled his eyes and swiped a hand through the air as if batting away a fly.

'Am I dismissed?' she said coldly. He didn't answer and he didn't look at her either. She knelt beside the body and quickly muttered a prayer. 'I ask you, White Witch, I beg you, to bless this man's passing and protect his soul. Please watch over his family. Don't let them starve.' She whispered the last words. Then, she got up and left the clearing.

She had a restless feeling in her stomach. She worried that he might pursue her but, as she created greater distance between them, the worry subsided.

Alexander remained in the clearing, pacing up and down for some time. Then, with a deep sigh, he knelt down beside the body, pulled out the knife, closed Gerald's good eye, and left.

Iris arrived back at the castle before nightfall, just in time for her evening lesson with Master Hagworth. Eve was already at her desk, Lucian had pardoned himself and Thomas had not yet returned with their father. She patted her hair down in place and sat beside Eve. When Master Hagworth materialised, he announced that the lesson would be, rather fittingly, about the Failed Rebellion. He asked Eve to list all the families who followed the Serpentine Wizard into battle, and grew aggravated when she could not.

'You are twelve years old, Eve! You should know this by now! Were you not paying attention to yesterday's performance?'

Eve began to stammer and splutter.

'Master Hagworth?' Iris interjected. 'The Failed Rebellion was almost a thousand years ago. Why are Mordarks and Mortenstones still enemies?'

Master Hagworth dropped his quill and threw his hands into the air in exasperation.

'Oh! If you even have to ask, I've clearly been a poor schoolmaster. I may as well give it all up now.' He sat down heavily in his chair. 'Iris, we are not unique. We pass our characteristics, our likeness, our history, our thoughts, to our kin. Do you understand?'

'So the Serpentine Wizard's kin are *all* like him? All evil?'

'Yes. All. It is in their nature.'

5. AGATHA

Iris watched as her father entered the courtyard and dismounted his horse. His lips were pressed into a hard line. He looked furious. Thomas and Saskian rode in close behind him, just as Lucian breezed into the yard from the castle, surrounded by servants. Iris felt a rush of excitement.

'Father!' Lucian said, opening his arms. 'Welcome home.' He clicked to one of the servants, who was holding a silver pitcher. 'Wine.' The servant poured the wine into a chalice and handed it to Lucian, who offered the cup to his father. Matthew slapped it from Lucian's hand. It fell to the ground with a clang and its contents splashed onto the stone and spread along the cracks like blood. Then Matthew struck Lucian hard across the face with the back of his hand.

The courtyard fell still.

'See me inside,' Matthew said calmly, striding away into the castle. The servants deserted Lucian and followed him.

Lucian looked around bemusedly. When he saw Iris, he glared. But Iris went on smiling. Even from where she was standing, she could see the angry welt on his cheek appearing, the last of his pride crumbling.

As everything sprang to life around them again, Josephine emerged from a side door into the courtyard and went straight to Lucian. She fixed her eyes on his cheek for a moment and then walked back to the door through which she had entered. Lucian stared after her. The red blotch on his cheek was gone.

Iris smirked, knowing he would hear, and then turned towards the stables to visit her horse. But, suddenly, her mother appeared behind her and gripped her arm tightly, sinking her nails into her skin.

'Did that amuse you? You are a malicious little whelp,' she spat. Iris pulled away abruptly and ran back to the castle.

Lucian was absent at dinner that evening. Matthew had taken up his usual place at the head of the table and the Ring of Rulers was back on his finger where it belonged.

'You look rather pleased with yourself,' Josephine said, looking at Iris with contempt.

Iris was surprised by the remark. She had not smiled once or even spoken a word throughout the meal.

'Something you care to share with us?' said Josephine.

'No,' said Iris, spearing a piece of beef with her fork. Josephine made a sharp hissing sound. Iris's cutlery was forced from her hands and sucked down to the table top. She looked up at her mother.

'I will not tolerate insolence. And I will not see you taunt Lucian again,' said Josephine.

Iris looked at her father in exasperation.

Matthew sighed. 'Josephine…' he said.

'Did you hear me, Iris?' said Josephine, ignoring him.

Iris stood up suddenly. Her chair screeched as it backed over the stone floor. 'Why can't you see it?' she shouted. 'Lucian's a monster!'

'Iris—'

'He is!' she cried at her father. 'Everyone sees it but her! You've told us all our lives that we're good, that it runs in our blood, but he's just as savage as…as the Mordarks!'

In an instant, Josephine picked up a knife and launched it across the table at Iris. Matthew stood and flung his arm forwards. The knife froze in the air above the table.

'Away with you! Now!' he said to Iris, who left the room, startled and angry, as Eve began to cry.

Matthew turned to Josephine, his face pale with shock. 'Do that again and you won't have hands.' He took the knife, threw it down to the floor and walked out of the room.

Josephine stood and looked at a servant before gesturing Eve with the flash of her eyes. 'Shut her up,' she said. Then she, too, departed.

Iris was confined to her bedroom for the next three days. Her siblings were not permitted to visit, her mother chose not to, and her father came in the evenings to bid her good night. And, each evening, when she refused to apologise, she earned herself another day's imprisonment. She spent most of the time lying on her bed, staring up at the white canopy, or sitting by the window and gazing across the Grassland at the Dark Forest. She thought about Alexander most of all. He was nothing like she had imagined. Master Hagworth had taught them much about the Dark Lands, where the Mordarks lived, and, when he was feeling particularly animated, he would tell tales of their monstrous, deformed faces and their translucent skin, through which a web of bold blue veins pulsed with black blood. The tales had held the four of them captivated in the schoolroom, though now she was sure she hadn't truly believed them all. But still it had shocked her to find that Alexander Mordark looked so very human. He was almost pleasing to the eye. But there was ugliness there, too; corruption, setting in. She remembered the way he had stared at Gerald Swampton's body. It was a fleeting moment, but one she had not missed. There was a look in his eyes, one Master Hagworth had spoken of in many of his lessons; he called it The Mordark Lust. They enjoyed death and pain. They craved it. She could hardly believe he had let her go.

But Gerald Swampton and his punctured eye did not leave her. She awoke in a cold sweat each night, her ears ringing with his scream, as moonlight streamed through the window and illuminated the same patch on the flagstones. He was still out there, dead on the ground, rotting, while she was tucked up safe in a feather bed. She thought about telling Thomas, when she was free to see him again, but, upon greater reflection, decided it would be better not to breathe a word. Perhaps he would sleep easier believing there was a chance Gerald had made it to safety in the Land of the Banished.

There were moments when she considered apologising, usually at mealtimes. She wasn't sorry, but her loss of privileges was taking its toll on her empty stomach, for she was forced to make her own food. Clueless about the ingredients necessary to make up any of the dishes that came into her head, often bowls of slop materialised on the table instead of the hearty stews and broths she had tried to conjure. By the third day, she summoned cheese and bread for lunch as well as supper, not caring, as she tore the crust off the warm loaf, that the cooks down in the kitchens had probably baked it fresh for the following morning and would now have to bake it again. But, every time her stomach growled or she thought of the cakes and custards and jams she could be enjoying, she reminded herself that it would be better to live forever on bread and cheese than to bend to her mother's will.

On the fourth morning, she awoke to a gentle knock at the door. As she sat up in bed, the door opened and her father and mother entered. Josephine looked dangerously happy. Matthew walked over to the Witchwood chair beside the fireplace; it had been a gift from Iris's late uncle when she was a young girl, carved from a Silver Tree in the heart of Mortenstone Valley. Her childhood Companion used to read bedtime stories to her from the chair. She watched, now, as her father brushed his fingers over the wood, as if summoning courage from it. He took a long, deep breath and, when he blinked, his eyes stayed closed a moment too long. Iris's stomach knotted with unease. She got out of bed and approached him. The stone floor was cold beneath her feet. She came to stand by the hearth in front of him, with the chair between them. Her mother was staring at him impatiently from the window.

'Iris,' he said, finally, his eyes fixed on the ground. 'Every young woman comes to an age when they must marry. Gregory Vandemere of the Low Lands is the best match we could hope for. The Vandemeres are, and always have been, loyal supporters. They're wealthy, they command vast forces… As you know, I visited the Low Lands recently and met with Eric Vandemere. And we came to an agreement. When you turn sixteen, you and Gregory will marry. Iris? Iris…'

Iris stood in a trance, too stunned to cry, or to speak. Of all the news her father could have brought her, this was the last thing she expected. Married, before Lucian? She was not ready. Matthew came around the chair and put his hand on her shoulder. It felt as heavy as a lump of stone and she sagged under the weight of it. He caught her and sat her in the chair. She looked up at him, but she didn't recognise him. This man was not her father. He couldn't be. Because her father would not betray her like this, her father would not send her off to market like a prized pig. She felt sick.

'The family will visit Mortenstone Castle at the end of the month, so you and Gregory can get to know one another,' Matthew said solemnly. Josephine came to stand beside him. Her lips grew tight and pinched as she suppressed a smile.

When they left, Iris slid off the chair onto the floor. After marriage, she would have to lie with her husband and bear his children. But what if she didn't love him? What if he repulsed her? What if he was cruel? What if she died during childbirth? Without another thought, she got up, took her cloak and fled.

*

Alexander Mordark sat on the trunk of an uprooted tree in the middle of the forest, as he had done every day since his encounter with Iris. She was a strong-willed girl. He liked that. And, though she had angered him, he found he wanted to see her again. She was much prettier than sour-faced Risella, who hounded him persistently at the castle.

He hadn't told his father about his encounter. She was from *over there*. Fabian would have insisted she be brought to him for interrogation, and they never ended happily. No, he didn't want his father laying hands on her. And he didn't want his brothers to know, either. He loved Vrax, but he knew he would do anything to impress their father, even if it meant betraying his brother. And Tobias… well, Tobias did as Tobias pleased.

When he saw her approach, he thought he had dreamt it. The birds had not stirred, the ground had not given voice to her tread. All was quiet and still. And then, out of the gloom, she came. Her fair hair flowed out from beneath her hood like silk. She walked across the clearing towards him. Before she reached him, she stopped and lifted her hood. When she looked at him, he went hot and cold and rose quickly like a nervous fool.

'Miss Swampton,' he said. She bowed her head and looked down. 'Is something wrong?' he asked, taking a step towards her. 'What is it?' He stretched out his arm to try and comfort her but let it fall back to his side again, thinking better of it.

'I can't go back there,' she said softly. 'You have to help me escape.' She looked up at him. Her eyes were red and swollen.

'You don't mean that,' he said. A tear slipped down her cheek. He watched it linger on her jaw and then drop to the ground.

'I do.'

'Why?' he said. She gave a strangled whimper and shrugged, shaking her head, her eyes brimming with fresh tears. 'Geraldine, you may think life where you're from is unbearable, but it could be worse. Much worse. You won't find refuge in the Dark Lands. They'll kill you the moment they learn you're from *over there.*'

She didn't answer. More tears fell and, somehow, he felt responsible for them. As he stood there, watching her cry, he felt an ache in his gut. She didn't know real suffering. He thought about how, every winter, the walls of Castle Mordark turned black with the relentless deluge of rain, and how the marshlands overflowed, and how they all succumbed to the Winter Sickness; how their clothes steamed when they stood by the fire, damp and stinking; how they used so much magic to mend leaks and repair the crumbling tower rooves, they were bedbound afterwards, sometimes for days, their bodies stiff, their heads throbbing from the exertion. And here she was, in her fine clothes - to think, even peasants wore fine clothes in The Light! - consumed by her own menial troubles. He gritted his teeth. But, as irritated as he was, something about her made him want to help, to stop the tears. Sighing, he took her hand, squeezing it reassuringly.

'Come with me,' he said. 'There's someone I want you to meet.'

They went deeper into the forest, walking in silence. Alexander knew the way. He had attached a memory to every tree, branch, root and nest, every pond, clearing and hideaway in these parts. They passed the tree choking with Rash Ivy; the pale leaves wound tightly around the trunk, which had begun to lean to one side as the years wore on. They passed an old den, made from branches that had been woven together. The roof was a blanket of black moss, sagging now. A band of outlaws had once resided there. Iris froze when she saw the structure, but he pulled her on. There was nothing to fear; those men didn't live there anymore. He and Vrax had smoked them out, though they hadn't needed much coaxing. They had come running, six of them or more, knives in hand, ready for a fight. But they hadn't seen Tobias, crouching behind the thicket of thorns, or the traps they had laid, ready to snap shut and crunch through the bones in their feet. They made a lot of threats, those men. Until the traps sprang. And, by then, he and his brothers were not feeling particularly merciful.

When they came to a well-beaten track, Iris looked over her shoulder warily.

'What?' Alexander said, stopping.

'You *will* kill anyone who comes after me, won't you?' There was a plea in her tone. She looked at him like her every hope depended on him.

'If you tell me what's going on, I will,' he said.

'Not now. I can't…'

'Then I can't promise anything.'

'This isn't a game,' she said, turning on him, her face so close to his he could see every lash that framed her blue eyes. He looked down at her feet; she was standing on the tips of her toes. 'You're useless,' she said, her mouth twisting into a grimace. 'You wouldn't know *how* to help.'

'What does it look like I'm doing?'

'Give me your knife at least, so I can protect myself.'

He backed away from her as she tried to snatch it.

'No.'

'Give it!'

'No.'

She stared at him incredulously. And then, in the distance, came a screech. Crows. She jumped with fright and looked over her shoulder again. There was a sad desperation in her eyes. Alexander sighed and pulled the knife from is belt, handing it to her. She wouldn't need it.

They walked on. A dull light filtered into the forest above the track, illuminating the way. Iris held the knife out in front of her and moved it everywhere she turned. She almost sliced into Alexander's arm, mere moments after he had given it to her. He stopped and asked for it back but she wouldn't give it. He left a wide space between them after that.

*

Iris looked around at the forest. Many people lived there, concealed from the world in the vast darkness. Most, she knew, were not the kind she would want to encounter without her magic, but she could hide from

51

them, too. She could hide from everyone. No one from The Light would venture this far in search of her and, if they did, they would never find her. As she contemplated a life in the shadows, her eye was drawn to something in the distance. Ahead, on the edge of the track, tucked away between two trees, stood a cottage. She stopped dead. Like the trees around it, the little house was crooked and appeared to list forwards, as if it were about to topple over onto the track. The roof thatching hung low over the walls, which were patched together with wood and mud and stone, and a small chimney puffed smoke out into the forest.

Alexander nodded towards the cottage. 'We're here,' he said.

Warm light spilled out from one of the windows. They walked along the track towards it. Iris began to wonder who might live there. In plain view of passing strangers and completely isolated, they would have to be fearsome, people others dared not cross. The thought made her feel ill-at-ease. She looked at Alexander. He seemed relaxed as he ambled towards the house.

When they reached the door, Alexander knocked three times and then turned to her, raising his eyebrows. Reluctantly, she lowered the knife and handed it back to him. As he slid it into his belt, there was a loud *click* and a thread of light appeared around the door. Slowly, it creaked open. Iris stepped back behind Alexander. There, in the doorway, silhouetted against the firelight, was an old woman. She was no taller than Iris, her back slightly hunched. She hobbled forwards, using the door frame to steady herself. Beneath the thick stole that covered her shoulders, she wore a brown smock that looked to have seen better years. Her grey hair was wound into a bun; the loose hairs stuck out around her face as if frozen in the wind. Her skin was pale and her forehead was lined with deep wrinkles, which seemed to smooth out when she saw Alexander.

'I wasn't expecting you, boy,' she said, with a voice like gravel. 'I've not gathered anything for supper if that's what you're here for.'

'No, I came to see you,' he said, bending down to embrace her. She smiled faintly before her flinty eyes found Iris over his shoulder. Her face hardened. Iris's skin prickled under the old woman's gaze. 'This is Geraldine,' Alexander said, standing back and nodding towards her.

Iris bowed her head and stared at the ground. There was a moment of silence. She could feel her cheeks burning. She glanced at Alexander, whose eyes widened, as if prompting her to speak. But, before she had mustered the courage to look at the woman again and greet her, she heard a low groan behind her. She spun around, her breath trapped in her throat, her hands scrabbling for Alexander's knife. But then she stopped. She could hear him tittering.

On the other side of the path, twisted and disfigured like its companions, and gleaming like a bright jewel amongst them, was a Silver Tree. Hundreds of intricate, weaving branches splayed outwards as far as they did upwards, encroaching on the neighbouring trees, encasing them in a web of silver. She stared at it, open-mouthed. There were Silver Trees in the Wild Garden at Mortenstone Castle, even more in Mortenstone Valley, but it seemed too pure a thing to be there, in the Dark Forest, surrounded by giants, clinging to them in the darkness. The tree creaked again, the way a ship creaks when the sea is pressing in around it. It made her feel better, to see something so familiar all that way from home; it was as if a piece of home was now with her. She felt a strange compulsion to walk over to it and rest her hand upon its bark. But the impulse left her as soon as it came. She turned, instead, to face the old woman, whose eyes flicked from the Silver Tree to her with deep suspicion. Her brow twitched, fighting off a frown, and she looked hard at Iris, as if she was searching for the answer to an unuttered question. Iris stayed completely still, trying to make her face as unreadable as possible, opening her eyes up wide. It was important to widen the eyes; wide eyes were trustworthy eyes, or so her father said. The woman's expression did not soften. She went on staring, staring, and then looked at Alexander sternly.

'Agatha, be nice,' he said.

The woman's eyes darted to Iris once more before she turned around and walked back into the cottage with a grunt.

'Come in, then!' she called impatiently. Alexander laughed under his breath and shrugged apologetically but Iris could not find the will to smile. He raised his arm, inviting her to go in first, but she stood rooted to the spot, waiting, until he gave up and went inside. She stole one last look at the Silver Tree and followed him over the threshold.

'Hip's been playing up,' Agatha said from an armchair by the fireplace, as she pulled a fur throw onto her lap. A black pot bubbled away over the flames, perfuming the room with the mouth-watering smell of roasting meat and broth. Above the mantelpiece were shelves laden with books, pans, knives and jars. Iris's eye was drawn to one on the bottom shelf, filled with a silvery liquid that shimmered in the firelight. Wooden cases with more books, weapons and bottles lined the right-hand wall. It was a homely, civilised living space.

Alexander moved to close the door. As he stepped back, Iris noticed a table on the left, behind the spot where he had been standing. Occupying one of the four wooden chairs at the table was a dark-haired boy, no older than five. He stared at her inquisitively through eyes wiser than his years.

'That's William,' Agatha said, looking at her expectantly.

'Hello, William' Iris said. The boy continued to stare after she looked away.

The fire spat a piece of wood onto the rug. Agatha smothered the glowing ember with the heel of her boot, wincing slightly as she lifted her leg.

'Come on then, let's be having it. What have you done now?' she said.

'I haven't done anything. But my friend, Geraldine, here, has run away from home. Home being *over there.*'

'And you want her to stay here, is that it?'

'Yes.'

Agatha was silent for a moment. 'Out of the question,' she said finally.

'Why? She'll pull her weight. You can cook, can't you?' he said, looking at Iris.

'I don't care if she can hunt deer with a stick! She can't stay.'

'Ugh!' he groaned, falling into the armchair opposite Agatha, who leant forwards and smacked him across the head.

'Enough of your cheek, boy!'

Alexander rubbed his head. 'Why?' he said.

Agatha didn't answer him. She stared at the flames, her mouth set.

Iris's heart sank. This had been her only hope. She backed away, dejected, and slipped out of the house into the forest.

*

Alexander folded his arms and watched sullenly as Agatha began to stoke the fire.

'I know it seems harsh, boy,' she said. 'She's a pretty one, and you, being a typical man, want to impress her, no doubt. But this isn't the way.

'You should go home, girl,' she called over her shoulder, 'before they start to wonder where you've got to.' She turned to look at Iris when no response came. Alexander looked, too. She was gone.

He stood and made for the door at once.

'Wait!' Agatha said, struggling to her feet. She put a hand on his arm. He was still angry with her and didn't meet her eye. 'Look at me,' she said. Frowning, he looked at her. 'Watch yourself with that one,' she warned, lowering her voice. 'She's a Mortenstone.'

6. AGE OLD ENEMIES

On the eve of the Vandemere visit, Iris sat up late in the library leafing through books. A storm raged outside; rain lashed at the windows in furious bursts, but the hearth glowed comfortingly and she pulled her chair close to the fire for warmth.

She had cried all the way home from Agatha's cottage. The very moment she set eyes on her, she knew the old woman would not help, that Alexander could not help, that she alone was responsible for her fate. The walk back to The Light had been excruciating. It was as if her legs were made of stone; each step grew harder than the last, every muscle burdened with weight she could hardly bear. She didn't want to return at all, to Mortenstone Castle, to her mother, to marriage. But, in truth, she was more afraid of living in darkness.

She moped for days, wandering the corridors aimlessly and refusing to attend lessons. She didn't speak to or even look at her father; her heart still stung with his betrayal. When she passed Lucian on the staircase, his sneers made her want to scream and throw herself over the railings just to wipe his smug smile away. Though who could say if it would.

Then, one night, it came to her, as she dreamed a familiar dream. Always, it was the same. Always, the baby's cries woke her. Only this time, upon waking, she did not feel sadness or fear, but hope. She snatched up her night robe, pulled on her boots and rushed down to the library, where she had remained ever since.

The library door creaked open. Iris didn't take her eyes off the book but she knew it was Thomas from his faltering footsteps. He cleared his throat to make his presence known, then dragged a chair over to the fireside and sat down opposite her.

'Why do you spend so much time here? You hate studying.'

'I have a need for it now,' she said, turning page after page.

'You have a need to learn *Historic Tales of the Non-Magical Folk*?' he said, lifting up the cover to read it. 'And… *The Myths and Mysteries of the Passage to the Land of the Banished*?' He looked confused as he put the second book back on the table. 'How is that useful?'

'There weren't any non-magical folk in the beginning. Did you know that?' Iris said, looking up from the book. 'Our ancestors stripped people of their magic and sent them off to die in the Dark Forest, just like father does. They had no food, no shelter or weapons and yet they made it all the way south to new lands. How? How did they survive?'

Thomas looked more perplexed now than he had when he asked the question. He shrugged and shook his head.

'Luck, I suppose.'

'No, not luck. They survived because there is a safe passage in the Dark Forest that leads to the Land of the Banished.'

'Iris, it's just a story—'

'No! It's true, I know it is. We could find it.'

'Find it? Have you gone mad? Mordarks roam the Dark Forest! And worse!'

'There is nothing worse than Mordarks,' Lucian said.

Thomas and Iris both started at the sound of his voice. He emerged from the shadows. The bookcase through which he had entered closed softly, concealing the secret doorway.

'I want to hear the rest of your story, Iris,' he said, smiling as he approached, his footsteps silent against the stone floor. He came up behind Thomas's chair and leant against it, watching her. His smile withered. 'You can't run from this marriage. You were born for the purpose of forging and maintaining alliances, all of you,' he said, gesturing Thomas as well.

Iris bit her lip and looked down at her book again.

'You are here to assist my rule and keep our family name strong. You cannot abandon your duty. So put the book away.'

When Lucian had gone, Iris sat back in her chair. She could taste blood in her mouth. Never fan the flame, her father had told her. But Lucian's burned regardless of what she said or didn't say.

'Do you remember when we were younger and we saw father banish that man and his family?' she said, staring into the fire.

'Yes,' Thomas said solemnly.

'Do you think they deserved it?' They sat in silence until, eventually, Thomas shook his head. 'Neither do I,' she said. 'And yet father still did it. And if he could do that, what might Lucian be capable of? He is the future of this family, which means there is no future. Lucian is no leader. He will destroy the family name with or without our help. Why should I stay? Why should I sacrifice my happiness, my life?'

'But you would risk your life searching for a mythical passage to a land that might not exist? Where is the sense in that?'

'The land exists. Merlin himself travelled there, many times,' she said, tapping the book of tales.

'*Many* times? And what of the Misty Veil? You must remember the poem - Master Hagworth made us recite it a thousand times at least! Is that not in your book?'

Iris remembered it well. All children knew the Poem of the Misty Veil, the magical border between the Dark Forest and the Land of the Banished, a border which, once crossed, could never be re-crossed. The poem told of countless tragedies – children who wandered through the veil, never to be seen again; lovers who, upon passing through its enchantment, lost all memory of their former lives and lived the rest of their days with empty hearts. The Misty Veil slipped between history and legend. Even Master Hagworth appeared to live in confusion about its existence. At times, he would denounce it as an old wives' tale and blame the "simple people" of Edgeton for fuelling the rumours; at others, he would talk of it in such a way that there could be no doubt it was real.

'It's only a poem,' Iris said, dismissing it.

'It's only a story,' said Thomas, nodding at the book. 'Why should that be true and the poem false? If Merlin did go, if anyone did, they did not return. So how will we ever know what stands on the other side? The myths you are looking at cannot be based on any real knowledge. They are made up stories for children.'

'Well, we shall see, shan't we? The Banished Ones left marks in the Dark Forest for exiles to follow. Help me look. If we can't find them, I will accept there is no path, no safe passage, no border, no lands south of the Dark Forest,' she said.

Thomas looked concerned. He leant forward in his chair and grasped her hands. 'Iris, this is your home. If the Dark Forest is the only way to get to where you want to go, you won't ever make it.'

But Iris believed she would. She had one year, time enough to find the passage. And, when she found it, she would follow it to The Misty Veil, she would cross the border, she would find the Banished Ones and be reborn into a world without Lucian. She smiled to herself at the thought.

'I'm going to bed,' Thomas said, looking solemn as he rose from his chair and walked away.

'Goodnight,' said Iris.

When he had disappeared through the doorway, she shook her head, pitying him.

'You'll see,' she whispered.

The castle was crawling with people the following day, as final preparations were made for the Vandemere visit. The Vandemere house colours were on display in every room and every corridor. Flowers, banners and tapestries were turned silver and black to welcome the family.

The dressmaker had created a purple gown for Iris and sewn a patch of silver and black cloth to the inside so that it rested over her heart. Iris resented it far less than she might have, now that she knew there wouldn't be a wedding. She would be far away from the realm before her sixteenth birthday. She had already begun to think about the note she would leave behind for her father and where she would hide it. The underside of the Witchwood chair seemed a good place. By the time he found it, she would probably have passed through The Misty Veil.

She descended the staircase to the entrance hall and went outside to wait in the courtyard. Thomas was already out there. She walked over to him, letting her new dress trail through the brown puddles. When she reached him, she smiled secretively. He blanched and leaned in towards her.

'What are you going to do?' he said.

'Nothing,' she said, still smiling.

'Iris!' called their father from the castle steps. 'Come and stand here,' he said, pointing to the space next to him. He, too, was wearing new garments. A rich purple cloak hung over his shoulders and pooled around his black boots. A Silver Tree had been stitched into the dark fabric of his tunic; the silver threads glinted as he turned to her. He looked very formal, and rather uncomfortable. She scowled and walked towards him.

As she climbed the steps, her mother emerged from the castle with Lucian, who sniggered when he saw her. He looked her up and down, slowly and deliberately, before moving to stand on the other side of their father. Iris gritted her teeth, reminding herself that she wouldn't have to endure any of them for much longer.

When the Vandemeres arrived, it was without spectacle. They rode in on horseback, Eric and his wife, Cecilly, at the front, followed by Gregory Vandemere and his younger brother, Edward, and their little sister, Angelina. They brought two servants with them, who rode alongside Angelina to keep her from falling off her horse.

Gregory was a serious-looking boy of Lucian's age, perhaps older. He dismounted quickly and approached them with his father, eyes fixed on Iris, who felt her cheeks burning and looked at the ground.

Eric Vandemere was short and stout, his hairline fast receding. He climbed the steps with the laboured breathing of a man who had spent too many years drinking and feasting. Gregory looked nothing like him; he was tall and dark-haired, like his mother and siblings. He strode up the stairs beside his father and they bowed and clasped Matthew's outstretched arm in turn. Then, while Eric exchanged pleasantries with Josephine, Gregory came to stand before Iris. He smelled of wood smoke, a result of many days on the road. She glanced up at him as he took her hand and kissed it firmly. His eyes stayed on hers.

'It is a pleasure to finally meet you, Iris,' he said.

Iris did not like her name on his lips. Something about Gregory and the way he looked at her made her feel ill-at-ease.

They dined in the Great Hall that evening. Iris was seated between Gregory and his brother Edward, whose tireless attempts to make her laugh with boyish humour left her irritated and exhausted. Edward was a buffoon. Gregory was only marginally more tolerable because he hardly spoke. But he stared. Longing, sideways stares that made her want to shrink into her own skin.

Lucian, Matthew and Eric Vandemere leaned in together to talk at the adjacent table. Lucian looked over at Iris and Gregory frequently throughout their conversation. This put Iris off her food. Something was brewing. Matthew was nodding. Eric and Lucian were smiling. Then Matthew clapped a hand on each of their backs and rose to his feet.

'I have an announcement!' he declared. The room fell silent. The knots in Iris's stomach began to twist. She caught Thomas's eye across the room; he looked troubled. 'My beautiful Iris and young Gregory here are due to marry next year in the spring. But, having met this fine, wise young man and seeing with my own eyes the connection he shares with my daughter, I have decided to bring the wedding forward. So, friends, guests, there will be a summer wedding. This year!' He picked up his goblet and raised it above his head. The room erupted with cheers. The musicians chimed in with their instruments, playing jolly songs and flitting about the room like dancing fairies.

Iris was deathly still. Toasts were made in her honour and men and women approached her table to offer their congratulations. Gregory shook their hands and clanged his goblet against theirs. But Iris made not a sound, moved not a muscle. And no one noticed.

She escaped the hall before the dancing commenced and climbed the stairs to the second floor. Her father was waiting for her behind a pillar at the top of the steps. She turned away as soon as she saw him but he rushed towards her and turned her back to face him.

'Iris! Iris, I have my reasons. I didn't want to do that back there. When you're old enough to understand, I'll explain why,' he said. He looked as though he had aged ten years in a day.

'If I'm not old enough to understand, I'm not old enough to marry,' she said, her eyes glistening with tears.

'Oh, Iris,' he said, pulling her close and resting his chin on her head. 'I'm sorry. It is a curse to rule.'

In the morning, as Iris made her way across the entrance hall towards the castle doors, she jumped with fright as Gregory came out of the shadows, where he had been lurking. He took her hand.

'I missed you last night. I had hoped we might dance. But perhaps it is best to save it for our wedding day,' he said, standing rather too close.

She noticed how slimy his bottom lip looked, and that there were stray, dark hairs between his eyebrows. And she thought suddenly of Alexander. He was more handsome than Gregory. He didn't repulse her. Her heart began to flutter as she thought of him.

'May I escort you to breakfast?' asked Gregory.

'Uh, no, I'm sorry. Would you tell my father I've gone back to bed? I'm feeling out of sorts,' she said, pulling her hand free. Gregory looked concerned. 'I didn't sleep well last night.'

'I will tell him. Rest, my sweet,' he said.

She listened as he went into the dining hall and announced that she would not be joining them for breakfast.

'Where is she?' said Lucian. He sounded suspicious.

Iris left the castle quickly.

∗

Alexander set out early that morning with Vrax and Tobias. Fabian had instructed them to walk through the Dark Forest to the Mortenstone border and report back on what they found.

'When you get close, split up. In case,' he had said. His parting words made for a tense journey. They were familiar with the forest, up to a point. Beyond that point, they knew not what traps the Mortenstones had laid. Fabian said they were evil and cunning, so the three of them would likely face a number of dangers.

Indeed, Alexander knew just how cunning they could be. Iris Mortenstone had tricked him, made him doubt himself and his family, with just a smile and pretend tears. He would never tell his brothers of his error, and he would not make it again. He tramped through the forest, setting his jaw against his anger. They were close now.

When they came to the Hang Man, a mighty oak with limbs that stretched low across the forest, Vrax held out his arm. They stopped and looked at each other. The Hang Man marked the furthest point any of them had ever ventured. An old, frayed noose dangled ominously from one of its branches. No bodies swung from it today, though several skulls littered the ground at the base of the trunk.

Alexander crouched and scanned the surroundings. Then, he picked up a stick and threw it as far as he could. It whistled through the air and landed with a dull thud. Nothing happened. Silence. Everything still.

Vrax looked at him and gave a small nod before lifting his leg to take a single step. Twigs snapped as his foot crunched down but no trap sprang.

They pushed on.

*

Thomas watched Iris steal away down Stone Lane from the window of his bedchamber. He had been afraid this would happen and hoping all night that it wouldn't. He didn't want to get her into trouble, but if it would save her life – for she would surely die in the Dark Forest – he had no choice but to tell their father.

As he prepared to leave, he noticed something in the corner of his vision that made him return to the window. Lucian was skulking off down the lane. Telling on Iris was one thing, but getting Lucian into trouble was a different matter, for he would never forget it, and he would have his revenge. Thomas's heart sank as he realised he could not go to his father. He would have to face the problem on his own.

He left his chamber for the place he had promised never to go, dreading what he would find there.

*

Iris tried to think like an exile. If she had been stripped of magic and forced into the Dark Forest with nothing but the clothes on her back, how would she leave behind a mark? She walked a little way, keeping the

Grassland in sight, and circled every tree she passed several times, inspecting it for clues. She grew frustrated when she couldn't remember which she had checked and which she hadn't. But her irritation quickly subsided when she heard footsteps nearby, slow and cautious. She froze, listening. The footsteps stopped.

Suddenly, a hand came down over her mouth. She screamed, but the sound was stifled. Alexander hauled her back against a tree, his hand pressed tight against her lips.

'I know who you are,' he whispered into her ear.

She tried to pry his hand away but he was too strong. It took all the effort she could muster to open her mouth wide enough to bite him. He released her instantly, cursing, calling her foul names.

She staggered away, but he came after her again, grabbing her by the waist and swinging her into a tree. She smacked against the trunk with a winded gasp. Alexander pulled her round to face him and held a cold knife to her throat.

'If you scream…'

'You wouldn't!' she said. Alexander pushed the knife into her throat, but when she began to choke he quickly pulled the blade back.

Iris looked into his eyes. She could see anger in them, hatred even, and something else… And it was that something that made her sure he would not harm her. Heart pounding, knees trembling, she seized his face and kissed him. He tensed up at once. But then he dropped the knife, pulled her into an embrace and kissed her back.

'Mordark scum!' came a shrill cry.

Iris drew back. When she saw Lucian running towards them with a dagger in hand, she screamed. His face was puce with fury. His eyes blazed. Alexander spun around and shoved her out of the way as Lucian lunged with the knife. Alexander ducked. Lucian drove the blade deep into the decaying bark of the tree behind him. The knife remained lodged in the bark and, while he struggled to pull it free, Alexander fumbled for his own knife in the dirt. Grasping it, he stood and kicked Lucian hard in the stomach, knocking him to the ground. Then he threw himself down on top of him and prepared to plunge his knife into Lucian's chest.

'Gut him! GUT HIM!' Vrax shouted, rushing out of the shadows.

'No!' Iris shrieked, crawling across the ground and grasping Alexander's shoulder. As he tried to shake her off, Lucian surged up and headbutted him and he fell backwards onto her.

Tobias appeared then, reaching them at the same time as Vrax. Together, they dragged Lucian to his feet and held on to his arms.

'Mordark scum!' Lucian shouted, writhing in their grasp as Alexander stumbled towards him with his knife.

'No! Stop! He's my brother! He's my brother! Please!' Iris screamed.

Suddenly, Thomas came hurtling out of the darkness and collided with Tobias. Both of them went crashing down to the ground.

Lucian punched Vrax in the side of the head, sending him sprawling.

'Run, Lucian!' Iris shouted. He took off without looking back.

Thomas scrambled to his feet. Tobias reached out to grab his ankle but Iris stamped on his hand.

'Iris!' Thomas cried as he, too, started to run.

She hurried after him, towards the Grassland, while Alexander and his brothers retreated.

7. THE DEAD SPELL

'MORDARKS! MORDARKS!' Lucian cried from the end of Stone Lane. 'Raise the alarm! Mordarks! Mordarks at the border!' he shouted, waving his arms at the guards in the tower.

The lane began to fill as people emerged from shops and side streets, drawn to the noise. Heads ducked out from under market stall canopies, and out of windows in the houses along the lane. The townsfolk stared at Lucian in bemusement. But when the bells of Mortenstone Castle started to ring, the confusion turned to panic. People began to scream as the name spread through the crowd.

Lucian ran for the castle, shouting as he went. 'Mordarks! Mordarks!'

Suddenly, he found himself caught up in a wave of frenzied townsfolk, all pressing towards the castle. He fought his way through, kicking, elbowing people aside, grabbing them by the hair to pull himself forwards. As he came to the front of the throng, he saw a troop of armed guards ahead, pouring out from the castle gates. Matthew Mortenstone was with them. When Lucian saw him in the distance, he pointed in the direction of the forest.

'Mordarks! I told you they'd come! I TOLD YOU!' he shrieked.

Matthew looked at him, seeming not to recognise him, but then his blue eyes widened. The moment stretched on. Lucian stared back at him, running as fast as he could, hearing only the rumble of feet, seeing only his father's eyes, growing wider, wider as the bells rang and the people came barrelling towards him. But it could only have lasted half a heartbeat. And then the crowd engulfed Lucian and his father disappeared from view.

*

Matthew and his men battled to create a pathway through the terrified townsfolk. They finally broke free at the end of Stone Lane. And that's when he saw them, running desperately across the Grassland. Iris and Thomas. He almost fell to his knees. What were they doing here? What had happened? The bells were ringing furiously. He ran towards his children, his panic rising with each toll.

'Are you hurt?' he said, grasping them and feverishly checking for any sign of injury.

'No,' Iris panted. Her face was as white as death.

The guards ran on towards the Dark Forest, drawing their swords. There was no time to waste, no time to fret.

'Get back to the castle!' Matthew said, pushing them both away from him and turning for the forest.

His silver breastplate rattled as he ran. His boots thumped against the hard ground. Blood thundered in his ears. He could see his men ahead, slowing before the border, lifting their shields. He ran through them with his hand raised, ordering them to stop. Then, he looked back over both shoulders. They were all staring past him, peering over their shields into the shadows, fear in their eyes. Pressing a finger to his lips, he signalled for them to advance. As he took the first step, an icy wind hissed through the trees. He held his nerve and resisted a shudder.

They slipped into silence, beyond the reach of the bells and the sounds of the city, the shouting, the screams, the panic. They moved through the darkness, seventy men as cautious as deer. When a twig snapped, they stopped and surveyed their surroundings, until Matthew waved them on.

The further they ventured, the more ragged their breathing became, the fiercer their hearts began to beat. Moving deeper. Consumed by shadows.

The city was in chaos that afternoon as townspeople demanded answers, exchanged stories and watched the guards moving back and forth between the castle and the border.

Matthew had returned from the forest. He stood on a platform in the middle of the square, trying to calm people with words of reassurance. But his voice was inaudible over the cacophony of questions, wails and prayers to the White Witch. Eventually, he gave up on soothing them.

'Silence!' he shouted. The crowd fell quiet at once. 'Do your memories fail you? You have no reason to fear. Merlin's spell protects us. Mordarks cannot cross into our lands, unless they wish to live out their days here slithering in the grass. You are not in danger!' he said, looking around at them all. 'The ancient spell of Merlin the Good remains strong!'

'But why are they at the border?' murmured an old, blind woman.

'They are not at the border! We have searched and found nothing but simple thieves, mistaken for Mordarks. You are all safe.'

'But what if…?' someone began to say, before abandoning their question.

'What if?' Matthew said, searching for the one who had spoken. 'What if we see a vile snake slipping through the grass?' he said, stepping down off the platform, his eyes flashing excitedly. 'Then we will rip out its guts and tear off its head!'

He left the square to an explosion of bloodthirsty cheers, his head held high, his face unflinching. But his façade disintegrated the moment he entered he castle.

'Where are the children?' he said angrily. When they materialised before him on the staircase, he flinched. 'What have I told you about just appearing out of nowhere? It's the height of bad manners! Don't do it again! Now, come with me!'

They went with him to the Great Hall, followed by six council members and a dozen guards.

*

Iris was badly shaken. Every time she shut her eyes, she saw them, restraining Lucian while Alexander staggered towards him with the knife. The memory of her helplessness stung her like venom. They would have murdered him. And all because of her. She had very nearly led her brother to his death.

Josephine was waiting for them in the hall. For the first time in her life, Iris saw that her mother was nervous. She wrung her hands over and over again until the doors closed. Then, she rushed to Lucian.

'Was it them? How many? How can you be sure?' she said, grasping his arms. 'What were you doing there?'

Lucian looked at Iris and her stomach dropped. He had seen her with Alexander. But, strangely, he said nothing. His whole body was trembling.

'It was them,' Matthew said, pacing over to the round table and sitting down heavily. 'The Mordark brothers. We caught up to them in the forest, not far from the border. I had an altercation with one, but he got away. There's no mistaking those eyes, though.' He looked at his children then. 'I don't want to know what the three of you were doing in the Dark Forest, but you will not go there again. Do you understand?'

'Yes, father,' they mumbled.

'Please go. All of you. I want to speak with Saskian alone.'

Iris felt a fresh swell of panic as she left the Great Hall. Which brother had her father fought? Was it Alexander? Had he hurt him? She slipped behind a pillar as the others walked away, crossed her hands over her chest and thought of the hidden passageway, picturing it clearly in her mind. When she opened her eyes, she was standing in darkness. She stumbled forwards, running her hands along the walls of the narrow passage, towards the door at the end. She opened it a sliver, enough to hear.

'…Is there another spell that can be cast?' Saskian spoke in a low, hushed tone. His words drifted into the passage, a dying echo. Iris pushed the door open a little further.

'It was a big spell. Some say it was the spell that killed him. It took all he had. I don't know if I have enough in me,' said Matthew.

'But, Matthew, you are Merlin's direct descendant. His power flows through you.'

'Some of it, yes.' There was a pause. 'I'm not as powerful as he was.'

'Then…what will we do?'

'I'm not sure. I don't know how much time we have. At the moment, they have no reason to believe the spell is broken. But those Mordark boys were close today, too close.' Matthew sounded agitated. 'It's as if they sense it. They're circling in, waiting for us to grow weak before they strike. Without that spell, they will come. Without it, we can't stop them.'

'And we can't ignore the disappearances,' said Saskian. 'The numbers have been rising steadily for months now. It begs the question, are they interrogating them? Recruiting them?'

'I don't know.' Matthew's voice was muffled as he covered his face with his hand. 'But Iris's marriage to the Vandemere boy couldn't have come at a better time. I'll need a large army.' He sighed and there was a long silence. Finally, he said, 'Tell Wingworth to recall the guards. I don't want them stationed at the border—'

'But, my Lord!'

'It will look suspicious. We must carry on as normal.'

'Very well,' said Saskian. 'But there is only so much longer we can go on pretending. The forest is dying, Matthew. And, I can assure you, it will fall.'

8. THE PROPHECY

Alexander and his brothers stood before Fabian. None of them dared meet his eye. Tobias's nose was broken and his face was covered in dirt and dried blood. Vrax was bleeding from his ear and Alexander's eye was blackened from his clash with Matthew Mortenstone.

Fabian observed them in silence from his chair. The longer the silence went on, the more uncomfortable Alexander became. Fabian tore off a hangnail with his teeth and spat it to the ground. Then, he looked up to the ceiling as if searching for the words he wanted to say. Suddenly, he smiled.

'Tell me everything,' he said.

'We got as far as the border. No traps have been laid,' said Vrax.

'No traps? Oh,' said Fabian, looking surprised. 'Then how did you come to be so bloody?' This time, when he smiled, it looked as if it pained him. 'Do tell,' he said, nodding eagerly. Too eagerly.

Vrax glanced at Alexander and cleared his throat. 'We came across the Mortenstones.'

Fabian looked up at the ceiling again. The corners of his mouth quivered.

'Three of them, in the forest,' Vrax continued. 'Two boys and a girl…and then Matthew Mortenstone and his men.'

Fabian curled his fists around the spikes on his chair. 'Did they know who you were?' he said, still gazing up.

'Yes,' said Vrax.

'And who did that to your face? The guards? Or the Mortenstone children?'

Vrax didn't answer.

'*HOW* could you let them do this to you?' Fabian shouted, lurching from his seat, the veins in his neck bulging. 'You come to me, drenched in your own blood, meek as mice! I raised wolves!' he bellowed, beating his fist against Vrax's chest. 'I sent you to spy, to bring back information.' He pointed a long, pale finger at Alexander. 'I did not send you to attack the Mortenstones, to make yourselves known, to bring war to our doorstep when we aren't ready for it! You've exposed our intentions! You've exposed our weakness! Get out of my sight, or I'll throw you all into the Worgrim pit and be done with it!'

From the corridor outside the hall, they heard Fabian shriek with rage.

'Do you think they'll come?' Vrax said.

Alexander shook his head. 'No.'

Tobias grabbed a tuft of his own hair and pulled it, pacing up and down. 'We aren't prepared,' he said anxiously. 'If they do come…'

'It won't be our fault. Father sent us. He knew the risks,' Alexander said.

'It doesn't matter whose fault it is. If they come, we're all dead,' said Vrax.

Alexander didn't care if they did invade. He didn't care if they tore down the castle, if they killed his father, even. Whatever happened, whether he died tomorrow or lived for another ten years, one thing was certain - he would never see Iris again. She would never return to the Dark Forest now. It was all over, whatever it had been. And that thought made his heart unbearably heavy.

When he arrived at Agatha's house that evening, he slumped against the wall, not bothering to knock. Agatha opened the door at once, stepped outside with her hands on her hips and then sighed loudly and went back into the house. She returned with a wet cloth moments later. William followed, carrying a bowl of water.

'What happened this time?' she said, bending to wipe the blood from his chin.

'Father sent us to the border this morning and we were seen.'

'Who did this to you?'

'Matthew Mortenstone.'

Agatha stopped mid-dab and lowered the cloth. 'Matthew Mortenstone? He came into the forest?' she said, looking around uneasily. Alexander nodded. Agatha dropped the cloth into the bowl and stared up at the trees. 'Why would he do that?'

'I don't know,' said Alexander.

'Hmm.' She seemed distracted. Alexander watched her closely. 'Do you feel it?' she said, turning to look over her shoulder.

'Feel what?'

'There's a change coming, boy. The birds are unsettled. The rabbits stay in their burrows in spring. The forest knows.' Agatha looked around suspiciously. 'Mortenstones in the Dark Forest…' she went on, shaking her head.

'It won't happen again. She won't come anymore, not after this morning.'

'But her father might,' Agatha said. 'Mortenstone filth.' She spat at the ground. 'He's the one to worry about. He could march through this forest with five thousand men.'

'He could… But why would he? There's nothing to gain on the other side.'

'Maybe so,' she said. 'But if it's revenge he's after, then there's everything to gain.'

After a long silence, Agatha sighed and got to her feet, using the doorframe to steady herself.

'It's getting dark now, boy.'

'I'll stay here a while,' Alexander said, resting his head against the wall.

'There's still a bed for you here if you want it,' she said, steering William back into the house and closing the door.

Alexander listened to them climb the rickety staircase. He heard the bed creak as William climbed into it, and Agatha's low, gravelly voice as she told him a bedtime story. When she left William's room and went to her own, Alexander felt the house grumble with each heavy step across the floorboards.

When all was quiet again, he looked out into the gathering darkness. The Silver Tree on the other side of the path groaned in the wind. Its aged branches looked tired, its bark duller than it had once been. He stared at it for a moment and then closed his eyes and drifted to sleep.

*

Iris was woken early in the morning by her father.

'Put on your cloak. Your lesson is outside today, in the Wild Garden.' He spoke gruffly and she could tell by the look on his face that he was still furious about what had happened the previous day.

'Father–'

'Be quick about it. Master Hagworth is waiting for you in the entrance hall,' he said, turning and leaving the room.

Iris could hear the commotion in the streets below from her window, as guards marched back and forth between the castle and the Grassland and townspeople grew as agitated as they had done the day before.

Suddenly, her father came striding back into the room. He looked at her sternly and then lowered his gaze.

'I am very disappointed in you,' he said. 'Your brothers almost died trying to save you yesterday. And I almost lost three children. I hope you didn't do it to punish me. I deserve a lot of things, Iris, but not that.' He paused, shaking his head. Iris felt too ashamed to look at him. 'I know you won't disappoint me again,' he said, finally. And with that, he quietly walked out of the room, leaving her to wallow in her guilt. The fire crackled and spat in the hearth, but its warmth did not reach her.

Down in the entrance hall, Master Hagworth stood with his hands clasped together behind his back, an impatient look on his face. He was wearing a bulky black cloak and long, mud-spattered travelling boots. Lucian, Eve and Thomas were waiting beside him in their deep-purple hunting cloaks. Lucian looked at Iris sourly as she came down the stairs.

'At last!' Master Hagworth said with a hint of annoyance. 'Hurry, Iris, we've a walk yet to the Wild Garden – and this lesson *will* begin on the hour.' He stared at her over his hooked nose reproachfully as she came to a standstill in front of him. Iris tried to look apologetic, but with Lucian in her periphery, eyes glistening with hatred, all she could do was grit her teeth and force her lips into a hard line.

The Wild Garden stood on the edge of the castle grounds. To get to it, they walked for a mile through neat lawns filled with flowers and old stone statues, across a curved bridge, which hung over a vast, steaming natural pool, and through a small woodland.

As soon as they passed out of the woodland, Master Hagworth began to root around in the inside pocket of his cloak. There was a jangling sound and then he pulled out a set of ancient keys. He selected the longest, largest key and held onto it firmly. Up ahead, Iris could just make out the entrance to the Wild Garden. The wall seemed like a great, ominous shadow in the fog that enveloped it. She could see the barred gate but nothing beyond, except whiteness.

The Wild Garden was a place over which two winds met; the warm wind from the west and the icy east wind that blew in from the Dark Lands. And so the garden was shrouded in a thick, eternal fog.

Master Hagworth stuck the key into the keyhole and jiggled it until it unlocked with a loud *click*. Then he planted his feet and pushed the gate open with a huff of exertion.

'Come on,' he said, ushering all four of them inside and closing the gate again.

The cold bit through Iris's heavy cloak and she shivered. It had been years since she had set foot in the Wild Garden; she had forgotten how the cold here chilled even the blood. In the castle, adding logs to the fire could take the edge off a draft. Here, the cold was different. Here, even a thousand furs would not keep the bones from shuddering.

The cloud of fog that hung over the garden was descending slowly, curling around the trees and hugging the uneven ground. Master Hagworth marched forwards, leading them down a bumpy slope, made perilous by the wet grass and stones that came loose from the earth and fell away at the lightest touch. Lucian cursed furiously under his breath every time he slipped or stumbled.

'Why are we here?' he protested angrily after he'd fallen for the sixth time. His cloak was filthy, his hands red from clutching sharp rocks every time he lost his footing.

'Quiet!' Master Hagworth said. But, not long after, when they had descended the slope, he stopped and turned to face them. 'We have exactly one hour of good visibility, so let us begin.' They looked at him as if he had gone mad; the Silver Tree, standing less than ten feet away, was but a shapeless, murky shadow. 'Today, you are going to learn about the music of trees,' Master Hagworth continued. 'And who better to teach you than—'

Eve cried out as a man materialised in front of them. He was tall and slender with short, curly black hair and lively purple eyes. His face twitched slightly when he blinked – and he blinked so frequently, it was all Iris could pay attention to. His ears were large and pointed and his head snapped this way and that as he angled the ears towards the many different noises that came to them in the Wild Garden. Iris found herself imitating the elf. Tilting her head to one side, she listened to the whistling of the wind and the distant caw of a crow. The elf's bright eyes darted between them all. He smiled a wide smile, bearing small, white teeth, and gave a bow. Master Hagworth looked at him disapprovingly.

'Bink,' the elf said, in a voice as soft as his young face. 'I am Bink.'

'Yes, yes,' Master Hagworth said irritably. 'As I was saying, elves have an ear for music, so, naturally, they make rather good music teachers,' he said. 'Your father believes you will take a lot of useful information away from this lesson. Music was, after all, one of Merlin's great loves and this garden his place of refuge. Soak it in. It is just as much a lesson in history. I shall leave them in your hands, Bink,' he said, nodding to the elf. 'If you need me, I shall be over there by the Silver Tree.'

When Master Hagworth left them, Bink's eyes narrowed and he regarded each of them carefully.

'Close your eyes. Tell me what you hear,' he said.

They closed their eyes.

'Wind?' Thomas said.

'Wind. Yes,' said Bink. 'What else?'

'Birds,' said Iris. Bink concurred and then fell quiet again. Iris opened her eyes. The elf was staring at her expectantly. She glanced at her siblings. Thomas and Eve had their eyes closed still; their faces were scrunched up as they strained to hear. Lucian was looking at Bink sullenly and shrugging, in no mood to continue the task. Then, he frowned, at the same time Iris heard something…else.

Bink looked from one to the other excitedly.

'Yes?' he said.

'There's a…creaking sound,' Iris said. It was distant, but it was there. A deep groan, like an arrow being stretched taut against a bow, and then silence. She had heard the sound before. Bink nodded slowly, looking pleased.

'Yes, Iris. That is tree music.'

'Tree music?' Lucian said incredulously. 'That's not music. It's nothing but groaning.'

'Maybe to you. I think it's beautiful.,' Bink said. Lucian stared at him with distaste. 'Every tree has a story, you see. When they sing, they are telling us that story. You have not yet learned to interpret their language. Where you hear creaking, I hear much, much more. Although, I must say, it is a little easier for us elves. We are born with the understanding. But it is possible to learn. Merlin learned. Your grandfather, Rambulus, learned. I taught him, in fact.'

'You?' Iris exclaimed. 'But you're…'

Bink smiled.

'Too young?' he offered. 'I am ninety-six years old, which is young for an elf, but old to you, I should think.'

Iris gawked at him. Her father's advisor, Saskian, was an elf, but he looked old and withered. She couldn't begin to imagine how old *he* might be.

Bink looked surprised. 'You did not know this about elves?' he said.

'*I* did,' Lucian said. 'Iris never listens. We've had countless lessons on elves with Master Hagworth.'

Iris blushed. She vaguely remembered a lesson on elves. She had been more interested in the pictures.

'Well,' continued Bink, 'now you know, Lady Iris. Now, where were we? Ah, yes, trees!' Lucian rolled his eyes. Bink saw this and turned to look at him. 'Merlin the Good valued their voices. You've all heard of his prophecy, of course. But did you know it came to him through a Silver Tree?' The bored look on Lucian's face melted away. 'Oh yes,' said Bink. 'Follow me!' Suddenly, he disappeared.

'Where did he go?' Thomas said, as they stared around in the fog.

'Here!' came Bink's voice. 'Over here!' He was standing beside the Silver Tree Master Hagworth had retreated to. 'It was just like this one!' Bink said as they approached, running his hand over the shimmering silver bark.

'But not this one?' Iris asked.

'No, not this exact tree. The tree that spoke to Merlin was in Mortenstone Valley, near his home, I believe. Legend tells he had been dreaming about this tree for years and years. And then, one day, he found it.

And when he touched it…' Bink clutched the tree with both hands and gasped, his eyes widening. They all watched him, enraptured.

'Enough with this nonsense!' Master Hagworth snapped, rushing out of the fog.

'What did he see?' said Eve, ignoring the schoolmaster.

'The White Witch!' Bink said in a voice just above a whisper. 'And the War of Light and Darkness.'

'Stop this at once!' Master Hagworth shouted. 'You are here to teach them about tree music, not to fill their heads with silly stories.'

'They aren't stories. The White Witch *is* coming. Father believes it,' Iris said, as though that settled everything.

'No man, not even a powerful wizard like your great ancestor, can foretell the future. We place far too much faith in old tales,' said Master Hagworth. 'We are going back to the castle.'

'But we haven't—' Iris began, but Master Hagworth cut her off.

'Your teacher has chosen not to teach you, so it falls to me to fill your heads with facts. This lesson will continue in the schoolroom. Good day, *Bink*,' he said scornfully.

As he marched them away, Iris looked over her shoulder apologetically. Bink smiled faintly through his disappointment, before he vanished into the fog.

As Iris stumbled back up the slope, she heard the loud groan of a tree and, somewhere further away, another tree answering its call.

Master Hagworth's foul mood did not dissipate back at the castle and they spent the remainder of the lesson reading silently from books. When they were finished, he snapped his tome shut, sending dust scattering in all directions, and disappeared without a word.

'What's wrong with him?' Thomas asked.

'I don't know,' said Iris distractedly as she rose from her seat. Throughout the lesson, while Master Hagworth had sighed and huffed, she thought about Alexander. She had kissed him. He had kissed her back and, for a moment, she felt as light as a cloud. Happy and free and full. And then it had all come crashing down. Lucian had followed her. Of course he had followed. She should have known he would. But, even now, as he glared at her across the schoolroom, she knew he could not have seen everything. If he had, she felt sure he would have told their mother.

That afternoon, she watched from the castle steps as Lucian and Thomas rode out of the courtyard with the Vandemeres and a pack of hunting dogs, bound for the Wild Wood, in search of a stag to butcher and boast about at dinner. Normally, she would have resented being left behind while they went off on an adventure. But, today, their departure brought her nothing but relief.

She went to the library and pulled a book of old legends from the bookcase, ready to brandish if anyone stopped her and asked what she was doing. But no one questioned her on her way out of the castle, nor did they notice her on Stone Lane, which was more crowded than usual. She overheard a baker telling a group of people that the guards had been marching to the border every hour to run checks; one of them had barged past him, knocking him to the ground without a word of apology.

She stopped at the end of the lane and looked across the Grassland, scanning the border. Then she smiled to herself. There wasn't a guard in sight.

Alexander was splitting logs outside Agatha's house. Every time he swung the axe, he pictured Matthew Mortenstone's face and sliced each log clean in half. His eye was swollen and bruised and there was a deep gash above his brow. Beads of sweat trickled down his forehead, burning the wound. As he stopped to wipe his face with his sleeve, he heard a rustling sound further down the path. He fumbled for the axe. It was stuck firmly in the chopping post. More rustling, louder now. Something was out there, moving closer. He tugged and tugged. Just as he wrenched it out, Iris emerged from behind a tree and came onto the track, tipping her hood back. The knots in his stomach eased. He lowered the axe.

'Sulking?' she said when she reached him. She leaned in to look at his eye and winced. He turned his face away. 'I'm sorry,' she said softly. 'For what he did to you.'

'It's not your fault,' he said to his shoulder. He could feel her staring at him. He moved back to the chopping post, placed a log on it and brought the axe down. Iris jumped back as the wood splintered.

'Ouch,' she said suddenly. Alexander looked up and saw her spinning around to look at the Silver Tree.

'What?' he said, tossing the axe aside.

'Something just… What is that?' she said, running her hand over a contraption protruding from the silver bark. When he saw what it was, he laughed.

'That's the secret to Agatha's youth,' he said, gesturing the wooden funnel that was sticking out of the tree trunk like a short, bony finger. 'She fashioned it herself. She bleeds the tree and drinks the fluid. You lift this little trap,' he said, sliding up a thin, smooth rectangular segment of wood. For a moment, nothing happened. And then out began to trickle a pale, silvery liquid. 'Try it,' he said. Iris looked unsure. 'I used to drink it all the time. Just don't let her catch you. She doesn't like sharing it.' Iris glanced uncertainly at the house. Alexander cupped his hands beneath the funnel and watched them fill with the strange water. Then he drank it in three gulps. It was oddly sweet and refreshing. It had been years since he had enjoyed this drink, and now he remembered why he had gone to such pains to sneak it when Agatha wasn't looking. 'It's good,' he said.

Iris looked at the house again and then cupped her hands and collected the liquid in them. As she began to drink, there was a sudden squeaking sound as Agatha's front door opened. Iris jumped away from the tree and quickly wiped her mouth. But it was only William. The boy closed the door carefully behind him, took a few steps towards them and then stopped. He stared at them inquisitively, until Alexander, pitying him, finally said, 'Come on then, William. You're strong. You can help me carry these logs in for the fire.'

William looked pleased to be included and marched dutifully towards the pile of wood, arms swinging at his sides.

Iris waited outside while they transported the firewood into the house. She seemed wary of Agatha and asked Alexander not to tell her she was there. He found this odd; she was brave enough to wander through the Dark Forest alone, but too terrified to face an old woman.

Agatha was snoozing in her chair by the fire, an empty wooden cup sitting in her lap. On the mantelpiece stood a half-empty bottle of the same silver liquid he and Iris had just extracted from the tree. Alexander smiled to himself.

When he stepped back outside, it was almost dark. Iris was sitting in the dirt, leaning against the Silver Tree. She seemed sad. Her lips were turned down at the corners. He felt a pang of sorrow then, looking at her. His throat ached. He wanted to put his arms around her. But he also wanted to throttle her. She was one of them. She could never be his. They would always be enemies. He traipsed over to the tree and sat down next to her. His arm tingled where it touched hers. It wasn't fair. He banged his head against the tree in frustration.

'Why? Why do you have to be a Mortenstone?' he said. Iris looked startled. She stared at him, wide-eyed, and then turned her head away and sniffed.

'I won't be for much longer,' she murmured.

'What do you mean?'

'I'm going to marry Gregory Vandemere of the Low Lands,' she said.

'You can't!' he snapped, a burning anger rising in him as he imagined another man's hands on her. No. If he couldn't have her, no one else could either. 'Don't marry him!'

'I don't want to. I have to,' she said. 'The wedding is in the summer. By next summer, I'll probably be a mother.'

'No!' he shouted, pulling her around to face him. He shook her. 'No,' he said again. Her eyes brimmed with tears. He felt something blocking his throat and tried to swallow it down. His eyes stung as he stared at her. Iris was his. She belonged to him. He leaned in and pressed his lips to hers. Her tears wet his cheeks, trickling down them as if they were his own.

'Come inside,' he said, brushing his fingers against her neck. 'Agatha will have gone to bed.'

'Alright,' Iris whispered, her breath hot in his ear. Alexander stood up and pulled her with him. She held onto him so tightly, he gave her a small nudge of reassurance and brought her hand up to kiss it. Then he led her across the path and into the house, closing the door quietly behind them.

Outside, not a breath of wind stirred the air. But, in the still quiet, on the edge of the path, the Silver Tree began to sing.

9. A MOTHER'S BLOOD

Iris awoke before first light when the floorboards above started to creak. She shook Alexander.

'I have to go,' she hissed, springing from the bed and pulling her boots on.

'It's fine. It's only Agatha,' he mumbled, rolling onto his back and rubbing his eyes. Iris fastened her cloak, picked up the blanket that had fallen to the floor at threw it at him. Then she opened the door and peered into the sitting room. It was dark. The floorboards above had fallen silent. She waited, staring into the room for any sign of movement. When she was sure no one was there, she looked at the front door, outlined by the faint morning light that seeped in through the gaps around the frame. As she prepared to run for it, a hand seized her shoulder. She gasped.

'What are you doing?' she said, turning back to Alexander, who was standing behind her, grinning.

'I'm going with you,' he said.

'Be quiet then!'

They tiptoed across the living room. When Alexander knocked into one of the wooden chairs, she gave him a murderous look. She had only opened the front door a fraction when it began to squeak. She didn't dare open it any further and squeezed through the small gap, signalling for Alexander to do the same.

When they were outside, she darted away along the track until Agatha's house was out of sight. Alexander ambled on after her.

'I have to get back!' she called, stopping to catch her breath. Alexander continued towards her slowly.

'Iris—' he said.

'It's morning already! If the servants come and my bed is empty…' she said, feeling dizzy at the thought.

'Fine, go,' he said when he reached her. Iris scowled at him and he broke into a smile and kissed her on the forehead. 'Here, I want you to have this,' he said, slipping his hand into his pocket and pulling out a smooth blue stone. 'I always carry it with me. It matches your eyes.' He handed the stone to her. She took it and held it tightly.

'Thank you.'

'When will I see you again?'

'I don't know,' she said anxiously, backing away from him. 'Soon. I need to go!' And with that, she hurried off into the forest and became lost amongst the trees.

When she came to the border, she stopped and looked out across the Grassland. The castle was but a shadow on the hill, turrets, sharp as needles, poking holes in the night's sky, letting daylight bleed out.

Stone Lane was slowly waking from its slumber. She could see movement in the fading darkness - a white market stall canopy, flapping in the wind; a cart horse dragging supplies down towards the Snake's Head Inn; a woman, leaning out of an upstairs window to beat a rug against the wall, and… a man? Her stomach clenched tight. Was it a trick of the shadows, or was there truly someone standing at the end of the lane, watching her? She stepped back behind a tree, her heart pounding. If there was someone there, they would report to her father before she made it halfway across the Grassland. And, if there wasn't, and she walked through Stone Lane unnoticed, how did she ever hope to get past the guards at the gate without raising suspicion? How would she answer them, when they asked her where she had been? How could she stop them from telling her father, their Lord? No, it couldn't be done. Time was running out. Any moment now, the maids would come into her bedchamber to light the fire. There was only one way. She had no choice. Nervously, she moved out of the forest, crossed her arms over her chest and thought of her bed.

She felt a touch of wind and opened her eyes. She was standing in her bedchamber. It was dim; the fire had not yet been lit. She had never travelled this far before with magic. A small part of her had thought she wouldn't be able to. But she had done it. It had worked. She sighed with relief. But, as she did, she felt suddenly strange. Her head began to throb, the pain starting behind her eyes and moving back like a wave beneath her skull. Her body ached as if a lump of stone had been tied to every muscle, every bone and tendon. Blood coursed her veins like poison, burning, itching, stinging. And heavy. Her blood felt heavy, thick. It oozed through her body, weighing her down. Her fingertips bulged with it. She tried to unfasten her cloak. Her hands worked lethargically. The cloak finally fell to the ground with a *flumpfh*. She crawled onto the bed and retched but there was nothing in her belly to vomit. She didn't have the energy to pull back the covers, so she lay there, willing the dreadful feeling away.

*

Matthew was sitting in the courtyard with Eve. It was a pleasant morning. The sun was up, warming the back of his head as he listened to the familiar clinking of the blacksmith's hammer and the nearby clopping of hooves. He looked at Eve, perched quietly on a milk stool, staring at her thumbs. Her Companion lurked in the doorway of the servants' quarters, watching her mindfully.

Matthew made a clicking sound with his tongue to get his daughter's attention. When she looked at him, he held out his hand. In his palm was a white feather.

'See?' he said. She nodded, her eyes fixed on the feather. He pinched it between his thumb and forefinger and gave a fast, sharp blow. The feather vanished. He opened up his hands and looked all around in astonishment, lifting each foot, leaning down to search for it beneath his stool. Eve laughed and clapped her hands together softly.

Suddenly, a maid came skittering out of the castle, her skirts bunched in her fists.

'My Lord Mortenstone, come quick!' she exclaimed, bounding down the steps towards him. Two stable boys paused in their duties to watch. 'It's Lady Iris! She's terribly unwell. She's… she's… You must come!'

'Send for the physician,' Matthew shouted, charging past the maid up the steps and into the castle.

He burst into Iris's bedchamber and felt cold all over the moment he saw her, lying there on the bed, her face pale and waxy.

'Iris,' he said, moving to her bedside to place a hand on her head. It was warm. There was no fever. 'What is it?' he said, falling to his knees. 'What's the matter?'

Iris's eyes drifted lazily to his. She stared at him blankly for a moment and then her lids closed. He pressed his fingers to her neck to feel for a pulse. Her heartbeat was strong. Her breathing was deep and steady.

The physician entered the chamber moments later. He was a round man, whose vast stomach put the buttons on his waistcoat under significant strain. He paused when he saw Matthew. Then he remembered himself and bowed. The bald patch on his head gleamed in the firelight.

'My Lord Mortenstone,' he said.

Matthew stood and stepped aside. The physician passed him and moved to the foot of the bed, breathing heavily. He set down a large case, opened it and pulled out a thick pair of spectacles, propping them on his nose. Then, he lifted out a bulbous silver pendulum and moved around the side of the bed to dangle it over Iris. The pendulum began to swing in circles above her body, slowly at first and then with furious speed. He held it there a moment longer before snatching it up and putting it back in his case. 'Hmmm,' he said, tapping his lips with a plump finger. 'She's suffering from exhaustion. The girl used magic to transport herself a substantial distance.'

'Then she'll be well again soon?' said Matthew.

'Only time will tell, my Lord,' said the physician. 'The further she travelled, the longer her sickness will last. I advise that she travel shorter distances in the future, until she is strong enough, experienced enough, to go further,' he said, closing his case. 'Ensure that she rests and drinks plenty of water,' he said. Then he bowed again and departed.

Seven days passed and Iris's condition did not improve. Matthew tried to find out where she had been but it was impossible. In her waking hours, she was too weary to speak, and when she did try, her words were slurred and incomprehensible. That did not stop Josephine from voicing her suspicions, however, and she this did at every opportunity.

'The Dark Forest, that's where she's been, the wretch,' she would hiss.

But Matthew refused to hear it. Iris had promised him she wouldn't go back there. He trusted his daughter. And yet…

On the eighth day, he went to Iris's bedchamber at dawn and sat in the Witchwood chair by the fire, gazing at the flames, wondering if he was to blame. Was it because of the marriage? Had she been trying to escape? Had she made herself sick on purpose?

Eve arrived soon after, quiet as a mouse. He wouldn't have noticed her, had the door not creaked when she closed it. She went to the bed and stroked Iris's hair gently with the back of her finger. They sat in silence, the flames crackling and dancing in the hearth. Then, there was another creak. He looked up. The room was bright, sunlight flooding in through the window. Afternoon already. The time had slipped by. He blinked, dazzled by the light. Thomas had come into the chamber and was standing by the bed.

'Look,' Eve said, holding up a blue stone. Thomas walked around to the other side of the bed where she was sitting and looked at it, turning it over in his hands.

'Where did you find it?' he asked. Eve tilted her head towards Iris. 'Well, put it back,' he said.

Matthew watched them, smiling faintly. They came every day to see her. They were good children with kind hearts, both of them.

Lucian had not come.

*

When Iris awoke, she sat up and looked around the bedchamber. The room was empty. Her cloak was gone. And her boots. She was wearing a white gown with long sleeves.

She remembered the terrible feeling, the heaviness, after she had transported herself to her bedchamber from the Grassland. She remembered her father sitting on the bed, and Eve stroking her hair. But was all foggy, the edges of those memories blurred.

She felt better now. Her head ached a little, but she could stand it. Nothing would ever be as awful as what she first endured.

'Hello?' she said. No one answered her call. She fell back onto the pillow and closed her eyes.

Suddenly, there was a sharp click as the door opened. An aged maid came in, walked to the bed and pulled back the covers. She moved Iris's legs to the side, inspected the sheets and then put everything back with a grunt. Iris stared at her in surprise as the maid left the chamber. Why would she do that? What was she looking for? And how did she hope to find it under the covers? She let her eyes fall shut again, feeling suddenly overcome with drowsiness. Then, she sat bolt upright.

Her blood had not come.

Her hands started to shake. Her blood had not come. The maid was searching for blood. The maid always searched for blood, when it was time. And she always found blood. But, today, the blood had not come. It was time and the blood had not come.

When Eve came to visit later that morning, Iris beckoned her over.

'Eve, I need you to do something for me,' she said, trying to keep her voice steady.

Eve's face lit up. 'You're feeling better!' she said.

'Yes, yes, I'm better,' Iris said impatiently. 'Eve, I need you to get me something. Can you do that? I need you to go down to the library and bring me *The Book of Old Magic*. It's a big green book. It's very important. But you mustn't get caught – I want to impress father with a new trick, and we don't want to spoil the surprise, do we?'

'Can I learn one, too?' asked Eve.

'Yes, you can. But only if no one sees you.'

When Eve returned with the book, Iris sent her away for another one. And, while she was off searching for it, Iris flicked through the pages and found the spell that would save her.

The next morning, when the maid came to lift the covers and inspect the sheets, she found a dried patch of blood on the linen and on Iris's nightgown. With a satisfied grunt, she held her hands over the stains and they disappeared. Iris felt instantly lighter. It had worked. She had deceived them. And won herself time.

As the weeks turned to months and her blood still did not come, Iris lost all hope that it would. As much as she tried, she could not ignore the truth any longer. She was with child. She lay awake every night, thinking about what to do. The Vandemeres would be returning soon for the wedding, which meant that, any day now, the dressmakers would come to measure her for her dress. They would find out, if she let them see her body. They would tell her father, her mother…

If she could just sneak back to the Dark Forest to ask for Agatha's help. Agatha would know how to remove the baby; she knew about herbs. But Iris did not have the luxury of freedom anymore. Her mother had guards watching her. Three of them. They followed her every move, from the moment she left her bedchamber each day. In the corridors, in the courtyard, at the spice stalls, at the gown shops, at the book shop, at the bread stand, there they were, ten paces behind. She couldn't give them a reason to believe she was behaving suspiciously, so she never wandered to the end of Stone Lane, never walked anywhere too quickly. But time was running out. A small bump was beginning to show. Whenever she looked at it, she felt physically sick. She needed Agatha.

One grey morning, as Iris was walking around the courtyard, she heard something that made her stomach lurch - a volley of hooves, beating against the cobbles along Merlin's Way. The guards in the towers began to shout, and the guards at the gates moved aside. Time was up.

The Vandemeres burst into the courtyard, flanked by a dozen outriders in silver-plated armour, who cantered around in circles, carrying the Vandemere standard of two open hands encasing an orb of light. One of them almost knocked Iris down as she retreated towards the castle. This couldn't be right, she thought with rising panic. They were early, far too early. They weren't expected for at least another week.

Two wooden carriages rattled through the gates then, pulled by giant cart horses that screeched as they were forced to a halt, white foam frothing at their mouths. Another stream of horses followed the carriages through the gates, filling the courtyard until there was almost no room left to move.

Inside, the castle was in total disarray. Frenzied servants were darting in every direction, scurrying up the stairs to prepare rooms, calling for Lord Mortenstone to be informed. Trays laden with cold meats, breads and fruits were carried up from the kitchens into the dining hall. Iris could hear the scrape of tables being hastily dragged together to create ample seating for the party. Wine and ale were rushed out to the courtyard, spilling over the sides of the pitchers as flustered servants ran with them across the entrance hall.

Iris made for the staircase. She took the steps two at a time. *Boomfh, boomfh, boomfh* came the clunking footsteps of the guards close behind her. She climbed faster, light as a nymph, feeling triumphant as they fell further behind.

She was breathless when she reached the second floor. She walked a little way along a corridor before pausing to lean against the wall, her chest rising and falling heavily. Suddenly, she felt a twinge. She froze. Another twinge. She brought a hand up to her stomach, her heart thumping wildly, the sound filling her ears. The child was moving. Her head began to spin. The guards clanked along the corridor towards her, but she didn't move on. She stood there, feeling her baby shift about inside her, and realised she couldn't end its life. It was strong. It kicked against her hand, hard. She smiled, her eyes swimming with tears, a dreadful ache in her heart. No one could know. And, when it arrived, she couldn't be its mother. But that didn't matter. As long as it lived.

She heard raised voices then, coming from her father's antechamber. Wiping her tears, she walked along the corridor and stopped outside the door to listen. The guards followed noisily.

'Shhh,' she hissed, turning sharply. They stopped mid-stride and fell silent.

'…She's up to something. I know it,' she heard her mother say. 'If you don't keep an eye on her, she'll cause chaos like she did the last time. Do not pretend, Matthew. You are no fool. She was in the Dark Forest. And if we don't follow her, she'll go there again!'

'What would you have me do? Follow her for the rest of her life? Call off the guards!' her father shouted.

Iris looked over her shoulder. The guards exchanged a look of uncertainty.

'I'll talk to her,' Matthew said in a voice of controlled calm. 'She won't go back there if I ask her not to.'

Josephine laughed coldly. 'You will pay the highest price if she does.'

When Iris walked back down the stairs, the guards didn't follow. She left the castle and slunk through the courtyard, drawing her hood. No one noticed her in the chaos. The carriages were being unloaded. Stable boys were struggling with three or four horses each, leading them away to the stables with difficulty as the skittish creatures snapped and butted one another. Iris glimpsed Gregory Vandemere, helping an old man down from one of the carriages. She hadn't seen him since she had fallen ill, and was, for the first time, glad that she had been.

This was her one opportunity, when all eyes were turned inwards, focused on the masses that had descended upon the castle courtyard. She walked through the gates into the square, which was packed with people straining to see into the courtyard. The guards, busy holding them back, didn't say a word as she brushed past them.

She hastened along Stone Lane, hesitating when she heard a shout. She looked up. In the distance, a Mortenstone guard was charging in from the Grassland on horseback.

'Move!' he shouted. Two women jumped out of his way as he advanced towards the castle.

Iris dashed into the nearest shop and slammed the door shut just as the horse cantered past. She sighed with relief. The low thrum of voices inside the shop died instantly. Iris turned and stared into the room. It was dim, the air hot and cloying. This was the precious stone shop. Dozens of curious eyes were watching her. She bent her head and spun around quickly to hide her face. But, as she did, there was a crackling sound. She looked down and gasped. Her cloak had swept through one of the dribbling candles on the small table by the door and a flame now licked at the wool. She gaped at it, horror-stricken, and then, quite suddenly, it extinguished itself. A woman standing by a table loaded with purple gems reached out and grasped her shoulder, pulling her away from the candle.

'Careful there. Hang your cloak up at the door. We don't want no more accidents,' she said. Iris turned away from the woman, muttered an apology, and left quickly.

Drops of rain had begun to spatter the cobblestones in the lane. Shop owners hurriedly pulled the wares they had outside on display back indoors. Iris bowed her head against the wind and walked. Now the raindrops were fat and heavy; they fell hard onto her hood and shoulders, as if someone was pelting stones at her from an upstairs window. She walked quickly and with purpose, glancing up at the Grassland ahead, as the first wave of thunder growled above her. At the end of the lane, she picked up her skirts and ran.

The heavens opened. Thick sheets of rain fell so furiously, she could hardly see anything in front of her. Her cloak grew heavy with water and the ties pulled at her neck. She slid over on the grass and felt a sharp pain in her wrist but pushed herself to her feet and staggered on. Running, running, running until she reached the forest.

As soon as she stepped beyond the border, she threw her hood back and unfastened the ties, letting the cloak fall to the ground. She doubled over, slapping one hand against a tree, and tried to catch her breath. When she looked up again, she felt an ominous chill in the air as it whistled through the trees. Her skin prickled. She picked up the cloak and fastened it again, the immense weight of it providing some form of warmth and protection. A twig snapped somewhere close by. She looked around wildly. There was no one there. Her heart began to thump faster. She found herself wanting to turn around and go back. But she couldn't go home, not until she'd done what she came to do. She couldn't be this child's mother. But someone else could… Swallowing her fear, she lifted her skirts above her ankles again and ran.

No light filtered through the leaves to illuminate her path and she tripped and stumbled her way along. When she looked back, the Grassland was hidden completely from sight.

Suddenly, a man jumped out from behind a tree and she ran straight into his arms. He grasped her tightly and turned her around, pressing himself against her back. He smelled rancid. She froze in terror.

'I like that dress,' came a voice from the shadows. And then a second man emerged, walking towards her with a toothless grin. 'Looks expensive, don't it, James?'

The man holding on to her put his face to her neck and breathed in. 'Mmm… I can smell the wealth.' His bristly beard scratched her skin and she shuddered.

'I reckon she's got a few hidden jewels under that cloak,' said the second man, smiling lewdly as he approached. Iris stopped breathing. He came up close in front of her, so close she could smell his stale breath, feel the rotten warmth of it. As he put a hand up to stroke her face, she heard a sudden burst of footsteps and a rush of movement blurred across her vision, followed by a strangled scream. The man fell to the ground in front of her with a knife buried in the side of his head.

The other man released her immediately. Alexander turned, eyes fixed on him. The man held up his hands and took a step back.

'I-I-I'm sorry. I didn't mean no 'arm. I'll go, I'm sorry! I'm—'

Alexander lunged forward, thrusting the knife between his eyes before he had a chance to scream. The man collapsed onto his back, twitching, and then fell still.

Iris's knees gave way. Alexander crouched down and put a hand on her shoulder but quickly withdrew it when she flinched.

'It's alright. You're safe,' he said. 'Don't look at them. Come on, let's go.' He helped her to her feet and steadied her when she swayed.

They walked in silence. Iris tried to compose herself. Her hands were shaking. Every shadow, every falling leaf, every whisper made her jump. She knew what those men would have done to her if Alexander hadn't come.

When, finally, she calmed herself enough to remember the reason she had come to the forest, she reached out a hand and stopped him.

'I need to tell you something,' she said.

Alexander looked at her expectantly. 'What?'

'I'm…' Her heart began to race. She couldn't say the words.

'What?' he said again.

'I'm…with child.'

The silence was excruciating. For a time, he didn't react at all, didn't appear to have heard her. He stood there, quite still, staring blankly. His lips parted but he said nothing. Iris watched him, a lump forming in her throat.

'I…What?' he said, frowning in confusion.

'I'm with child,' she said again.

Alexander looked at her stomach, which was poking through her drenched cloak, and his frown melted away.

'Say something,' she said.

He went on staring at her rounded belly. Then, he shook his head, smirked, and walked on.

'Where are you going?' she cried, staggering after him. 'You can't run away. Stop! STOP!'

He stopped abruptly and turned back to face her. He wasn't smiling anymore. He looked angry.

'Don't you know what this means?' he shouted, a vein swelling in his neck. 'Mordarks and Mortenstones can't breed. That thing will be cursed!' He jabbed a finger into her stomach. She backed off and put a protective hand over it.

'It's not a *thing*, it's a child!'

'And what will you do with it? Raise it in your castle? Perhaps I should come and live there, too, and we can be a family,' he said mockingly.

'No, I—'

'What then? Do you want me to take it? My father would love that. A Mortenstone grandchild to feed to his Worgrims!'

'No,' she said, holding her stomach tightly. 'I thought that…Maybe Agatha could look after it.'

Alexander's eyes widened. He looked at her as if she had gone mad.

'It's the only way to keep it safe!' she said, stepping towards him. 'She'll do it for you, I know she will. She loves you.'

Alexander squeezed the bridge of his nose. Iris came closer and grasped his forearm.

'Will you come with me? I need her to take it from me. Today. Now. I can't go back until she's taken it. They'll find out. She has to take it now, or the dressmakers will come and—'

Alexander backed away in horror.

'Iris, you have lost all sense!'

'Don't you see? This is our only chance!' she said. 'I won't have another opportunity to come here. It has to be now. The child is strong enough!'

Alexander laughed incredulously. 'What child? It's a monster! Why would Agatha take in a monster?'

His words stung. Iris drew a sharp breath.

'It's not a monster,' she said, wishing he had felt it moving, knowing he would feel differently if he had. He would know, then, that it wasn't cursed, wasn't monstrous in any way. She cupped his face in her hands and forced him to look at her. 'It's our child,' she whispered.

His expression softened. He closed his eyes and sighed. Then he placed his hands on hers and gently brought them down from his face. When he opened his eyes again, they were cold.

'Kill it,' he said.

10. REVEROFS

'You disobeyed me, Iris!' said Matthew, pacing back and forth in the Great Hall. He could feel his blood boiling but tried to keep calm. Iris was slumped in a chair, staring at nothing. Her eyes were red and swollen from crying. He would have words with the guards who dragged her along Stone Lane like a common thief, though he didn't believe that was the reason for her tears. 'Why? Why did you go there again? Answer me!' he said. Iris shrugged indifferently. He slammed his fist on the table, incensed. 'Do not treat me with such disrespect!'

Iris didn't seem to hear a word he said. She didn't flinch, didn't blink, didn't move at all.

'Put her in the dungeon,' Josephine said over his shoulder.

'Quiet!' he barked.

'It's what she deserves,' she said, striding past him towards Iris. 'Get up,' she said, standing over her. Iris didn't stir from her trance. 'Get. Up.' She plucked at Iris's cloak and then began to pull it. Iris resisted, planting her feet on the ground, leaning back in her seat. Josephine grabbed the cloak with both hands and gave a hard tug, dragging her off the chair. The cloak's neck ties unravelled and it dropped to the ground.

Silence.

Matthew staggered forwards, his eyes wide as he stared at Iris's round stomach. He couldn't believe what he was seeing. It couldn't be… Not Iris… Was it some trick? Some magic?

'What is this?' he said in a voice barely above a whisper.

Iris burst into tears and crossed her arms over her middle to conceal the bump.

'You filthy girl,' Josephine said, backing away from her, ashen-faced. 'You're no daughter of mine. Disgusting creature. Down to the dungeon with you!'

'Who?' Matthew said, looking Iris dead in the eye.

'Father—' she pleaded, as Josephine continued to curse her.

'Filthy, filthy, wretched—!'

'WHO?' he bellowed. Josephine fell silent. Iris snivelled and sank back into the chair. Her golden hair fell over her face.

'Alexander Mordark.'

She murmured the name so softly that, at first, he thought he had imagined it. He stared at her, trying to understand what he had heard. Slowly, Iris brought her head up to look at him. Her eyes were brimming with tears of shame. And, suddenly, it all made sense. Her relentless desire to return to the forest; the Mordark brothers lurking at the border; the weeks spent bedbound with exhaustion from transporting herself with magic. As he fit all the pieces together, they formed a monstrous picture, a picture he could not refute. The ground moved from under him. He fell to his knees. Iris and Alexander Mordark. His head began to spin. He felt as if he had been kicked in the stomach with a steel-capped boot.

'Leave,' he said breathlessly, too appalled to look at her.

The chair screeched as she backed out and ran for the doors at the end of the hall.

Matthew stayed on the floor, still reeling, long after she had gone. Josephine sat at the round table. She pulled at the silver chain around her neck, withdrawing a low-hanging pendant from the bodice of her dress, and began to tap her long nails against it. The tapping and the spitting of the fire were the only sounds that filled the room.

'Saskian,' he said quietly, when the tapping became insufferable. In an instant, the old elf materialised before him, his head bent to one side, his large eyes scanning the room before settling on Matthew.

'My Lord,' said Saskian, looking alarmed to see him sitting on the floor.

'Send for the physician. Escort him to Iris's bedchamber. Then bring him to see me.'

'At once, my Lord,' said Saskian, inclining his head and vanishing.

Matthew scratched his beard absentmindedly, staring across at the fire. Then he sighed and let his hand slip from his face to his lap.

'I've fought in battle, quashed civil wars, watched men die,' he said, turning to Josephine. 'But I have never felt as frightened as I do tonight. Our daughter, Josephine…and a Mordark!'

'Send her away,' Josephine said. 'She can be treated, discreetly, and return for her wedding with Gregory Vandemere. Send her now, before word gets out. The physician will need to be silenced.'

Matthew rubbed his temples and turned back to the fire. 'Let's hear what he has to say first,' he said.

They received the physician in the Great Hall that evening.

'Can something be done?' Matthew asked, rising from the floor as the man approached. 'Can you put an end to it?'

The physician looked grave and paused to carefully select his words. 'The girl is too far along for me to forcibly remove the child without there being…complications.'

'What complications?' said Matthew.

'To terminate the pregnancy at this stage would cause the girl a great deal of pain and, quite possibly, bleeding I might not be able to stop.' The physician hesitated, pulled out his handkerchief and squeezed it. 'My advice would be to see the pregnancy through and send the child away when it is born.'

'That's not possible,' said Matthew. The physician looked perplexed. Matthew glanced at Josephine and sighed heavily. 'The child is a Reverof,' he said. 'Fathered by Alexander Mordark. Cursed.'

The physician's mouth fell open. 'My Lord…I…I…this cannot be!'

'So, you see,' Matthew said. 'The child cannot live.'

'The child *must* not live,' the physician concurred. 'It is a destiny that spawns evil. It will endanger us all. My Lord, forgive me, but I think the child should be expelled immediately, no matter the consequences for the mother.'

They went to Iris's bedchamber in the dead of night. Matthew could hear her crying from the other side of the door. He stayed behind with the physician as the four cloaked figures, who had arrived at the castle moments before, entered the room. All was quiet.

'Iris Mortenstone, we have come to take you away,' came the gentle voice of one of the cloaked figures.

Iris gasped.

'Who are you? Don't touch me. No! No!' she shouted.

Matthew heard the terror in her voice and it made his gut wrench. He held his nerve. It was the only way. It had to be done. She could not stay in the castle in her condition. She had to go, now, before the Vandemeres or the maids or anyone else saw her. He turned to the physician.

'I will not have this child torn from her. I won't risk her life. And neither will you. If anything happens to her...' he said, his voice shaking.

'She will be looked after in the valley, until it is time, my Lord. I will deliver the child safely and dispose of it myself. And I shall return your daughter to you good and well,' he said. 'None need know.'

Iris screamed then, a loud, piercing sound that chilled Matthew to the core.

'Father! Father, help me!' she cried.

Matthew smashed his fist into the wall in frustration. She was afraid. This was wrong. The whole thing was wrong.

The physician eyed him cautiously. 'It is for her own good, my Lord.'

Iris screamed again, but the scream was cut short by the sound of a struggle. Thrashing, banging, screeching. Matthew could take it no more.

'Stop. Stop them!' he shouted.

The physician looked at him incredulously. 'But, my Lord—'

'Now!'

The physician hurried into the bedchamber and returned soon after with the cloaked figures, tall and thin and white-skinned. Elves of Mortenstone Valley. Their hands, which they held clasped in front of them, were deathly pale against their black cloaks and, etched onto the top of each, just below the knuckles, was a faint red circle. The mark of healers. The elves would care for Iris well in Mortenstone Valley, and with kindness - Matthew knew this. But even so, he could not do it. Not this way.

'Go. Away with you. Say nothing of this,' he said. The elves gave a small bow and vanished instantly. Matthew approached the physician then, and spoke in a low voice. 'You will stay. I will have rooms prepared for you. Do not speak a word of this to anyone in the castle. Is that clear? You'll dangle from your toes in the dungeon if you do.'

The physician swallowed hard and nodded. A bead of sweat trickled down his forehead as he looked from Matthew to the doorway of Iris's bedchamber.

'But the child… it must not live!'

'I know,' said Matthew. 'But I cannot force my daughter out of bed and send her off into the night alone and afraid. I will explain to her what needs to be done. She deserves that much.'

'If she stays here, my Lord, they will all find out,' said the physician, looking anxious. 'I cannot be held responsible if they do. I won't say a word, but if anyone *sees* her, there is no hiding it.'

Matthew turned and walked away, leaving the physician staring after him. The man was right; one look at Iris and everyone would know. And then what? What of the alliance with the Vandemeres? What of the great army he needed to build? What of the future? One of Merlin's spells had already run its course. How long would it be before the rest did, too? How long before the old magic was no more and their enemies returned with a vengeance? He had to make Iris see why she must go to the valley and why, once born, her child could not live. All their lives depended on it.

'Send for schoolmaster Hagworth at first light,' he said to a passing servant as he went wearily to his bedchamber.

*

Master Hagworth received the news of Iris's condition in grave silence in the schoolroom. He did the best he could to mask his horror from Matthew, who sat across from him at Thomas's desk, dark shadows beneath his eyes.

'She has to go willingly,' Matthew said in a hushed voice. He scratched his beard anxiously. 'I'm afraid of what she'll do if I force her. I don't want her to… I don't want to push her too far,' he said, his gaze suddenly far-off and troubled. Master Hagworth nodded with understanding. And, when Matthew looked at him again, it took him by surprise to see the sheer desperation in his eyes. No longer a lord or a ruler, but a man, a father, lost. 'Will you help me?' he asked.

'It is my duty to serve you, my Lord Mortenstone,' said Master Hagworth. 'And my honour.'

A fire was lit in a small anteroom next to Iris's bedchamber. Master Hagworth used his magic to summon a desk and two chairs from the schoolroom. Then he sat and waited for his pupil.

When Iris appeared in the doorway and he saw her stomach protruding from her nightgown, he felt in his heart a terrible sadness. She was still a child, her cheeks full and plump with youth.

'Sit, Iris, sit,' he said.

Iris walked to the desk and sat down. She didn't meet his eye.

'I have spoken before on this matter, but never in depth. I think it is best I start at the beginning,' he said, leaning forward in his chair. 'Centuries ago, after the

112

Failed Rebellion, Merlin the Good cast two powerful spells to keep the Dark Families out of our realm. Up grew the Dark Forest, separating the Dark Lands from The Light and blocking all magic from within,' he said, resting a hand on the desk. Iris's eyes darted to it. 'That was the first spell. The second was far darker. The second made certain that the outcasts could never return to The Light. If they tried, they would turn into monstrous serpents. It was powerful magic. Many believe these were the spells that killed Merlin,' he said solemnly. Then he paused and folded his hands in his lap. 'But there was another spell, one that remained undiscovered until after his death. A spell that ensured Merlin's blood and the blood of his enemy would never mix to secure a lasting familial line. A Reverof is the name we give to children born of Mortenstone and Mordark blood. They are the Cursed Ones, Iris. History has record of few. And, of the few, even fewer survived birth. They are not meant for this world. They are not meant to live. Those who did bore the mark of their curse. They were cruel, malicious and cold of heart. They could not love. Death followed them wherever they turned. And so, they were isolated and, eventually, in all cases, cast out, passing into legend. It is a tragic fate, but one they are destined to meet. Mortenstone and Mordark blood must not mix. You are a kind girl, Iris. You've always been kind. Wouldn't it be kinder to spare your child from a life of sorrow, and others from its malice?'

Iris instinctively brought a hand to her stomach, shielding it from him. Master Hagworth sat back in his chair and sighed.

He had failed.

*

Matthew made his way down to the dining hall to see Eric Vandemere. There, he would broach the subject of postponing the wedding between Gregory and Iris. He had a nervous feeling in his gut. He had thought all night about what he would say, how he would say it, and decided to keep the reason vague. Iris was unwell and needed time to recover. Yes. Providing he delivered the words convincingly, Eric wouldn't ask to know the details - he hoped.

The castle had awoken. Maids and servants scuttled about to begin the day's duties. Matthew stopped every person he saw and told them no one was to tend to Iris. Master Hagworth would be with her now. For good measure, he sent a guard to stand outside the door and make sure no one entered.

Wedding decorations had already been put up in the corridors. Matthew ducked his head as he passed beneath the low-hanging rows of white banners above the stairs to the entrance hall. Suddenly, he heard the sound of wheels scraping against stone. A carriage was moving out of the courtyard, drawn by two black horses. Outriders were flanking it on both sides. It was one of Eric Vandemere's carriages. Matthew moved faster down the steps, his stomach beginning to tighten with unease. And then he heard the scraping wheels of the second carriage. When he came to the bottom of the stairs, he started to run. Across the entrance hall, out into the courtyard, up to the gates, where the guards stood looking at each other in confusion as the second carriage rattled away through the square, headed for Merlin's Way. Matthew blinked. Why were they leaving? He turned to the sound of clattering hooves behind him. Riding out from the stables, side by side, were Eric and Gregory Vandemere, followed by a dozen of their men.

Eric stared at him in disgust as he approached. 'My Lord,' he said, stopping his horse before the gates. 'I have heard the news. We are leaving at once. I will not have my son wed to your daughter. Did you really think you could hide this from us?'

Matthew's heart was pounding. He could only shake his head in bewilderment. How did they know? Gregory's nostrils flared as he bowed his head to Matthew. Then his eyes moved to the square beyond the gates and, setting his jaw, he dug his heels into the side of his horse. The creature bolted, stirring up a wind that blew Matthew's hair across his face. He took a step back. Eric inclined his head reluctantly, kicked his own horse and, before Matthew could utter a word, rode out of the castle gates behind his son.

Matthew stood in stunned confusion. But when he noticed the guards' gazes shifting to something behind him, he turned around – and gasped. Iris was standing in her nightgown on the castle steps, her round stomach sticking out for all to see.

'What are you doing?' he said, rushing towards her. 'What have you done?'

Iris stared at him defiantly. 'I won't let you take it. I won't let you kill it. Now they all know. I don't care. You can't smuggle me away and take my child!'

Matthew could feel the sweat streaming down the back of his neck. Everyone was staring at Iris now, mouths falling open in astonishment.

And then Lucian came out of the castle, his dark hair limp with grease. He looked mildly surprised to see Iris standing there in her nightgown, in full view of the courtyard. As he circled around her, his eyes dropped to her stomach and his face fell. A heavy silence settled over the courtyard. Lucian shook his head in disbelief, his eyes wandering up to meet Iris's. Then, he spat at her feet.

Matthew lifted his chin and strode up the steps towards them both, his boots clicking against the flagstones, the sound rising around him, filling the silent courtyard. *Click, click, click.* When he reached them, he paused and then walked on, back into the castle, without a word.

As the months wore on, Eric Vandemere finally came around and offered his second son, Edward, to Iris. Matthew had no choice but to accept. It was an insult, but his daughter had been spoiled - no man could be expected to offer his first son. Even though he told them it wasn't her fault, announced publicly that his poor innocent girl had been attacked in the Dark Forest, it made no difference. She had been spoiled.

Iris was larger than ever now. She was on his mind every moment of every day. He asked after her constantly. But he couldn't stand to be in her presence, looking upon her stomach. It made him think of the cunning Mordark boy and wish he'd killed him when he'd had the chance.

*

Iris heard them, muttering outside her bedchamber, thinking she couldn't hear. She sat on the bed, staring at the door, as the voices grew louder.

The physician had finished his morning examination and remarked, begrudgingly, that the child was strong, after it kicked against his hand so violently its foot protruded from Iris's stomach. But Master Hagworth was bickering with him now on the other side of the door, telling him to check again.

'If I say the child is strong, the child is strong,' said the physician.

'The likelihood of a stillbirth is so high it verges on total certainty,' Master Hagworth retorted. 'I have pored over the records for *months*. There is a pattern. And, according to the pattern, that child should be weakening in its mother's belly as we speak.'

'Would you like to go in there and check yourself, Hagworth?' snapped the physician.

'Perhaps I should, if all we have is *your* word for it.'

'Stop!' said another voice, firmly. Iris sat up a little straighter. Her father was out there with them. The physician and the schoolmaster fell quiet. But, after a short time, they began to speak again, in hushed voices. Iris heard only small fragments of what they were saying, but what she did hear made her tremble with fear.

'…Who will be the one to do it?'

'…never forgive me…'

'…has to be done.'

'…cursed...'

'…dispose of it… Wild Garden…'

Iris hugged her arms around her stomach. She didn't want to give birth. She wanted her child to stay safe inside her, where no one could take it or hurt it. She screwed her eyes shut, tried to block out the voices beyond the door, and prayed silently to the White Witch. Let the child live. Protect it from them all. Show them they needn't be afraid. Because they *were* afraid - her father, Master Hagworth, the physician, the maids, everyone. But she wasn't. And, if they let her love it, one day soon they would all see that it wasn't a monster after all.

The next morning, a flash of lightning woke Iris with a start. She sat up in bed, looking straight at the window. The clouds outside were black. As the thunder followed, she realised the baby had not kicked. She put a hand on her belly to check for movement and felt none.

She opened her mouth to call for the maid, when a searing pain sliced through her body. She fell back against the pillows and gasped as the pain intensified. She felt as if she was slowly tearing in half from the inside. When it became too much, she screamed.

Three maids came rushing into her bedchamber and each cried out in horror as the bedsheets turned red with blood.

*

'Sir! Sir! Come quick! Lady Iris…It's Lady Iris!' exclaimed the servant boy as he burst into the physician's bedchamber. The physician jumped out of bed at once. The time had come. His hands shook as he hurriedly dressed himself. He shouted for the boy to bring water and rags to Iris's chamber. Then he snatched up his case and ran.

He could hear the screaming from the staircase as he raced up to the second floor and along the corridor towards Iris's bedchamber. As he came to the door, it swung open and a panic-stricken chambermaid ran out and grasped his arms.

'There's blood everywhere!' she cried hysterically. 'The delivery maid said you're not to come in, but there's so much blood!'

Delivery maid? He pushed her out of the way and barged into the room.

Iris was sprawled on the bed, her hair drenched with sweat, her nightgown dark with blood. He went straight to the gaunt woman sitting at the foot of the bed. She wore a black dress and her black hair was pulled tight into a bun. Her lips were thin and pressed together in a hard line as she piled fresh rags between Iris's legs.

'What is the meaning of this?' he said.

The delivery maid looked at him sharply. 'Leave,' she said. 'I have stopped the bleeding. You are not needed.'

'I am delivering this child!' he shouted.

'No. I am,' she said, mopping the blood from Iris's inner thighs with a wet cloth.

The physician's face flushed pink. 'This is an outrage! I will not—'

'Stand in the corner. And be quiet,' she said, without a second glance.

He raised a shaky finger and pointed it at her furiously, when Iris shrieked with pain and began to claw at the bedsheets. Scowling, he backed down and stomped over to the corner of the room as the women fussed and ran back and forth with wet cloths and smelling salts. *He* should have been the one to deliver the child. Had he not earned the right? Had he not spent every day with Iris, examining her and the child? He folded his arms. But, as he continued to watch, a cold feeling trickled down his spine. The thunder rumbled outside. The rain pelted the window. And, suddenly, he was glad that he would not be the first to touch the cursed thing that would soon be pulled from Iris Mortenstone.

The door flew open. Matthew was halfway over the threshold when the delivery maid shouted, 'No!'

Another maid hurried to the door and shoved him back out. 'My Lord, this is no place for a father. Beg your pardon. The delivery maid insists,' the young maid said breathlessly, and she closed the door again in his face.

*

'Push it out, Iris!' urged the delivery maid. The other maids stood around the bed, holding her legs, looking at her, their mouths moving rapidly. But Iris hardly heard anything they said. Their voices seemed far away, as though they were speaking to her through a stone wall. She was so tired. She wanted to sleep. She whimpered and let her head fall back onto the pillows.

'…almost there!'

'…Push… Lady Iris, push!'

'Don't give up now…very close!'

As if a battering ram had come crashing through the stone wall that separated them, there was a sudden burst of sound. Iris heard them shouting her name, encouraging her, their voices loud and shrill. *Push. Push. Push.* She felt their hot hands grasping, shaking her. She brought her head forward and bore down with all her might, squeezing their hands, feeling their bones shift as she gripped tighter and tighter.

The moment the child slipped out, the agony subsided and she collapsed onto the pillows.

Solemn looks were exchanged around the room in the silence that followed. The maids abandoned their posts and gathered around the delivery maid at the end of the bed. They all looked down at the blanket in her hands. The delivery maid stared at Iris gravely and then turned to the doctor.

'The child lives,' she said.

11. ENOLA

'Her name is Enola,' Iris said, offering up the bundle to Matthew, who leant across the bed to take her.

The girl had blue eyes – Mortenstone blue – and the same delicate nose as Iris, but her hair was black as night. She stared at him fixedly as he rocked her, never blinking. It was not the curious gaze of a newborn baby, but one of cold awareness. She looked deep into his eyes, almost as if she knew him and everything he was thinking, as if she was penetrating his mind. He looked away, feeling uneasy, and stared at the delivery maid, who was sitting over by the fireplace folding a pile of old blankets. She gave him a regretful look and then returned to her work, eyes lowered to the floor. When he turned back, Enola was still watching him. A prickling feeling ran up his neck, making the hairs stand on end. He handed her back to Iris, who stared at her daughter adoringly, and gave her a kiss on the forehead. She was pale, dark shadows encircling her eyes.

'You must rest,' Matthew said. When she looked at him suspiciously, he sighed. 'No one will take her from you while you sleep, I promise you.'

Iris looked down at Enola, still frowning. And Matthew noticed, as the child turned her face towards Iris, that there was a patch at the back of her head through which a streak of white hair grew.

'Well?' said Josephine as Matthew entered their bedchamber later that morning.

'A girl,' he said, taking off his boots.

'Not that!' she spat. 'Is it gone?'

'No.'

'Well get rid of it! Soon!'

'Josephine,' he said, a warning in his tone. She closed her mouth and returned to her sewing, violently thrusting the needle through the cloth. 'I don't think it would be so terrible to let Iris bond with the child for a day or two,' he said. The words tasted bitter on his tongue. Josephine stared at him, her eyes wide with horror. Then she got up, tossed her needlework into the fire and stormed out of the chamber, slamming the door behind her.

Lucian barged in moments later, his face white. 'You cannot mean it! Father!' he said, striding over to him, his hands balled into fists. 'Let it stay? Here?'

'Knock next time, Lucian.'

'Father! Get rid of it! I won't let Iris manipulate you anymore. It has to go! You're risking our relationship with the Vandemeres. You will insult them if you let it stay. If we offend them again, we'll lose them and their men. Then how will you ever build your army? Father, take control!'

'Lucian, I will strike you if you don't leave!'

Lucian snorted with exasperation and left. As soon as the door closed, Matthew sank onto the bed and shut his eyes, pulling the fur throw up to his shoulders. The storm raged on outside, battering the castle walls. The sky was growing ever darker. And he felt as weary as if he had been awake for a thousand years.

There was a quiet knock at the door. Saskian entered.

'My Lord, the physician is asking whether he should… *proceed* with the arrangement, regarding the Reverof girl.'

'No,' Matthew said, sitting up quickly. 'No, tell him no. Not yet. I don't…I don't think I can do it.'

Saskian did not seem surprised. He nodded thoughtfully and approached the bed, perching on the edge beside him.

'And you know what this means?' he said.

'Yes,' said Matthew. He knew what was at stake. 'But even so, I can't.'

Saskian sat in silence for a long time. Then, the smallest hint of a smile appeared on his lips. 'Perhaps *She* is coming,' he said, looking at him knowingly. 'Perhaps it was all meant to be this way, my Lord.'

'What do you mean?' said Matthew.

'War will come, that is certain. And, when it does, we won't win. Darkness will befall us, cast its shadow over our land, as your great ancestor foresaw. We will suffer, my Lord. We *must* suffer. For then She will hear us. And She will come to save us. It is the prophecy.'

Matthew stared at him. Could his wise old friend be right? He wove his fingers together and sat in quiet thought, wondering whether any of the choices he had made thus far had ever been his own.

*

Lucian walked soundlessly along the corridor to Iris's bedchamber and paused outside the door. His heartbeat quickened as he took hold of the handle and carefully pushed the door open.

Iris was asleep, her hand draped over the side of a cot next to the bed. Lucian moved cautiously across the room and stood over it. The child was awake; it stared up at him and kicked out its legs. It was sickening. He clenched his fists and gritted his teeth.

'Lucian, what are you doing?' came a panicked voice. He looked up. Iris had woken. She sat upright in bed, wide-eyed with fear. He stared into her eyes as he lowered his hand into the cot and stroked the child's head. 'Don't hurt her,' she said, her voice shaking. He pinched the child's cheek lightly. Then he took a step back from the cot, turned around and left the room in silence.

He would like to have thrown it from the window before his sister's very eyes, listen to her scream as the child plummeted to its death. And he would do, one day, when their father was no longer there to protect it.

The following morning, Lucian awoke to the sound of clanking metal. He sprang from the bed and rushed to the window. Below, at least fifty guards were marching along Stone Lane towards the Dark Forest, suited head-to-toe in silver armour, holding longswords in front of them, blades pointing to the heavens. They walked in uniformed rows. *Crunch, crunch, crunch.* Their steel boots rattling. Behind them walked three horses, dragging carts filled with firewood, rolls of canvas, barrels of wine and ale, and servants.

Lucian dashed to the trunk at the end of his bed and threw it open, seizing breeches and a tunic and pulling them on hastily. He slipped his feet into his boots and ran from the bedchamber.

He raced down to the entrance hall, out into the courtyard and through the square, crossing it in four strides, running down Stone Lane towards his father, who was standing at the bottom, looking out across the Grassland.

'What's happening?' he asked breathlessly. His father turned his head towards him but his eyes remained fixed on the guards and the carts as they shrank into the distance.

'I'm posting men along the border. The Dark Forest is off limits to all. Entry is punishable by banishment. This arrangement is to be permanent.'

'Why?' Lucian said, bewildered.

'I must protect my people,' said Matthew. 'There are dangerous people in the forest.'

Lucian watched him closely. There was something his father wasn't telling him. He was avoiding his eye, combing his fingers through his beard anxiously. Why did they need protection? Why did he care now if anyone died in the Dark Forest, when he never had before? No. This wasn't about them. This was about Iris. He had always favoured her, always paid her special attention. But this? All this to prevent her from returning to the forest? It was madness.

Across the Grassland, servants were jumping down from the carts and pulling out the rolls of canvas and long wooden poles. Lucian watched as they thrust the poles into the earth and backed away, raising their arms, palms facing upwards. One roll of canvas unravelled and flew high into the air above them before falling gently down over the wooden poles. And, just like that, the first tent was erected. Lucian gritted his teeth.

'When is the wedding?' he said as the servants began on the second tent.

'Soon,' said Matthew distractedly.

'Good,' Lucian said. But it wasn't good. It wasn't enough. Edward Vandemere was not heir to the Vandemere army. He looked at his father with contempt. His weakness had cost them dearly. Iris had cost them dearly. He hoped she did go back to the Dark Forest. Then his father would be forced to banish her - and the snake spawn she had birthed.

Iris woke again to silence from the cot. She leaned over and looked in. Enola was wide awake, staring up at the ceiling. Then, suddenly, her head rolled to the side and she looked at her with eyes of ice. Iris recoiled slightly, a nervous flutter in her stomach, but quickly moved back to the cot again, pushing the feeling away. No. She wasn't afraid. She loved her daughter. She brushed her fingers over her soft cheek and smiled at her, but Enola remained expressionless.

It had been months now. Months and no smile, no laughter, no tears. Months of silence. Months of listening to the maids whispering in the corner of the chamber. "Peculiar", they called her. "Strange." None of them looked directly at the girl; it was as if they were afraid the curse was catching.

Iris stuck out her tongue and pulled a face. Enola looked away, disinterested, as three sharp knocks sounded upon the door. Iris's head snapped up.

'Who is it?' she said, pulling the bedcovers up to conceal her nightdress. The door opened. Her father came into the room, followed by the delivery maid. Iris stared at the woman in surprise. She hadn't seen her since the day Enola was born and presumed she had returned to wherever it was she came from. Draxvar, perhaps, judging by her paleness.

Her father looked at her gravely and her heart began to race.

'Iris—'

'No!' she shouted, snatching Enola from the cot. 'No, don't hurt her. Go away!'

'I'm not going to hurt her, Iris. Listen to me. It's time. She can't share your chamber when you're married. Maid Morgan here will look after her down in the lower rooms. She will be her Companion while she grows up,' he said, nodding towards the delivery maid, who bowed her head.

'She'll hurt her,' Iris said, staring at Maid Morgan coldly.

'She won't.'

'How do you know? You don't know her! She might!'

Matthew looked at the maid apologetically.

'Maid Morgan is the daughter of Francis le Fay,' he said. Iris fell quiet, forgetting whatever it was she had been about to say. 'This is a great honour for their family, as it is our honour to have her here,' he continued. 'I doubt very much that she would do anything to harm Enola. Wouldn't you agree?'

Iris glanced at the woman quickly. The le Fays of Latheera were an old family, an important family. But how was she to know? She couldn't help thinking, even now, that this Morgan le Fay looked too stern and battle-worn to be one of them.

Matthew came closer to the bed and lowered his voice.

'I have shown you great leniency in these last months,' he said. 'I have allowed you to keep your daughter here in the castle, against the advice of my council, your mother and my own better judgement. Do not challenge me now, after all I have done for you.'

Iris felt a stinging pain behind her eyes and her father became a blur as they filled with tears. Her throat tightened. Her heart ached. But she didn't resist when Maid Morgan plucked Enola from her arms and carried her out of the room. When her father bent down to kiss her, she turned her face away.

The wedding day crept up on Iris like a snake in the grass. Before she knew it, she was standing in her bedchamber, staring vacantly out of the window as four maids fastened her purple gown.

Eve danced around with excitement. 'Do we get to keep these dresses?' she said, flitting past the other bridesmaids, who were sitting on the bed, their feet dangling over the edge. Iris didn't answer her. But for the maids' skirts swishing, the fire spitting and Eve's shoes tapping against the floor, no one made a sound.

As she left her chamber and began the long walk along the corridor towards the staircase, she noticed movement in the corner of her eye and turned her head. There, standing at the top of a darkened stairway that led down to the lower rooms, was Maid Morgan. She held Enola to her chest and offered a small smile. Iris nodded and returned an even fainter smile, feeling a stab of jealousy as she walked on.

A single bell began to ring. The sound drifted down from the bell tower, fading as it reached her ears. *Dong.* The dying echo replaced by another. *Dong.* Summoning her, not in celebration, but in duty.

Her father met her at the foot of the stairs and offered his arm. She took it, her hands trembling. The servants lined the corridor and bowed as they passed them, each beaming with excitement, eyes roving over her gown, over the jewels glinting in the fabric of the hem. Iris could hear the din of voices rising in the Great Hall as they approached. And then the bell stopped ringing. They halted outside the doors and waited while maids and dressmakers hurriedly straightened out the folds in her dress and veil, pulled up the bridesmaids' stockings and flattened their hair with spit, before arranging them into rows of two in order of height. In that moment, briefly, as the frenzy unfolded around her, Iris thought of Alexander, standing there in the clearing, as vivid as if he were in front of her. But the Dark Forest was another world away now.

With heart-stopping suddenness, the music began. Iris's stomach lurched. Her father glanced sideways at her and squeezed her hand as the choir began to sing the *Song of Merlin the Good*.

'For the realm,' he said.

Iris's mouth was so dry she couldn't speak. She looked ahead and swallowed hard as the doors opened. A sea of heads turned. Her father began to walk. And she was walking, too, the music blasting in her ears, the choir singing over it, projecting their voices from the end of the hall. Walking, walking, slowly, tentatively, under the Mortenstone and Vandemere banners, which rippled above their heads in the cold draft. She smiled tightly at the faces leaning out into the aisle to get a proper look at her. She didn't recognise any of them.

As they neared the end of the aisle, the music began to build, the singing grew louder, and Iris looked dead into Edward Vandemere's eyes. He was standing in front of the choir, staring at her in awe. His older brother, Gregory, was at his side, looking as if it was the last place he wanted to be. He glared at her as she approached and then turned around to face the minister, encouraging Edward to do the same with a nudge.

When she reached the end of the hall and came to stand alongside Edward, the music swelled. The entire orchestra held its final notes and let them ring out across the room. Her father lifted her veil and squeezed her hand one last time before handing it to Edward.

Then, a sharp, sudden silence.

The fat minister, whose purple robes were too small, stepped forward and closed his hands around theirs. He cleared his throat and the hanging skin under his chin wobbled.

'We are here today to witness a bond that only death can break!' he declared. 'It is my honour to conduct this sacred ceremony.' He turned to Matthew and bowed. 'My Lord Mortenstone.'

Matthew nodded and took his leave to join Josephine in the front seats.

'Edward Vandemere, Iris Mortenstone,' the minister continued, 'you come together in the presence of the congregation to make a vow of loyalty, love and kinship to one another. Repeat after me: I make this vow, this unbreakable bond, to the person here before me. My love, my life, all that I have, is reserved for only thee.'

Iris hesitated before she spoke. She could feel her mother's eyes burning into the side of her head and, from the corner of her eye, saw Lucian's lips moving as he mouthed the vow. She muttered the words without sentiment, while Edward stammered his way through nervously. When they were done, the minister tightened his grip on their hands and closed his eyes. His own hands were warm and clammy.

'Here, in the Great Hall of Merlin the Good, I bind these two in life.'

Iris felt a tingling sensation in her fingers and it grew painful as it spread up her arm, through her veins. She looked at Edward, who seemed to be experiencing the same pain. He half-smiled through a grimace. Suddenly, the feeling vanished. The minister let go of their hands and beamed.

'The enchantment is cast. You are man and wife.'

Iris felt nothing but emptiness as the cheers filled the hall. She was bound forever to Edward, who leaned in and kissed her on both cheeks, smiling happily. Alexander crept back into her thoughts but she pushed him away. She could never be with him again. It was too late. All too late. It seemed a lifetime ago that she had plotted her escape, convinced herself that she would find a passage to freedom.

Dreams had a way of seeming absurd in the plain light of day, when night was long behind them.

12. MORTENSTONE VALLEY

The following winter, Iris gave birth to a son, Jacobi. And, the winter after that, a daughter, Rose. Both children had her eyes and golden curls. In fact, they didn't look much like Edward at all, which pleased her; though, in truth, she did not find marriage unbearable. Edward was a fool, but fatherhood seemed to agree with him and the children found hilarity in his silliness and loved him for it. Often, she would catch herself laughing when he was entertaining them. She didn't love him, but she was fond of him. He was a good man, a good husband, a good father.

Enola remained in the lower rooms of the castle, in the care of Maid Morgan. Iris would not admit it but she was glad the girl was not sharing a nursery with Jacobi and Rose. Where they were sweet natured and kind, Enola was devious and sullen. It was frightening sometimes – menacing, even – to glimpse her dark, unwavering stare from a shadowy corner of the chamber; her blue eyes, cold as the winter frost. Something lurked behind those eyes, something vicious. Iris knew this because the physician had stopped visiting. He refused to set foot in the castle again. He said Enola had attacked him when he came to examine her and he had the scars to prove it. Maid Morgan had insisted that he was lying or exaggerating; it was almost as if she was trying to protect Enola, as if she was trying to be a better mother to her than Iris. But, no matter, they all knew the doctor was telling the truth. Even if he hadn't shown them his wounds, they would have believed him.

With each mounting incident, Iris found herself thinking more and more of Alexander. Did he think of her, or ever wonder what became of their child? Did he regret the last words he spoke to her, when Enola was still growing in her belly? A *monster*, he had called her. *Kill it*, he had said. And, in her most shameful moments, Iris wondered if she should have listened to him.

*

Matthew descended the stairs to the castle basement and headed for Enola's chamber. It was dark in these passages, with few torches and no windows to offer any light. Already, he couldn't stand it. The ceilings were low and the air felt close. He wanted to march back up to the ground floor and take a long, deep breath, fill his lungs. It would do Enola good to get outside, he thought. Staying down here all day would drive anyone to distraction. Could he blame her for attacking the physician? She needed fresh air. The trip he had planned could not have come at a better time.

He knocked twice upon the door and entered the bedchamber. The room was dark, like the hallway. Four torches blazed in their brackets at intervals around the room, throwing shadows across the stone floor. A fire roared in the hearth; Maid Morgan was sitting in a chair beside it, sewing a hood onto a black cloak. She rose from the chair quickly when she saw him and bowed dutifully. Enola was sitting on the floor in the corner, fiddling with a wooden doll. Her hands stilled for a moment as he entered and then went on bending the arms of the doll.

'Hello, Enola,' he said, crouching down in front of her. Enola continued to play as if he wasn't there, but moved the toy further away from him and then shuffled around completely, so that her back was to him. He smiled, staring for a moment at her white streak of hair. He rubbed his cheek thoughtfully. Curses always left their mark. He was reminded, then, of the note that had arrived at the castle the previous night, scrawled hurriedly across a piece of parchment. *These vicious outbursts will only become more violent and uncontrollable. The curse grows with her*, the physician had warned him. And, looking at her now, Matthew could not deny that, in the weeks - or had it been months? - since he had last come to visit Enola, the white streak had certainly expanded.

'Would you like to see a bit of magic?' he said, flicking his hand upwards and conjuring a small horse from wisps of white smoke. He flicked his hand again and sent it prancing about the chamber. Enola looked around and watched intently over her shoulder. But, when the horse evaporated, she returned to her toy without a word. Matthew stood and turned to Maid Morgan. 'I would like to take Enola to Mortenstone Valley with the other grandchildren tomorrow,' he said. 'She will travel separately, with you. I will have guards escort you both. You are to leave before dawn. It's not far - half a morning's ride on horseback at most. Home in time for supper.'

It would be an educational expedition, he believed, an opportunity for his grandchildren to learn about where they came from - all three of them. They would enjoy it too, he hoped. Josephine and Lucian had refused to come, just as he expected. And he was all the happier for it.

Maid Morgan nodded. 'I shall prepare her travelling things,' she said.

'Very good,' he said. As he took a step towards the door, there was a sharp, sliding noise, the sound of something coming loose, and, in a blur of orange, a torch fell to the ground where he had stood. He turned slowly and looked at Enola. She was staring at him darkly from the corner. 'Missed,' he said. Maid Morgan rushed forwards to pick up the torch but he held out a hand to stop her. Next moment, the torch jumped up from the floor and slotted back into its bracket on the wall, the flames reigniting themselves. 'Tomorrow, then,' he said, eyes fixed on Enola. Maid Morgan nodded and bowed again.

When he left the chamber, he hastened down the darkened corridor, putting distance between himself and Enola. His heart was beating furiously. And, for a moment, he felt afraid.

They gathered in the courtyard at dawn. Master Hagworth filled his horse's saddlebags with blank parchment, quills and ink, for the children to draw and write about the things they saw, and waited patiently for them all to mount their horses.

Iris emerged from the castle, carrying Rose in her arms. The child was peaceful in her thick woollen blanket, nestled against her mother's chest. Jacobi followed, helped down the steps by a maid in a violet cloak.

Matthew strode into the courtyard from the stables. When he saw Jacobi, he grinned and dropped to one knee. Jacobi ran straight into his arms.

'I have a surprise for you. Would you like to see?' Matthew said. Jacobi nodded. 'Wait here, then,' he said, standing and walking back to the stables.

When he returned, he was sitting astride his black Latheerian horse, which walked majestically towards Jacobi, unbridled and unsaddled, its long neck arched, its blue eyes bright as jewels. The creature dwarfed the other horses in the courtyard. Matthew held onto its mane with one hand. As the horse came to stand before Jacobi, it tossed its head and grunted.

'This is Wistor. He's been my friend since I was your age,' Matthew said, patting the horse's neck. 'Say hello to my grandson, old boy.'

Wistor drew his head around to regard Matthew, then turned back to Jacobi, bent his right leg and bowed. Jacobi squealed with delight. Matthew chuckled.

'Now, close your eyes, Jacobi. It's time for your surprise,' he said, and he looked over his shoulder and nodded. A young boy emerged from the stables with a sprightly black foal. 'Open!' Matthew said. Jacobi opened his eyes and his jaw fell open. He began to jump up and down with excitement as the stable boy led the foal right to him. 'Quickly now,' Matthew prompted the stable boy, who had paused to watch Jacobi. Remembering himself, the boy plucked Jacobi from the ground and swung him onto the foal's back. Suddenly, the animal went still. Jacobi frowned, looking confused and unsure. And then he, too, fell still. Matthew watched avidly.

*

As Iris stared at Jacobi and the Latheerian foal, she felt a sting of disappointment. They were rare creatures, enchanted creatures, expensive creatures. She remembered the day she had been given hers. Lareena, white as snow, fresh from the mountains of Latheera, legs strong from the long journey to Lambelee. She had been bonded to Lareena when she was three. She was too young to comprehend much about the world, but old enough to understand the significance of the moment a barrier between them dissolved and the horse's thoughts found hers.

Iris looked at her father bitterly. He caught her eye and quickly climbed down from his horse and came to her.

'What is it?' he said.

'Enola wasn't given one,' she muttered.

'Iris, come now, it wouldn't be proper. I won't insult the Vandemeres.'

'Then why did you ask her to come today? Why did you include her?'

'Iris—'

She turned her back on him.

'Iris,' he said again, a caution in his voice. 'I will not insult the father of your children.'

'You've insulted him already by keeping her here,' she said.

The foal had begun to skip about in circles, with Jacobi laughing on its back. The stable boy looked flustered as he tried to keep hold of him. Iris heard her father sigh and felt instantly guilty for snapping at him. She understood why he couldn't treat Enola like the other two children. She couldn't blame him. And, what was more, even if Enola had been legitimate, it would have been wrong to give her a gift like this. A creature as pure as a Latheerian horse didn't deserve to be tainted by her dark thoughts.

'Mount your horses. We are leaving!' Matthew called, walking over to the foal. Iris almost gasped as he removed the rope from around its neck.

'What are you doing? He can't ride it by himself!' she protested, handing Rose to a maid and striding after him.

'Of course he can!' Matthew said.

'He's only two. He doesn't know what he's doing!'

'He'll be three soon. I was his age when I first rode Wistor. It's better to start them off young. Riding will become second nature to him,' he said, tossing the rope aside.

'But he'll fall!'

'Then we'll put him back on. Iris, don't fret. No harm will come to him,' he said, giving the foal's nose a rub before walking back to his own horse and hoisting himself up onto its back.

'How do you know that?' she said.

Matthew turned to Master Hagworth. 'Master Hagworth, you have a Seer's blood. Will any harm come to my grandson?'

Master Hagworth straightened up in his saddle. He looked affronted.

'My Lord, what my father claimed to be and what he really was are two different matters. Perhaps if he had dedicated as much time to reading and furthering his mind as he did to providing false insight into people's futures, he might have made something of his life and met his end in a comfortable bed instead of a ditch outside a tavern,' he said curtly, the vein in his forehead throbbing.

Matthew seemed surprised by the outburst. Iris was not; she knew by now never to mention Seers to Master Hagworth. It was a sensitive subject. She had found herself on the receiving end of the schoolmaster's wrath countless times before for such impudence. Her father bowed his head apologetically.

Master Hagworth flushed with embarrassment.

'Forgive me, my Lord, forgive me,' he said. 'Lady Iris, I will personally ensure that no harm comes to young Jacobi today.'

Iris backed down. She trusted Master Hagworth. He was a man of his word.

'Hold his mane like this,' she said to Jacobi, folding his hands around the hair at the nape of the foal's neck. 'Don't let go,' she added, before leaving him to mount Lareena, who had just ambled, unaccompanied, into the courtyard from the stables.

Thomas and Eve hurried down the castle steps, followed by four servants, who were laden with sacks of bread, cheese and ale for the journey. Matthew sighed impatiently and his horse began to fidget.

'Quickly, quickly,' he said to them. Eve stopped in her tracks and looked at him in dismay, clearly horrified to have been made the focus of everyone's attention. Iris tutted under her breath at her father. Eve's Companion ran down the steps after her and put an arm around her shoulders to calm her nerves as a jittery, chestnut-coloured Latheerian horse came careering through the courtyard, its blue eyes wild, and skidded to a halt before Eve. But Eve made no move to climb onto its back. She covered her face while her Companion soothed her, speaking to her softly. Matthew pinched the bridge of his nose and closed his eyes, but said no more as he waited.

When, finally, everyone had mounted their horses, Matthew nodded to the guards, who opened the gates. They filed out behind him. Iris rode at the front with Rose. Thomas, Eve and Eve's Companion rode beside her, followed closely by Jacobi and Master Hagworth, ten guards, four servants, three stable boys and two lady's maids.

After a hard ride across open fields, they reached the outskirts of Lambelee and the steep descent into Mortenstone Valley was suddenly upon them. Trees clung to the hills, bent and warped over time as they struggled to remain upright.

Master Hagworth had his work cut out for him trying to keep Jacobi on the foal, which was as nervous as its new master on the crumbling slope. It tripped and staggered and almost fell to the ground completely when its hoof clipped a stone. Jacobi started to cry and begged to ride with Iris on her horse, but Matthew would not allow it.

'The first ride is the most important,' he said. 'He cannot abandon him.'

They rode on, along wide tracks that snaked through the valley's forests. Sunlight seeped through the delicate green leaves, making everything around them glow with warmth. Jacobi quickly forgot about his fear, so enraptured was he by the wild, dappled deer, the rabbits and the streams and the great, lolloping valley dogs that bounded alongside them. Iris beamed as she watched him and gently shook Rose, who was leaning against her on the horse, sleeping. She woke with a start.

'Look,' Iris said, kissing her daughter's soft cheek. Rose leaned forward eagerly to stare at the large brown mushrooms with fat stems and spotted tops on the edge of the track. 'Do you know what they are?' Iris whispered. As she spoke, a small, winged creature flew out from under a mushroom top, flitting left and right before disappearing behind a tree. Rose gaped after it. 'Oh, look!' Iris exclaimed. 'A mushroom fairy.'

As they pushed on, the slope became gentler, the ground underfoot fern-covered and springy. More and more mushrooms lined the path, some reaching as high as the horses' flanks. The fairies buzzed around them, wings beating rapidly and glinting with light. They filled the air like golden dust. Rose reached up and tried to catch one as it passed overhead but Iris brought her hand back down.

'Be careful, my love,' she said softly.

When Matthew called for them to halt, Iris looked up. Over his shoulder, she could see several horses standing together further down the track, their reins fastened to tree branches. In front of them stood Maid Morgan, Enola and three Mortenstone guards, who looked utterly bored. Iris's horse shuddered and jerked its head back suddenly. She could feel the creature's distress and it began to make her own heart beat wildly.

'Lareena,' she said firmly, as the horse backed into Master Hagworth's gelding. She held tight onto its mane. *What is it?* she asked silently. Enola's image flashed across her mind and, as it did, she felt another swell of panic. Lareena's panic. She took a sharp breath. Her horse was afraid of Enola. *It's alright*, she thought, *it's alright*, but Lareena only continued to back up.

Master Hagworth was shouting at her now; his horse was growing agitated, stamping its hooves as Lareena pushed against it.

Iris slid down off the horse quickly, pulling Rose with her.

'Sorry!' she said, skirting around her father, who had come to help them. Master Hagworth shouted after her, ordering her to come back and control the animal. But she didn't want to be near Lareena just now. She wanted to be as far from her as possible.

'Enola!' she said cheerfully, walking along the track towards her, heart still racing. Enola's eyes drifted past her to the commotion behind. Iris didn't look back. Lareena's fear troubled her. She had made a blood bond with her horse when she was three years old. How, then, could the creature be afraid of Enola? Was she not half Mortenstone? Was she not of Iris's blood? It didn't make sense. And yet it did.

She knelt in the fern and placed Rose next to her. Then she took Enola's hands.

'Are you warm enough?' she said. Enola did not respond; she didn't even look at her. Iris glanced at Maid Morgan, who averted her eyes, pretending not to have witnessed the exchange.

'Come, Enola. Master Hagworth has exciting spells for you to learn,' said Matthew, striding past them. 'Jacobi, keep up,' he called. Jacobi stumbled after him. Master Hagworth followed, hands filled with parchment and quills. He looked at Iris angrily and then raised his chin and walked on. Enola pulled her hands free with a hard tug and went after him.

Iris got to her feet as Thomas and Eve reached her and together they led Rose towards the others, who were now gathering around a tree stump by the side of the path. Master Hagworth put the parchment and quills on the ground and dusted his cloak; he cast Iris another scathing look as he did so. Iris sat next to Eve on a bed of moss and pulled Rose onto her lap. Thomas stood behind them, arms folded, watching, as Matthew picked Enola up and sat her next to Jacobi on the tree stump.

'Do you know where we are?' he said. Jacobi shook his head. Enola remained expressionless. 'We are in Mortenstone Valley. Do you know why we call it that?' Jacobi shook his head again. 'Because this is where our ancestors are from. Where we are from. Do you know who our most famous ancestor is?'

'Merlin,' said Jacobi.

'Very good. Merlin Mortenstone. Merlin the Good. And Merlin was born here, in this valley. Did you know that?'

Jacobi's mouth fell open. 'Where is his house?' he asked, looking thoroughly excited.

Matthew chuckled. 'Well…Mortenstone Castle was his home, where we live now. But the house in which he was born is far away, deep in the heart of the valley. We won't go there today.'

'I want to see it.'

'One day you will. I will take you there. Both of you. And Rose. Would you like that?' Matthew said. Jacobi nodded vigorously. Rose copied her brother.

Matthew's eyes flicked to Enola, who stared but didn't answer, and then he looked away, turning to the schoolmaster. 'Master Hagworth, please begin the children's lesson.'

Master Hagworth came forward and knelt in front of them. He stared at each of the children in turn over his spectacles. Then, he held out a quill horizontally and took his hand away. The quill remained, suspended, in the air. The children watched it intently. Suddenly, the quill dropped. But, before it hit the ground, it stopped again, hovering above the moss. Master Hagworth leaned forward.

'That is mind magic,' he said. And he reached out and picked up the quill, pointing the feathered end at them. 'Where I come from, this is the magic we are born with. We use our thoughts to control the world around us. It takes much practice and skill. In Draxvar, they use blood magic,' he said. 'Any spell or enchantment requires a drop of blood, or more, depending on the spell. In the Low Lands, they use hand magic. A swish of the hand,' he said, swiping his own hand through the air, 'is what it takes to make things happen. In Edgeton, spells are spoken. Incantations, we call them. The easiest magic to perform,' he said, a derisive smile twisting his lips. Iris heard her father laugh. 'And do you know what kind of magic they are born with here in Mortenstone Valley?' Master Hagworth continued, leaning even closer and looking at them conspiratorially. The children stared at him, enraptured. 'All of it!' he said. 'Everything. A Mortenstone is born with the ability to command mind, blood, hand and spoken magic. That makes you stronger and more powerful than anyone else, but only if you practise. If you do not master your magic, then others can master you.'

The children absorbed Master Hagworth's words unblinkingly. He sat back, looking quietly pleased with himself.

Iris remembered the day she had received the same lesson from the schoolmaster. He told it exactly as he did now, with the same theatrics, the same trick with the feather. And one day, when they were old enough to understand, he would tell her children the whole story. He would tell them about the family who shared the valley and its magic with the Mortenstones. He would teach them about that family's rebellion and the events it set in motion, and how those events changed the course of history and the realm they might have known.

'Now, here is what I want you to do,' said Master Hagworth, taking two quills and handing them to Enola and Jacobi. 'We will start with some simple hand magic. Using your hands, I want you to make your quills float. You must concentrate. Gently bring your hands over the quill. Do you feel that? There should be a pulsing feeling in your palm. Focus on that feeling. Make it grow. Now, move your hands up. Ah!' he exclaimed, as both children lifted their hands and their quills rose from their laps and hovered in the air. 'Very good!'

'Look, Mama!' Jacobi said, smiling with delight.

'I see! Well done, Jacobi!' Iris said, clapping.

'When you are older and stronger, you will be able to make the quill float with a single thought,' said Master Hagworth.

'I want to do it now!' Jacobi said impatiently.

'Ah, but you cannot, dear boy. Not yet. Mind magic is a gift that will come to you when you are nine, perhaps older. I was eleven - a late developer.'

Iris and her father exchanged a look. Enola had mastered mind magic before she could walk.

'Now, here is your next exercise. Take this parchment here,' said the schoolmaster, handing each of the children a sheet. 'Go and find somewhere quiet to sit. Wait for the first creature you see. Then draw it. Make it a detailed drawing. And then come back to me and tell me four things you noticed about that creature. Off you go,' he said, shooing them away. They climbed down from the tree stump and went off in different directions. Maid Morgan followed Enola and a young lady's maid accompanied Jacobi.

When they were gone, Matthew, Thomas and Master Hagworth discussed their growing concern over the illegal trade of Latheerian horses across the border, while Iris and Eve threw up armfuls of leaves for Rose to run beneath.

'Throw them higher, Iris!' Eve cried, laughing as freely as Rose as she launched the leaves into the air and ducked under them as they fell.

Iris glanced at her sister distractedly and then returned her attention to Lareena, who had begun to paw at the ground in the distance. As one of the stable boys attempted to soothe her, she grunted and snapped at his hand. Iris dropped the leaves she was carrying.

Suddenly, there was a flash of white light. And a scream.

Without a second thought, she was running, running in the direction Enola and Maid Morgan had gone, running down a moss-covered hill with her father, sliding and stumbling, blood rushing in her ears. They emerged onto a twisting, uneven path and stopped. Maid Morgan was sprawled on the ground with her hands over her face. Enola was sitting calmly, further along the path, surrounded by smoking debris. Iris stared at it for a moment. And then she realised what it was and backed away, her mouth falling open in horror. Blackened mushrooms were strewn across the track. The little fairies that inhabited them lay scattered on the ground around them, contorted in all sorts of hideous ways. Dead. All dead. Their skin was grey. Their delicate wings scorched. Their little eyes vacant.

Iris ran to Enola, grabbed her by the arms and shook her. 'What have you done?' she shouted.

Thomas and Eve came crashing down the hill onto the path, with the guards and stable boys close at their heels. Eve began to scream when she saw the bodies.

Iris felt the forest spinning around her, the trees merging into one green blur, Eve's screams ringing in her ears. And, over the screaming, the nearby howl of a valley dog, followed by a cacophony of distant barking. Word was spreading. She looked at her father, who, hearing the sound, straightened up.

'Ready the horses,' he called to the stable boys. They looked at him blankly. 'Now!' he shouted. The boys turned at once and ran back up the hill, passing Master Hagworth as he stepped down onto the path.

Iris grabbed Enola's hand and began to drag her away. The creatures of the valley would descend upon them soon if they did not move.

Matthew scooped Maid Morgan up off the ground. Her eyes were red and swollen, her cheeks streaked with tears. And then her head drooped and lolled to one side. She had fainted. Matthew handed her to the guards.

'Take her. Put her on a horse!' he said. Then he turned to Thomas. 'Get Eve back to the horses!'

Thomas wrapped his arms around Eve's waist and began to haul her, screeching, up the hill. She struggled and fought against him. When he dropped her, Matthew ran to help him and together they carried her.

Halfway up the hill, Iris hesitated, looking back at Master Hagworth, who had not moved.

'Master Hagworth! We have to leave now!' she cried. But Master Hagworth didn't appear to have heard her. He was kneeling on the ground, staring at the bodies of the mushroom fairies. Exasperated, Iris ran back down the hill towards him, leaping over Enola's discarded piece of parchment. 'Master Hagworth!' she called, as the schoolmaster reached out and touched one of the dead creatures with the tip of his finger. Suddenly, his hand shot back as if he had been shocked. He fell backwards and shrieked, his eyes twitching, flickering, jerking wildly. 'Master Hagworth!' Iris shouted, reaching him and sinking to her knees to cradle his head in her hands. Master Hagworth drew long, rasping breaths and stared up at her without recognition. And then, slowly, his expression changed. A haunted look crept over his face. 'What is it?' Iris said. The schoolmaster grasped her arm. She helped him sit up and, as she did, his eyes locked onto something over her shoulder. She followed his gaze to Enola and looked between them as they stared at each other. And then she noticed that Master Hagworth's hands were trembling. She studied the old man's face; in his eyes, she saw a thousand fears.

The next day was Enola's fourth birthday. Iris fled the castle to Stone Lane in the morning to escape the incessant whispering, without visiting her daughter. Everyone had heard about what Enola had done. The very air felt toxic with the tale as it passed from person to person. Iris felt bitterly ashamed. For years, she had told them all Enola would be different, not like other Reverofs. And she had been wrong. It wouldn't be long, she imagined, before her father finally sent Enola away. There was a reason her mother and Lucian looked so happy. There was a reason the elves, who had tried to take her before, had been called back to the castle. And there was a reason her father had not asked for any items of clothing to be packed for Enola. Iris only hoped that when they disposed of her daughter – and they *would* dispose of her – that they did it quickly and

147

painlessly, that the deed be done by somebody, anybody, other than the physician who had been so desperate to do it years before.

She stopped halfway along the lane and watched two guards amble in from the Grassland. After years of sitting around in the camp down by the border, with nothing else to do but sleep and eat and rut with serving women who lived in the tents beside theirs, they had grown lazy and fat. The guards barrelled into the Snakes Head Inn. Iris stared absentmindedly at the door as it swung shut behind them. Then, suddenly, she felt a tap on her shoulder. Startled, she turned around and looked down into the bright eyes of a young boy, no older than ten. His clothes were heavily stained and covered in muck, like his face. She almost gasped when she realised who he was.

'William?' she said. 'What are you doing here?'

William glanced warily at the people passing by and leaned in to whisper, 'I have a message for you, from Alexander. He wants to meet. Tonight.'

13. THE FINAL FEAST

Alexander sat on the floor of his mother's bedchamber with a goblet of wine. The furs on her bed were folded neatly, the clothes in her chest untouched. A fire flickered in the hearth, throwing warmth into the icy cold air, and candles burned on the mantelpiece. It was as if the room waited for her return. Fabian had never treated her well. He had been cruel and chipped away at her spirit, day by day, until there was nothing left but a shadow of a woman with lost hopes and broken dreams. Alexander often wished his father would take her place in death, though, as the years wore on, it seemed to him that his wish was sustained purely out of habit. Because, in truth, it was impossible to miss her when she had so faded from his memory. Already, he had forgotten the sound of her voice. Soon, he would forget her face, too, for his father kept no portraits of her. There would come a day when she was simply gone. And that day was fast approaching. He could feel it.

He stared at his reflection in the mirror on the wall and took another mouthful of wine. Then, he stood up unsteadily. The wine began to spill; he tipped back the goblet to save it but lost his footing and fell, landing on the wine-soaked flagstones with a wet slap. The goblet rolled across the floor into the leg of the desk. He looked at himself in the mirror again and smiled crookedly, the way Fabian smiled. And then he started to laugh. And laugh. And laugh. And laugh. He could hardly breathe as he stared at himself, on his hands and knees, face spattered with red wine.

Two servants came rushing into the chamber and bent down to help him to his feet. When they finally got him up, they exchanged a look of unease. One of the servants snapped his fingers; the red stain on the flagstones vanished and the goblet disappeared, transported to the kitchens deep beneath the castle. Alexander tried to protest but his words were incomprehensible.

The servants propped him up on their shoulders and escorted him to his bedchamber, where they lowered him onto the bed and piled blankets and furs on top of him. They stoked the fire and lit candles before they left.

It was dark outside when he awoke. A boy was shaking his arm timidly.

'My Lord, you asked me to wake you when it was time,' the boy said. Alexander's skull felt tight and his head throbbed painfully. He tried to get up but collapsed back onto the pillow under the weight of the furs. He looked at the boy again and slowly began to comprehend his words. He felt a twinge in the pit of his stomach and sat up suddenly, remembering what he had to do.

'Get me my cloak,' he said. 'And something to clear my head.'

The boy went off and returned, almost instantly, with his cloak and a small, thin vial of green liquid. Alexander pulled out the cork with his teeth, spat it onto the bed and drank. His vision became sharp and focused once more and his headache disappeared. He felt light and fresh again, but the knots in his stomach remained. His hands shook as he fastened his cloak.

'Do you want me to accompany you, my Lord?' said the boy.

'No.'

*

'He's preparing to leave, my Lord. But he's been drinking wine. Lots of it,' said the boy.

Fabian's lip curled into a snarl. He stood and walked to the window, staring out into the night. It did not surprise him; Alexander had been in a wine-induced oblivion for almost four years. But, tonight, it was unacceptable. He was relying on his son. Tonight, their fate depended on him.

He had beaten Alexander with his own hands when word had reached him about Iris Mortenstone's pregnancy. Could there be a greater betrayal than that of a son fraternising with the enemy? And, worse, Alexander had tried to deny it. When the child was born, Fabian had beaten him again, the memory of his son's disloyalty stinging him afresh. But, after that, they heard no more of the Reverof girl - dead, most likely, he thought - and his anger drained away. The years slipped by without incident, each season as bleak and cold as the last. And then, at the end of the wet summer just passed, his men made a discovery. They found a Mortenstone Castle maid romping with a Mortenstone guard in the Dark Forest and captured them both. Fabian learned from the maid that the Reverof child still lived, that she was a strange girl, deviously clever, and prone to vicious outbursts that unnerved the bravest of men. But what intrigued him most of all were the girl's extraordinary abilities. The maid told him that, by the age of three, the girl had more power than a grown witch or sorcerer. A cruel and dangerous child, it seemed. And yet Matthew Mortenstone had allowed her to remain in his castle. Why, when she was illegitimate? Why, when her very existence undermined his authority? The maid did not know. But the answer came to him soon enough. Matthew Mortenstone had a weakness – his daughter, Iris. And if she ruled his heart, then she ruled The Light. And if her heart belonged to Alexander, then perhaps he had been too harsh on his son. Maybe Alexander had the power to win back their lands. The more he thought about it, the surer he became. And now, tonight, it would all unfold. He would do what no Mordark had yet achieved. If Alexander succeeded, if he lured Iris Mortenstone into the forest and held her captive, they could demand what they wanted most from Matthew Mortenstone. They could force him to lift the border spell. And they could fight him at last for what was rightfully theirs.

Fabian watched from his window as a torch was ignited and a figure carried it down the sloping hill towards the Dark Forest. When the figure stopped and turned and he saw Alexander looking back at him over the flickering flames, he smiled.

'Ready the men,' he said to the guards behind him.

∗

As Alexander walked along the path towards Agatha's house, he sensed a stillness in the air, as if a great breath had been drawn. All was quiet. The forest was listening. He heard a sound and swung the torch to the side to see a lump of bark crumbling away from a tree. He stared for a moment and then continued, heart pounding, one hand clenched tight around a length of rope.

He rapped on Agatha's door three times and it opened immediately. Agatha poked her head out, looked left and right and then waved him inside hastily. He doused the torch in a bucket of water and went in.

Iris was standing by the fire. He stopped when he saw her. His heart started to race. He felt hot and cold at the same time. Beads of sweat formed on his brow. He had half expected her not to come. But there she was before him, unchanged and yet different. The youth had gone from her face; her cheeks were hollow, her bones sharp and prominent. She was a woman now. He couldn't meet her eye. He had behaved terribly the last time they had met. He had hurt her, abandoned her. And now they were together again and he was going to do far, far worse. He could feel her watching him and held the rope behind his back.

Agatha pushed him forwards, firmly.

'You asked her to come. Now tell her what she's doing here.'

Steeling himself, he raised his head and looked Iris in the eye.

'How are you?' he said sheepishly. Before he had the chance to blink, Iris had crossed the room and slapped him hard across the face.

'That's enough!' Agatha said, stepping between them and pointing a crooked finger at Iris. 'The boy came to make amends. Strike him again and—'

'It's alright, Agatha. Leave her,' he said. A red welt had begun to appear on his cheek and it burned like fire. He blinked away a tear and faced Iris again. But, when he saw that she was crying, he dropped his gaze to the floor.

'It's been four years. Four years and I've heard nothing. Why now?' she said in a choked voice.

Alexander shrugged. The rope was coarse in his hand. He brought it round to his side. He needed to do it. Now.

'You're everything they say you are, you know,' Iris said suddenly. He froze. 'You're cold-blooded. You don't care about me or our daughter, only yourself.'

'That's not true!' he said hotly. 'I care! Of course I care!'

'Liar,' she said. She tried to move past him to the door but he clutched her arm and pulled her back. 'Let go!' she said.

'I wanted to see you again. I wanted to see her. You could have come and you didn't!' he shouted, tightening his grip on her arm.

'Come? So you could kill her? Do you think I'm a fool?' she said, wrenching her arm free. And then a strange look came over her face, the anger seeped away, leaving an expression of calm resignation in its place. 'You'll get your wish soon enough. She's going to die tomorrow. My father has given the order.'

Alexander's stomach lurched. 'What?' he said, staring at her in disbelief.

When he first heard that his daughter had been born, he had felt a rush of relief he hadn't expected to feel. He asked anyone he came across in the Dark Forest for information about her – what did she look like? Was she being cared for? He felt vulnerable, too, as though another part of him were living just out of reach, out of his protection. But those fears were lessened somewhat because he knew Iris would look after her and fight for her, as she had done the last time they had met, when he had told her to kill their unborn child.

'Iris, you can't! Don't let him kill her. You're her mother!'

'You don't know what she's like,' she said.

'You're her mother!' he repeated. 'Protect her. Hide her away. Take her away! Bring her here!'

Iris shook her head and a few tears slipped out, dropping onto her cloak. 'I tried to love her. I did. I tried and tried for years,' she said, sniffing and wiping her eyes. 'But she's a monster. I didn't want to believe it but she is. See for yourself if you want. Come tonight. There won't be another time. Come tonight and see.'

'Come where?'

'The castle.'

'I can't come to the castle.'

'You can,' she said.

'If I cross the border, I'll—'

'It's no longer bewitched. The spell ran its course.'

There was a loud clatter as Agatha, who had moved back to the fire, knocked her cup off the mantelpiece, spilling silvery liquid all over the rug on the floor. She stared at Iris, aghast.

Alexander let go of the rope; it fell to the floor with a soft thump. He looked at Agatha and then Iris.

'You're sure?' he said.

'My father said so himself. That's why it's guarded,' she said. 'Will you come?'

He nodded. 'Do you still have the stone I gave you?'

'Yes.'

'Hide it somewhere out of sight. I can transport myself to wherever it is.'

Iris's eyes lit up. She nodded vigorously. 'I'll go on ahead!' She hurried to the door and paused briefly to turn and look at William, who was sitting on the stairs, peering through the gaps in the railing. 'Thank you,' she said.

The moment the door closed behind her, Alexander pulled it open and ran out after her.

'Iris! Wait!' he shouted. Iris stopped further along the path and looked around. 'I'm sorry,' he said.

She stared at him for a moment and then her face softened and she smiled sadly.

'So am I,' she said.

When she had gone, Alexander turned back for the house and saw Agatha standing on the path in the light of the doorway, holding the rope.

'Is there something you need to tell me, boy?'

'No,' he said, and he began to walk past her into the house.

'You have never been any good at lying,' she said. 'Listen to me. Don't go over there alone. It could be a trap.'

Alexander stopped and looked at her over his shoulder.

'I'm not going alone,' he said.

*

Enola was fast asleep in her bed when Iris entered the chamber. Maid Morgan was snoozing on a chair by the fire. Iris went straight to the bed, drew back the covers and gathered Enola in her arms. As she turned to leave, she was startled to find Maid Morgan awake and standing in front of the doorway with a fierce look on her face.

'Your service is no longer needed,' said Iris.

Maid Morgan looked affronted. She straightened up and unfolded her arms.

'It is my duty to look after her,' she said.

'Your service is no longer needed,' Iris said again, pushing past her and leaving through the open door.

She climbed the back staircase to her own rooms and went to the small chamber adjoining the children's nursery. There, she tucked Enola into a narrow bed and listened to the fire crackle comfortingly in the hearth. She wondered if she should wake her but decided against it for now.

As she watched Enola and smoothed out her hair, she noticed a small bump in the breast pocket of her nightgown. Slowly, she slipped her fingers into the pocket and pulled out the blue stone. She stared at it in the firelight. She hadn't noticed it was missing. How long had Enola had it for? The stone was warm. As she turned it over in her hands, it grew warmer still. Soon it was hot, so hot that she dropped it on the floor. She rose from the bed and bent over the stone, watching, as it began to judder and glow from within. She stepped away quickly as light burst from the stone, illuminating the room. She covered her eyes. The light faded in an instant and, when she brought her hands down, Alexander was standing in front of her. He didn't seem real. When she thought of him, she thought of the forest, of Agatha's house. Here, he looked out of place. He stared about the room in wonder, like a boy who had found his way into a full pantry.

'It's nice here. No damp,' he said, running his fingers over the gold candlestick on the mantelpiece.

Iris reached out and clasped his hand tightly. Then, she glanced over at the bed. Alexander fell completely still. He stared at the little mound beneath the blankets in silence.

'Come,' she whispered, leading him across the room. His hand began to tremble in hers when they stopped beside the bed and looked down at Enola. Iris smiled up at him, suddenly overcome with emotion. This would be the first and last time he saw his daughter. She almost didn't want to wake her because, in that moment, Enola was a perfect little girl, sleeping peacefully, the picture of innocence.

Suddenly, the nursery door opened and Jacobi appeared behind it. He looked afraid when he saw Alexander.

'Mama?' he said. Iris rushed over to him and picked him up.

'Shhh,' she said soothingly, kissing his head. 'Back to bed.' She left the room with Jacobi in her arms. He stared at Alexander over her shoulder as she went.

When Iris returned, she walked to the door by the fireplace and opened it a fraction, peering through the gap into the corridor beyond. When she was sure no one was there, she closed it and walked back over to the bed, perching on the edge to stroke Enola's hair again. She would have to wake her. Alexander needed to see what she was truly like. She closed her eyes for a moment. Then, filling with dread, she tapped Enola once, twice, three times on the shoulder. Her eyes opened. With sorrow in her heart, Iris turned to Alexander – and gasped. He was gone.

She rushed to the door, which stood ajar, threw it back on its hinges and burst into the corridor, looking all about. She ran to the gallery and looked down from the balcony. Panic seized her as she saw Alexander disappearing along the corridor below.

'Alexander!' she hissed, running down the staircase after him. She caught a glimpse of his shadow as he turned the corner at the end of the passage. 'Stop!'

*

In the dining hall, the feast was well underway. The Vandemeres had arrived at Mortenstone Castle that very day, as well as the Doldons of Draxvar. Matthew had invited the Doldons to the castle to reprimand them for a severe punishment they had issued upon a Draxvarian sheep farmer. It was their right, as stewards of Draxvar, to punish law breakers, but this particular sentence was too severe in his opinion. It was said that life in the cold North hardened a man's heart and, hearing of what they

158

had done, he believed it. No crime was worthy of such a barbaric punishment, no man deserved to be used as bait on a dragon hunt. No, they would need to be spoken to – but tactfully so. They were not an exceptionally intelligent family, nor were their powers as advanced as the Vandemeres', but even he did not think he would be quick enough to duck Alastair Doldon's fist in the heat of the moment, and brute force could kill a man just as well as magic. Subtlety was key. He had another plan to ensure that the family remained loyal, too. He was going to promise Thomas to one of Alastair Doldon's three girls. He thought he would let Thomas decide which one. But the announcement could wait.

The Vandemeres were in good spirits. They ate and drank heartily and regaled the table with tales from the Low Lands. The mood was contagious. Josephine had smiled twice before the second course had been served. Matthew looked at her fondly. It pleased him when she was like this, and he suspected it had a lot to do with Iris's absence.

He sat back in his chair and sighed. Iris. She was always there, in the back of his mind. How would she react, he wondered, when her daughter was sent away in the morning, never to return? He suspected she knew what was going to happen, but she hadn't come to speak to him or to beg for Enola's life.

He had made many mistakes as a father, but the one thing he did not regret was the chance he had given Iris to bond with her child. Surely, she would not forget that. He had allowed her more freedoms than most fathers, allowed her to realise for herself that Enola was beyond love and help. And he had lived, ever since, knowing that his advisors, his family, his people thought him weak. But it was worth it. For Iris.

*

The voices from the dining hall grew louder and more boisterous as Alexander approached. He stopped outside the doors. His body shook with anger. He clenched his teeth. Matthew Mortenstone had given the order to kill his child. And Iris was going to let him do it.

He saw Iris from the corner of his eye, running towards him along the corridor.

A sudden bout of raucous laughter erupted from the dining hall. He held out his dagger.

'Stop! No!' Iris screamed.

In one swift motion, he threw open the doors and stormed into the dining hall. He ran straight to the head of the table, raised his dagger and plunged it into Matthew Mortenstone's heart.

Iris burst into the room and screamed when she saw her father in his chair, the knife buried deep in his chest. Alexander looked at her coldly and then folded his arms over his chest and vanished.

He felt the wind on his face and opened his eyes. He was at the border. Without looking back, he ran into the forest, all the way to the Hang Man, where Vrax and his men were waiting, ready to receive their hostage.

'Where is she?' Vrax hissed.

'I don't have her,' said Alexander.

Vrax stared at him incredulously. 'What do you mean? What about the plan? Why—'

'We don't need her. The border isn't enchanted. Just go!'

14. INTO DARKNESS

Iris sank to the floor in despair as her father's head fell back against his chair, eyes vacant, and blood began to seep through his tunic. In the candlelight, the silver serpent on the dagger's handle glinted.

There was a moment of complete stillness. The fire in the great hearth roared, the food on the table steamed, but no one moved, no one spoke, no one breathed. They all stared at the space where Alexander had stood in stunned silence. Matthew Mortenstone was dead.

'Mordarks,' Josephine said in a strangled whisper, turning to the horrified faces around the table. Then, clutching her chest, she sprang from her seat, wild-eyed, and screamed the name at the top of her lungs. 'MORDARKS!'

The hall exploded into life. Guards poured in and began to shout, disappearing back through the doorway, some vanishing into thin air. Alastair Doldon launched himself across the table, growling with rage. Plates and glasses smashed as he landed heavily on the other side.

'Find him!' he bellowed and, whipping a knife from his belt, bolted from the hall. Gregory Vandemere followed him.

Eric Vandemere rose from his chair in a daze, staring first at Matthew and then Eve, who was clawing at her own face, her screams shrill and piercing, scratching until her skin turned red with blood. But no one tried to stop her.

Iris watched them, watched as Thomas walked to the head of the table and touched their father's lifeless arm, watched as Edward Vandemere rushed towards her, knocking a chair aside as he came. He was saying something but his voice seemed far-off. He fell to his knees, grasped her shoulders and said it again, shaking her, but his words were no clearer. She stared at him blankly, until a guttural cry rang out, filling the room, overpowering even Eve's screams. Lucian. Iris looked past Edward to her brother as he pushed himself to his feet and began to stagger around the table, drawing rasping half-breaths, holding onto the backs of the chairs as he went. He stopped beside their mother and stabbed a finger at Iris from across the table.

'Seize her!' he shrieked, his chest heaving as he summoned the strength to repeat his order. 'Seize her now! She let him in. She led him here!'

Suddenly, hands were grabbing at her, dragging her up from the floor, while others held Edward back. Iris didn't struggle. And, when Edward had been restrained, she went without protest.

Two guards took her across the courtyard to a black, studded iron door. While one of them heaved it open, the other took a torch from a bracket on the wall. Then, they led her down to the dungeons, into darkness.

Faint moans disturbed the quiet as the prisoners were roused by the heavy thud of the guards' boots. Iris saw their withered forms in the glow of the torchlight, their outstretched hands grasping feebly at nothing as they reached through the bars. She wasn't afraid of them. She felt only numb, the image of her father, dead

162

in his chair, fixed in her mind. Alexander had betrayed her.

The guards flung her into an empty cell at the end of the passage. She fell to the straw-strewn ground with a gasp of pain and clutched her crushed wrist as the door clanged shut behind her.

Suddenly, the castle bells began to ring. The guards exchanged an ominous look and hastily locked the cell door before clambering back up the steps, drawing their weapons. As they opened the door at the top, Iris heard the screams from the courtyard and the distant roar of men. And then the door slammed shut and the cries were silenced.

Heart racing, she got to her feet and tried to force the cell door open with her mind, willing the lock to break, the door to collapse, seeing it before her eyes as if it had already happened. When that did not work, she shook the bars in desperation.

'Let me out! Please, let me out!' she shouted. But she knew no one would come. And she knew that whatever was happening out there was entirely her fault.

*

Hundreds of men in black armour surged across the Grassland from the Dark Forest. Screams filled the night as they reached Stone Lane and townspeople fled in terror towards the castle.

Vrax Mordark moved with purpose, obliterating everyone in his path as he stormed the lane ahead of his men. With the mere swipe of his arm, townspeople were snatched off their feet and thrown with bone-shattering force into buildings, their broken bodies falling to the ground motionless.

Lucian erupted from the castle with his mother close behind him. People were flooding through the gates, trampling the guards who were posted there, swarming the courtyard. He watched them, aghast; an endless stream, clambering over one another as they raced towards the castle doors.

'Close the doors!' he shouted to his mother. As Josephine turned back, he raced down the steps, fighting his way through the people until he was at the gates. He thrust his arms forward with all his strength and felt a cold wave rise up through him. The people pushing their way into the courtyard were suddenly flung backwards across the square, knocking others down as they fell. Lucian drew his arms in tight against his chest and the gates swung shut with a screech of metal. He stared as people got to their feet and rushed forwards again, the whites of their eyes shining in the moonlight. They clung to the gates; some began to climb in desperation.

'Help us! Help us!'

'They're coming!'

'…Mordarks!'

'Please… Open the gates!'

Lucian turned his back on them and looked around the courtyard for Eric Vandemere. The cries behind him became more frantic. When he saw Eric, stumbling around by the foot of the castle steps, he began to run, barging through a group of hysterical women and children.

'Call on your army!' he shouted. 'Now!'

Eric looked up. His mouth opened and closed dumbly.

'Get them here! Go!' Lucian bellowed. Eric nodded, half-stunned, swept his hands upwards through the air and vanished.

An orange burst of light lit up the courtyard. Lucian turned. Smoke and fire were rising into the sky from Stone Lane. The screams rang out in the square, and people were tumbling down over the castle gates into the courtyard.

'Lucian!' His mother was beside him now. 'Go with Thomas, up to the tower. Use all the strength you have to force them back! Your magic is strong. Force them back!' she said, pushing him away. He turned, ears still ringing with the screams. Thomas was behind him. They ran together up to the East Tower.

From the turret, Lucian looked down at the dark figures surging towards the castle. His breaths came fast and ragged. A cold feeling settled beneath his skull. There were too many of them. How could he hope to fight them all back? They were getting closer, closer to the castle gates. He glanced at Thomas, who looked at him with defeat in his eyes, and felt a swell of bitter rage. Iris had doomed them all.

Suddenly, a hand came down on both their shoulders. Lucian turned to see Master Hagworth standing behind them. His heart leapt with a strange and unexpected relief.

'Remember what I taught you. From the gut,' said Master Hagworth, his face hard and unflinching.

Lucian clenched every muscle in his body, straightened his back and focused on the men below, willing them to fall back, away from the castle, imagining it. As he did, he felt movement within him, a tingling feeling that turned suddenly fierce. His belly, his fingertips, his feet, his heart shuddered with the current that blistered through him, racing through every nerve and fibre of his being. He shrieked with the pain. Next to him, Thomas began to convulse.

Master Hagworth kept a firm hand on their shoulders. 'Keep steady!' he said.

Down below, it was as if the men had run head-on into an explosion. They were blasted backwards,

.

hurtling through the air out of the square, back and back and back, crashing onto the cobbles of Stone Lane.

One man remained, continuing on alone into the square. But before Vrax Mordark reached the gates, a torrent of arrows rained down around him. He hesitated, and only then did he appear to notice that his men were gone. He looked back in the direction of Stone Lane, as more arrows flew at him from the castle towers, but the arrows changed paths at the last moment, bending away from him and clattering on the ground by his feet. His magic was powerful, there could be no doubt, but it wasn't enough. The castle gates opened. Mortenstone guards poured out into the square. Outnumbered, Vrax spread his fingers and a ball of flames appeared, swirling ferociously above his palm. As he prepared to launch it at them, something astonishing happened. Men in steel-grey armour began to materialise in the square. Five men, fifty men, two hundred men, five hundred men. Eric Vandemere appeared with them; raising a sword up into the air, he released a guttural cry, which the men echoed, and began to charge. Vrax hurled the ball of fire at them and turned to run.

'Retreat!' he cried as he disappeared down the lane.

*

Alexander staggered through the forest, his legs burning with fatigue, so drained after transporting himself to the border that even his heart was beating weakly. He saw his father in the distance, torchlight illuminating his face so that it seemed to hang suspended in the darkness. As he moved towards him, he heard a low murmur of voices. There might have been a thousand men or more standing amongst the trees, their forms half-outlined in the faint glow of the firelight. A hush crept over the men as he passed. He felt their eyes following him as he walked the last excruciating steps to his father and collapsed at his feet.

Fabian bent low and put a cold hand to Alexander's cheek, looking searchingly into his eyes. 'Do we have our hostage?'

'No,' said Alexander.

Fabian's hand slipped from his cheek. He stared at Alexander blankly for a moment, then dropped his gaze. 'The blood?' he said.

Alexander looked down at his blood-spattered hands. He could still hear Iris screaming, see the horror in her eyes, as if she were standing there in front of him. 'I killed Matthew Mortenstone,' he said. 'The border spell ran its course. Vrax is advancing on the castle.'

Fabian stared at him for a long time. The torch flickered in the wind, throwing shadows across his face. Two identical flames danced in his hungry eyes. The forest was still around them, the men watching on in silence as Fabian grasped Alexander's hands and pressed them to his face, inhaling deeply, smearing Matthew Mortenstone's blood over his face. Then, eyes swimming with tears of triumph, he rose and turned to his men.

'The time has come to take back what is ours! At last, the enchantment has broken! Matthew Mortenstone is dead!' A ripple of agitation spread through the ranks. 'This night will be remembered for all time! Go forth and fight with valour! For Avalon!' Fabian shouted, raising a gloved fist into the air.

'For Avalon!' the men cried.

They cascaded past, a deafening rattle of shields and swords. Fabian screamed with laughter as they went.

Alexander watched through drooping eyes, feeling his head sink lower to the ground, unable to stop it.

When the men had gone, Fabian bent over and kissed him roughly on the head. 'Stand up, my son. Come, I want to see their faces. I want to watch them scream before I kill them all!' he said.

'You said you would spare Iris and my child,' Alexander said.

'Did I?' said Fabian.

'That was the agreement.'

'You didn't honour your part of the agreement.'

'I went beyond what you asked,' Alexander said, trying to rise, his stomach twisting with unease.

'Yes, you did. And now, because of you, Vrax is taking the castle without me. I should have been the first to set foot in that place. Me! The agreement no longer stands.'

Alexander pushed himself to his feet in anger, clenching his fists so tight he lost all feeling in his hands.

Suddenly, a hoarse scream punctured the silence. Alexander stiffened and turned towards it. Something was moving in the distance, and with it came a clanking sound. The sound grew louder, accompanied by the low, frantic beat of boots against earth. Shouting. That scream again. And then, out of the darkness, a man in black armour emerged, eyes wide, arms flailing, two arrows jutting from his back, screaming as he passed them, hurtling away towards the Dark Lands. More followed. A great mass of men, running for their lives.

'Retreat! Retreat!' Vrax's cry was unmistakable.

Fabian did not hesitate; he gathered his cloak around him, turned and ran.

Alexander tripped and stumbled as he fled. He felt as though he were no longer a part of his own body. He was an observer, a stranger, seeing through his eyes, watching the trees in the darkness rushing by, glimpsing figures as they overtook him, listening to the pounding of his heart, his gasps for breath, the thump of his feet as they carried him away.

When he reached the Dark Lands, he dropped to the boggy ground and vomited. Vrax came to him at once and rolled him onto his back, slapping his cheeks.

'Are you hurt? Can you hear—' But before Vrax could utter another word, Fabian was upon him, hauling him to his feet.

'Well?' he hissed. 'Alexander breached the walls of Mortenstone Castle on his own. Why couldn't you, with three hundred men at your back?'

When Vrax didn't answer, Fabian spat in his face and walked away in disgust. He went to stand beside a stout man of middling age, who was gulping down water from a ladle offered to him by a young, tired-looking woman.

'You went with my son. Did he fight bravely, like a true leader, or did he run like a frightened pup at the first sign of danger?'

The stout man choked on his water. He swallowed and wiped his mouth with his sleeve, looking entirely surprised to have been approached by Fabian Mordark.

'He led well, my Lord, given the circumstances. We were outnumbered,' he said, eyes darting nervously to Vrax.

'They were unprepared and they overpowered us. Now they know we are coming,' Fabian said with one eye on the Dark Forest, from which the wounded were still emerging. 'They'll bite back. We must all be ready.'

'Oh, we'll be ready, my Lord. This is only the beginning. We'll win the war. It's written in our destiny,' the man said. Fabian looked perplexed. 'The prophecy, my Lord. The time has come, I'm certain of it. The border is no longer enchanted. The old magic is dying… Merlin's magic—'

'Don't speak his name,' Fabian said.

'Forgive me! I only meant that, without the old magic to keep us from them, we'll have our war at last, as the prophecy says.'

Fabian rolled his eyes and began to move away when he stopped abruptly and turned back to the stout man.

'The prophecy states that a witch will rule after the War of Wars. Are you waiting for my demise? Waiting to pledge allegiance to a woman? To betray me?'

'No, my Lord—'

'Then what makes you so sure we will win?'

'I-I'm not... I don't —' the stout man spluttered.

'Then you believe we will lose? Have you so little faith in me?'

The man fell into a desperate silence and looked around for support. No one met his eye.

'Something wrong with your tongue, man?' Fabian said.

'I have faith we will win and you will rule, my Lord. No White Witch,' he said.

Fabian smiled, but the smile did not reach his eyes. He put a hand on the man's shoulder and ran a long, pointed fingernail up his neck and traced it along his jaw. Then, seizing the man's throat with both hands, he snapped his neck with a deft twist.

No one disturbed Fabian as he stood over the man's body. He was frowning, his eyes moving quickly as if he was working something out, piecing fragments together in his mind. And, suddenly, his mouth fell open. Stunned, and looking almost afraid, he strode back to Vrax and put his lips to his ear.

'If you want to redeem yourself, fetch me the Reverof girl,' he said.

Alexander's eyes flicked open. He saw Vrax nod. He tried to lift his head but it felt as heavy as stone. Then his eyes closed and shut out the world.

15. IRIS

Iris pressed herself against the wall of her cell, trying to find a footing on the slimy ledge that ran the length of the back wall. Her feet kept slipping down but she persevered, frantic with terror, as rats flitted about the dungeon floor. One ran over her foot and she screamed, and a chorus of laughter echoed through the darkness from the other dungeon cells.

'Please! Let me out!' she begged. No one answered. The laughter died away.

When she awoke, she was standing upright against the wall. She didn't know how long she had been there. Hours? Days? No one had come. Her throat was dry and her belly ached with hunger. The rats were huddled in darkest corner of the cell, a sleeping, quivering mass of filth that made her shudder all over again when she saw them.

There wasn't a chamber pot, nor rags or cloth of any kind, so she lifted her skirts, squatted in the corner and grimaced as she relieved herself and watched the liquid splash onto the floor and seep beneath her shoes. As she crouched there, she thought of her father, his glassy eyes, the dagger protruding from his chest. She had held that dagger once, in the forest. Had she known what it would be used for, she would have buried it in Alexander's chest instead. Or, at least, she hoped she would have. But, probably, she wouldn't. Her eyes stung with tears. She had always thought herself brave and strong. Venturing into the Dark Forest, confronting Alexander Mordark - her siblings would never have been so bold. But now she saw what her bravery had cost her. Her father was dead. Alexander had betrayed her. The people were under attack. And she was locked away in a dungeon, pissing on her own shoes. And she realised that she wasn't brave at all. She was nothing but a fool. A selfish, weak fool.

A jangling noise disrupted the quiet and a mangy-looking man came into view as he tramped down the dungeon steps and walked towards Iris's cell with a set of keys. Iris stood at once and pulled her skirts back down over her legs.

'Your presence is requested,' the man said, peering through the bars into the gloom of the cell as he jammed a key into the lock. Pulling open the door, he beckoned Iris forward.

'What happened out there? Are my family alive?' she asked, moving warily out of the shadows towards him.

'Your father's dead,' he said.

'And the others?'

'All fine,' he said, looking her up and down appraisingly.

'The Mordarks?'

'Gone. For now,' he said, staring greedily at her boots. 'They're nice. I'll be 'avin them.'

Iris pulled off her boots distractedly and handed them to him.

So, they had come. The Mordarks had crossed the border. Alexander had brought them here to kill her family, her children, to take her home away from her. But why hadn't he killed her? He'd had countless chances. Would he not have done it already, if he had wanted to?

The stench from the man's rotten teeth caught her by surprise as he smiled, stroking the boots affectionately before setting them aside in the corridor. Then he pointed to the ceiling and his eyes became wild with excitement.

'Up there,' he said. 'They're waiting for you.'

Iris followed a few steps behind the man as he made his way, barefoot, up the stairs, which were slick and wet with a foul-smelling black sludge. The man forced his shoulder against the door at the top of the stairs and it screeched open. A blinding light burst into the stairway. Iris shielded her eyes. She felt the man take hold of her elbow and pull her towards the open door.

The morning smelled of smoke and death. A bitter chill sank its teeth into her skin as she stepped out into the courtyard. She shivered and wrapped her arms around herself. All of the guards stationed along the parapet were looking out towards the square.

The man led Iris to the gates, where two guards stood, shoulder to shoulder, facing her. The guards came forward, took hold of her arms and turned around. Only then did she see what was waiting for her beyond the courtyard. In the square, surrounded by a silent crowd, was a pyre. And, rising from a small platform above it, was a stake.

The guards walked her out into the square and around the side of the great structure, which loomed above them, casting them in shadow. Iris's heart was beating wildly. She looked at the grave faces staring back at her as she passed; bloodied, withered faces, full of sorrow. And anger.

When she saw Lucian, standing in front of the pyre, her throat tightened and she fought back the urge to cry. His face was pale and haggard, his eyes cold. The guards stopped and pushed her forwards.

Lucian stepped towards her and stared at her with a contemptuous look that, for an instant, gave way to unbounded pleasure.

'You were always the disobedient one,' he said softly. 'I warned you, Iris. You can't say I didn't.' He exhaled heavily and looked up at the sky. The crows had begun to circle. 'You thought you were smart. But you aren't. Because you never learn. And now you have brought war and death to our door. You have betrayed your own blood. What can I do? Forgive you, as father would have, and end up in an early grave like him? No. I will not spend my life clearing up the destruction you leave in your wake. You want to see us all burn, sister. But you shall burn first.' He nodded to the guards, who seized her roughly and began to drag her towards the steps of the pyre.

'No!' she screamed, struggling to break free. 'No! Please!'

Thomas forced his way to the front of the crowd and clapped a hand on Lucian's arm. 'What are you doing? This was meant for father!' he said, looking up at the pyre as the guards pulled Iris to the top of the steps, kicking and screeching. 'Lock her in a dungeon, put her in the stocks, send her away – don't do this!'

Lucian shrugged his hand off. 'It's what she deserves.'

'No! Not this! Lucian—' As Thomas reached out to grasp Lucian's arm again, three guards took hold of him. He thrashed and fought against them but they held him firmly. Suddenly, he fell still and closed his eyes, his brows drawing together in concentration. But whatever magic he was attempting to use against them did not work. With a scream of frustration, he opened his eyes. Tears of blood streaked his cheeks and his neck ran red with the blood that gushed from his ears. Weakened and powerless to stop them, he pleaded once more, 'Lucian…'

'Thomas! Thomas, help me!' Iris shouted as the guards pushed her against the wooden stake and began to bind her to it with thick rope. Thomas looked at her and shook his head despairingly. 'Thomas,' she whimpered.

A guard picked up a torch and held his hand over the oil-soaked cloth at the end. As the cloth began to smoke, the other guard hurriedly climbed back down the rickety staircase.

Iris looked desperately at the crowd. Eve was screaming and writhing in the grip of a guard, reaching out for her, shouting her name. Her mother was staring up at the pyre behind Lucian. She looked straight through Iris with eyes of flint.

Iris looked away towards Stone Lane. Alexander would come. He would save her. That's why he had spared her life. He loved her. Any moment now, he would be here. She watched the lane, waiting for a figure to appear.

The guard tossed the blazing torch onto the pyre below. The crowd began to murmur as the fire caught on the wood and spread. In moments, it had engulfed the pyre.

Iris could feel the heat rising, hear the ferocious roar of the flames; she tore her eyes away from the lane, forgetting Alexander, forgetting everything but the fire.

People were weeping now and praying to the White Witch. Some looked away, most didn't, as the flames climbed towards Iris and jumped onto her white dress.

Iris screamed in agony. Smoke filled her lungs, fire licked her skin and, as she choked and cried, she saw Lucian through the haze, smiling.

Thomas vomited on the ground. Then he sank to his knees and sobbed to the heavens, which were black with smoke.

Suddenly, there was a loud *crack* from within the pyre. A scorching heat surged outwards into the crowd.

The screaming stopped.

16. FABIAN'S WAR

'You did it, Alexander. Now tell Vrax how to do it,' said Fabian.

The small group of men sat around a table formed from an old tree stump, mere metres from the fringes of the forest. All heads leaned in.

Alexander looked from his father to Vrax and found that he did not want to part with the information. He looked down at the table, staring at the hundreds of rings in the wood. When Fabian began to sigh exasperatedly, he spoke.

'There's a stone. If you can make it to the other side of the forest - you only need moments - think of the stone and you can transport yourself to it. It's in the castle, in the girl's bedchamber.'

'Very good,' said Fabian's cousin, Belfor, who then turned to Fabian, looking perplexed. 'Why not send him? He knows how to do it. He's been there before. He knows what the stone looks—'

'Vrax is going,' Fabian said, silencing Belfor.

Vrax leaned across the table. 'What does the stone look like? Have I seen it before?'

Alexander nodded. 'It was mother's. The one she kept in her chamber,' he said.

Vrax sat back and nodded slowly, remembering.

'Well it's settled then,' said Fabian. 'Vrax will—'

'Getting there is one thing,' Alexander interjected. 'But getting back… They'll have tripled their forces by now. It's impossible. Why risk Vrax's life on a Reverof?'

'It's quite simple. Vrax will bring along men who are dispensable. They'll provide a distraction while Vrax carries out his task.,' Fabian said. He looked over his shoulder at the men, who were encamped around small fires. 'Belfor, round up the weak. And select fifty strong men to assist my son, should the others die too soon. Tell them to hang at the back of the pack. We'll spare them if we can.'

Belfor rose from his stool, bowed hastily and departed, tramping across the bog towards the fires and the men around them, who looked half-dead already.

Fabian watched him for a moment before huddling back into the circle. 'We need to lure the Mortenstone filth into the forest. We know it better than they do. Lure them in and your men may stand a better chance,' he said to Vrax. 'But you, you must leave them there and go on to the castle alone. The filth won't notice you come or go – their attention will be on the fighting. When you return to the forest with the girl, keep far away from the battle. She is your only concern. Leave your men to lead the Mortenstones into our traps.'

'If they come as far as the traps, what stops them from marching straight here to us?'

'Alexander, if I wanted your opinion, I would ask for it,' Fabian said irritably.

'What if Vrax dies trying to take her?' said Alexander, feeling almost foolish as he uttered the words.

'Well,' Fabian said, waving a hand indifferently, 'thankfully, I have three sons.'

Belfor shouted something and the men looked up from the table, but not before Alexander saw his brother's jaw tighten.

Two hundred men stood shivering in the wind behind Belfor.

'They'll do,' said Fabian.

As Vrax set off with the men into the Dark Forest, Fabian watched with his arms folded, chewing his lip anxiously. Alexander could see that this mission was more important to his father than he was prepared to admit.

Fabian signalled Belfor to come forward and spoke quietly into his ear. 'Send another two hundred. And fifty bowmen. I want them up in the trees.'

Belfor frowned. 'But…We mustn't be careless. We could lose five hundred men over something completely—' Belfor stopped himself.

'Insignificant?' Fabian said. 'The child is family. I look after my own.'

Alexander exchanged a look with Belfor as Fabian returned his attention to the son he had sent marching off to almost certain death.

*

The townspeople had begun to filter out of the square beyond Mortenstone Castle, shaking their heads regretfully as the fire extinguished itself in the ashes. The skeleton frame of the pyre was all that remained, blackened and charred to a crisp.

Lucian stayed in the square, watching small pieces of the brittle frame float away in the wind. Soon, the air was full of ash flakes, drifting up to the heavens and away to the east. He was still gazing after them, following their ascent, when one of his father's advisors approached apprehensively and began to speak.

'My Lord Mortenstone,' the man said. 'It would be wise to triple the border forces, wouldn't you agree?'

Lucian responded with a vague nod. But the advisor didn't go away at once; he lingered, wringing his hands nervously.

'What?' snapped Lucian.

'My Lord, the Vandemere army travelled a great distance in the night and… the effects of such magic have proved dire. Eric Vandemere is gravely ill. I am told he will likely die come nightfall. And the exertion has incapacitated his men. They will not be ready to fight again for weeks, perhaps longer.'

Lucian turned to face the advisor, feeling the cold weight of his words settle on his shoulders. 'Then how will we defend The Light?'

'Alstair Doldon rides for Draxvar to bring reinforcements. I have sent word to Edgeton and Latheera. Help is coming, my Lord.'

'Not soon enough,' he said. 'What about the valley?'

'My Lord, there are no trained fighters in the valley.'

'Elves are fast learners.'

'My Lord, elves do not fight. They refuse to fight. We cannot make them—'

'We can. Send for them. And any man in the valley capable of wielding a sword.'

The advisor opened his mouth to protest when the castle doors swept open and Josephine emerged from behind them, her face drawn and pale. She walked calmly from the courtyard to the square, carrying a silver ring on a cushion of purple velvet. All around the square, people stopped to watch as she sank to her knees before the smoking ashes and offered the ring up to Lucian.

'The Ring of Rulers,' she said. 'May your rule be long and prosperous, my son.'

Lucian felt a prickle of excitement as his hand curled around the cold ring. He slid it onto his finger and stared at the tree engraved in the silver. He felt stronger, somehow. Powerful.

'Mother, ensure that this man sends word to Mortenstone Valley for the immediate enlistment of all men, boys and elves over the age of fifteen.'

Josephine bowed her head dutifully and walked away with the advisor.

'Wingworth,' Lucian called. Wingworth, head of the Mortenstone guards, and the ugliest man Lucian had ever seen - in a brutal, menacing sort of way - paced heavily across the square towards him. 'I have a personal matter I'd like you to handle,' Lucian said. 'The Reverof girl. Kill her.'

Wingworth left without a word, heading straight for the castle.

Lucian went back to admiring the ring on his finger, when a trickle of blood escaped from his nose. He wiped it away quickly, only for another trickle to slip from his other nostril.

'You performed extraordinary magic this past night. You would do well to rest. The body, as well as the mind, need time to heal.' Master Hagworth was standing beside him now, staring solemnly at the ashes. Lucian hadn't noticed him approach. He sniffed back the blood and swallowed it, tasting iron in his mouth. 'The people loved your sister, Lucian,' the schoolmaster continued. 'She was a kind girl. And she has been taken in the cruellest way imaginable. Was it wise? Was it worthy of the Lord of all lands?' he said, turning away from the ashes to face Lucian. His eyes were red-rimmed and inflamed beneath his spectacles; it was clear that he had been crying. 'If all you offer your subjects is fear and death, you will lose them. And how can you hope to lead when there is no one left to follow?'

Lucian had nothing to say to Master Hagworth. He looked away towards Stone Lane and kept looking that way until the schoolmaster gave up and walked back to the castle. Before Lucian had a chance to return his gaze to his silver ring, however, he saw something in the distance, half way down the lane. The family who had lived above the butcher's were being carried out of the smoke-blackened building on stretchers. Mother, father, daughter, sons – all dead. The stretchers were lined up outside the building alongside countless other bodies. A chorus of grief-stricken wails rent the air and lifted birds from the rooftops. Lucian turned back to the ashes as the townspeople mourned their dead, and cursed the schoolmaster under his breath.

*

As they came closer to the Mortenstone border, Vrax and his men moved with caution. Dead branches lay strewn across the ground, waiting for an ill-placed boot to crack them.

Vrax held up a hand, ordering the men to stop. Through the trees ahead, he could see daylight. He tightened his grip on his sword. They had arrived. He listened for a moment to the murmur of voices at the border and the clink of pots and pans. Alexander was right; the Mortenstones had increased their forces, but by how many, he could not say.

'All of you,' he said, turning to his men, signalling the first two rows. 'On my command, charge. Let them know you're coming. Draw them into the forest. And make sure you take at least one of them down with you.' The men looked troubled; this was a one-way journey. 'The rest of you,' Vrax said, looking to the larger group, 'spread out. Use the forest. Surround them, confuse them, and drive them to the—' His words died on his tongue. A strange, unsettling feeling crept up his spine. The noise from the border had ceased.

As he turned his head, an arrow zipped past his ear and into the throat of a man in the front line, who fell to the ground with a heavy thud. Then, in the distance, there came an almighty roar. By the time Vrax saw them, storming towards him through the darkness, brandishing swords and axes and glowing red pokers, it was too late. There was no time to follow his father's plan, no time to flee, no time to bolt for the border. Drawing his sword, he bellowed, 'Attack!' and ran towards the oncoming horde.

The two sides clashed with a crunch of metal, swords locking, armour colliding. Vrax severed a man's arm with a deft swing of his sword. Blood spattered his face and eyes. Half-blinded, he pushed on, seeing silver armour everywhere he turned. He and his men were outnumbered. Vastly outnumbered.

Suddenly, there was an eruption of wild, bloodthirsty cries behind him. Vrax looked back to see a wave of men in black armour surging into the battle. Hundreds of men, the strongest in Fabian's army. His heart leapt with relief and he threw himself at the next man with renewed vigour.

*

Alexander seized his chance. He had been following Vrax and his troop, moving silently alongside them in the darkness. And now, as he stood on the edge of the battle, watching as the Mortenstone guards abandoned their posts and charged into the forest, a gap opened up on the border. He shot out from behind a tree and ran towards it, narrowly avoiding an arrow that came at him from the side. He could see the buildings on Stone Lane and the castle at the top of the hill. He could hear the bells ringing. He was almost there. But, as he glanced to his left, he saw Vrax, surrounded by Mortenstone guards, lashing out at them with his sword, trapped. Alexander hesitated for only a moment. Then he ran on towards the border.

*

Enola sat concealed in the folds of the curtain in the unfamiliar bedchamber, where she had been all morning, ever since the screaming had started. In her haste to hide, she had left the blue stone on the floor by the fireplace. She wanted it, but she didn't dare come out and take it.

Maid Morgan had not come to find her and bring her down to the lower rooms, nor had she set out breakfast or laid a fire. The room was cold and quiet, save for the wind whistling in the chimney. Only, there was another sound now. A distant thudding. Enola stayed completely still as she listened. The sound grew louder. Footsteps. Someone was coming, marching with purpose, getting closer, moving faster. And then... silence.

The door burst open and the curtain was ripped from its rail by some invisible force. It fell in a heap on the floor, leaving Enola exposed, staring out across the room at the figures in the doorway.

Wingworth's hideous, twisted mouth broke open into a smile. The two men behind him looked on cautiously as he slid a knife from his belt. As he stepped over the threshold into the chamber, the blue stone began to glow.

'She's a demon, Wingworth! She's doing something!' one of the men behind him exclaimed, pointing at the stone.

Wingworth crossed the room in three strides and lunged at Enola just as the stone's light faded. He grabbed a fistful of her hair and dragged her to her feet. Then, he gasped and let her go, stumbling backwards, flailing his arms, his neck locked tight in Alexander's grip. The guards in the doorway snapped out of their stupor, drew their swords and leapt at Alexander. Enola fixed her gaze on one of them and clenched every muscle in her body. With a wet pop, the man's brown eyes exploded and he fell down against the bedpost, his brain bulging grotesquely through the empty sockets.

Alexander smashed Wingworth's head into the mantelpiece above the fireplace and then whirled around, whipping out his dagger, and slit the last guard's throat so fast that both men hit the floor at the same time.

Alexander stared momentarily at the body by the bed before wiping his face with his sleeve and turning to Enola. He looked perplexed. She stared back at him unblinkingly. The blood gushing from Wingworth's head pooled around her feet, warm and thick. Alexander walked towards her and bent down, so that his eyes were level with hers.

'Are you afraid of me?' he asked. Enola shook her head slowly. Alexander smiled and thrust the knife back into his belt. 'Good. We're going now,' he said, standing quickly and lifting her into his arms. He took the blood-spattered shawl hanging on the bedpost, wrapped it around her and carried her to the door. But then he stopped. Turning abruptly, he walked back to the fireplace, stepping over the bodies, and crouched to pick up the stone, which he wiped on his breeches and tucked into his breast pocket.

*

Alexander walked swiftly through the gloom, listening out for any other signs of life. None came. The distant echo of the bells drifted eerily through the empty corridors, which all stood in darkness. It was as if the castle had been long deserted.

He descended a set of stairs with Enola, grasping the handrail firmly. But, as he came to the next staircase and saw the castle doors standing open in the entrance hall below, he moved his hand to his knife. He walked slowly, eyes darting to every corner of the hall as he went. When he reached the bottom of the stairs, he made his way quickly to the doors and looked up at the parapet across the abandoned courtyard. It was unmanned. Something felt wrong. It was all too easy. Cautiously, he stepped out into the open.

The stench in the air hit him at once and he brought a hand to his mouth, resisting the urge to vomit. He knew the smell well. Burnt flesh.

'Look at me,' he said to Enola. 'Keep your eyes on me.'

He crossed the courtyard into the square. An old woman was kneeling in front of a mound of scorched wood and smoking ash. Her head was bowed. She was crying.

'Look at me,' he said again when Enola turned her head towards the woman, who had begun to mutter a prayer through her tears as they passed her. He walked calmly, looking ahead to the lane, when he heard something that chilled him to the core.

'Sweet, sweet Lady Iris. The pain is over. May your soul be delivered to the White Witch in all its purity.'

He stopped dead.

'What did you say?' he said, turning around. The woman did not respond. 'What did you say!' he shouted, striding towards her and grasping her face with a bloody hand, forcing her to look at him.

'Lady Iris. Sweet Lady Iris, born in light, taken in darkness.'

His legs gave way. He staggered backwards in horror. Not Iris. Not his Iris, who had stood before him only hours ago. He stared and stared at the ashes, the dying embers still aglow. It couldn't be. His heart thundered against his ribs so fiercely the sound filled his ears; soon, it was all he could hear. His throat began to close up; he couldn't speak, couldn't breathe. He had betrayed her, left her behind. And now she was nothing but ashes. If he hadn't come to The Light, if he hadn't killed Matthew Mortenstone, or told Vrax about the border enchantment, she would still be alive. He had killed her.

Enola tried to look but he quickly pressed her head to his chest with a trembling hand. As he did, he caught a flash of movement in the corner of his eye and turned.

Thomas Mortenstone emerged into the square from the castle courtyard. He paused when he saw Alexander and stared at him blankly, his arms limp at his sides.

'My sister's dead,' he said. There was a long silence. Then he spoke again. 'Why are you taking Enola?'

Alexander tightened his grip on Enola. 'She's not safe here. I need to take her away,' he said in a strangled voice.

Thomas shrugged. 'You won't get far,' he said, sitting down on the ground and crossing his legs.

Alexander backed away and, when he was sure Thomas was not going to pursue him, turned and ran down Stone Lane.

At the end of the lane, he stopped, leaned against a wall and tried to clear his head and think. A boy peered out through the window of the building opposite. His mother hurriedly pulled him away and he disappeared from view. Alexander looked further along the street. Dozens of eyes were watching him from the windows. He was out of time. Heart pounding, blood pulsing in his ears, he fixed his eyes on the Dark Forest in the distance and began to run.

Hundreds of tents crowded the Grassland, all deserted, pots still steaming, animal carcasses slowly being cremated on skewers over fires. He ran between the tents, using them for cover. He was almost there. He could see the men through the trees, hacking and thrashing at one another. The air vibrated with hoarse cries. Enola started to grow agitated. She wriggled and fidgeted in his arms.

'It's alright,' he said, pushing her head back against his shoulder.

Suddenly, an arrow shot out from the trees and landed at his feet. He abandoned his path and branched left. More and more arrows came at him as he ran. And, with a stab of blinding pain, one found its target. The arrow sank deep into his thigh and he came crashing down to the ground, dropping Enola. He cried out and smashed his fist against the earth again and again in anger. He tried to stand but his leg buckled and he fell back to his knees, jarring the arrowhead, and roared in agony. There was no time to waste. If they caught him, he would die and so would Enola. Steeling himself and clenching his teeth, he snapped the arrow shaft and threw it aside. As he stood, white pain rushed up his spine and his eyes welled with fresh tears, but he took Enola's hand and limped on into the Dark Forest.

The noise of battle died away as they moved deeper into the shadows. Enola's eyes were wide, glinting in the pinpricks of light that funnelled down from above. Alexander was drenched in cold sweat and, for an instant, everything around him turned black. When his vision returned, he led Enola to a tree and leant against it, disorientated, trying to catch his breath. Then, he stumbled onwards. Enola followed as he knocked into trees and tripped over their roots. He was exhausted, spent, but he would not fall until he got her there. To Agatha.

*

Vrax shoved two men out of his path when he spotted a gap in the trees.

'Cover me,' he shouted, darting for the border.

He crossed over into the Grassland and closed his eyes, thinking of his mother's blue stone. Nothing happened. He opened his eyes again to find himself standing on the border still. He tried again and again, until he heard a flurry of footsteps behind him. He turned just in time to defend himself against the sword that swung at him. The man holding it was tall and stocky. Vrax deflected the blade with the flick of his hand. The man, realising his mistake, had no time to return to the safety of the forest. Vrax crumpled his hand into a fist and there was a loud crunch as every bone in the man's body shattered. As he flopped to the ground, Vrax closed his eyes again and tried to transport himself one last time. When it did not work, he kicked the dead man in frustration. It was over. He had failed. He swallowed his fear and walked back into the forest, a doomed man.

*

As evening fell, there was a weak knock at the door. Agatha rushed to opened it and, when she had, she gasped. 'Good grief!' she said, taking Enola from a dishevelled Alexander. 'Come in. Close the door. Sit here, by the fire. William! William, fetch a damp rag.'

William was nine now, a handsome boy with kind eyes. He had come partway down the stairs and paused when he saw another child in Agatha's arms. Enola opened her eyes and stared at him stonily over Agatha's shoulder. Suddenly, he felt cold and lightheaded. He held onto the stair rail as a deep dread passed through him.

'William!' Agatha snapped.

William came to his senses and went back up the stairs for a rag.

As he rushed down to the living room, Enola's eyes followed him. He could feel her watching him, but he didn't look at her again.

Agatha placed Enola on a chair by the fire and then helped Alexander hobble to the armchair opposite.

'Where are you hurt?' she said, leaning over him. Alexander motioned his right leg. The arrowhead was embedded deep in his thigh. Agatha snatched the rag from William and wiped away the blood. Then she rooted around in a wooden box in her cabinet and returned with a vial of yellow liquid and a pair of pliers. 'This will sting,' she said. Alexander looked at the implement in her hand and gripped the arms of his chair.

When it was over, Agatha bandaged up his leg tightly.

'The dressing needs to be changed three times a day.' She turned to Enola then, as if noticing her for the first time. 'Who is this?'

Alexander stared at Enola for a moment. 'She's Iris's. And mine.'

'And where is Iris?' said Agatha. Alexander looked down at his feet and didn't answer. 'What have you done, boy?'

Alexander dropped his face into his hands and started to cry. Agatha wrapped her arms around him.

'It's alright, boy. It's alright.' She looked to William, who was watching with unease. 'Lock the door. Douse the lamps,' she said.

Agatha cradled Alexander long after his tears had dried. 'What will you do with the girl?' she asked.

William saw Enola's hand twitch from where he sat at the foot of the stairs. He bit his nails anxiously in the silence that followed.

Alexander sat forward and looked from his daughter to Agatha. 'Will you look after her?'

William couldn't stop himself. He got up and emerged from the shadows, to remind Agatha that he was there, that she already had someone to care for. Agatha put a warm hand on his shoulder and squeezed softly, deliberating. William tried to make his objection obvious to her without Alexander noticing, but his pleading stare was overlooked.

'Alright. She can stay,' Agatha said finally. William felt as if the rug had been ripped from beneath his feet. He clung to Agatha unsteadily. 'Careful!' she said, stabilising him. 'He's tired. I think that's enough excitement for one day. To bed!'

Defeated, William walked to the stairs and began to climb them slowly. As he reached the top, he heard Alexander talking in a hushed tone.

'If anyone comes looking for her…'

'I won't let anything happen to her,' said Agatha.

'But *if*—'

'*If* anyone comes looking, I'll take her to The Passage.'

191

'That must be the last resort. Only if there's no other way.'

'There is no other way, boy. You know that. You know what she is. Without her mother to protect her, she has no future in The Light. And she won't fare any better in the Dark Lands. With me, she's safe. But if they come here, there won't be anywhere else to turn. I'll take her to The Passage. But I can't go with her.'

'What about William?'

There was a long pause.

'Mmm,' Agatha mumbled.

William backed away from the stair rail. He didn't know who 'they' were or why they might come for the girl. He didn't know what The Passage was or where it led. But he knew he did not want to be sent there with Enola.

'Perhaps,' Agatha continued. 'I should warn you, though, boy. Be under no illusions here.' She spoke in a low voice, as she did when she was delivering grave news. 'If the time comes and they must go, they can never return.'

PART II

Twelve years later

17. THE CURSED ONE

Enola entered Agatha's house quietly, holding a sprig of Rash Ivy behind her back. She had plucked it from a hedge using an old rag to protect her fingers. The leaves on the sprig were as black as a raven's wing and, in the centre of each, ran a thin, green vein, through which its poison travelled.

William was sitting at the table hunched over a book, his back to her, broad and tight with muscle from years of hunting. Agatha called him the Prince of the Forest; she was always making a fuss when he returned with deer or wild rabbits strung over his shoulder, remarking on the succulence of the boar he killed as if he was responsible for its tenderness. But she never thanked *her* when *she* caught anything. Agatha ignored William's bouts of sulking, but when *she* sulked, the old hag couldn't scold her fast enough. She humoured William when he spoke of his desire to leave the Dark Forest, but when *she* expressed her wish to venture beyond the shadows, Agatha would snap at her like a dog. Enola loathed her for it. As she loathed William.

She approached him silently and brandished the Rash Ivy. In one swift stroke, she reached over the back of his chair and rubbed the dry, prickly plant on his neck. William shrieked and jumped up from the chair, clamping a hand over his neck as it began to erupt in angry red blotches.

'You evil—!' he cried, picking the book up off the floor and hurling it at her. Enola ducked out of the way and ran for the door. William went after her.

*

Agatha was awoken from her nap by the commotion. She got to her feet with the help of her stick and shuffled towards the door, grumbling.

Outside, shrinking into the distance down the forest path, was Enola, followed closely by William. Agatha sighed. Enola was always tormenting him. In all her life, she had never seen so many tears. It saddened her. Before Enola came, William was a contented little boy. And, ever since, he couldn't wait to get away. He dreamed of leaving home, leaving her. But she couldn't blame him. Enola was a wretched little thing, hair as black as death, eyes as cold as ice. It unsettled Agatha to even look at the girl for too long; she was unnatural, cursed. There was darkness in every word she spoke, every breath she breathed, every smile she smiled.

She remembered the time she had marched her out into the forest to punish her. Enola had been no older than six; she had bitten William and drawn blood. Without a word, Agatha had taken her by the wrist, led her to a tree and tied her to it. 'A feast for the wolves,' she had said to her. Then she went back inside and waited. William was distraught; he pleaded with her to let Enola go - the bite hadn't hurt that much. 'I'm not really going to let the wolves eat her,' she told him. 'I'm teaching her an important lesson. She's safe. But we don't want her to think she's safe.' And she recalled how a cold feeling had crept up the back of her neck when she heard it. A deep growl. She went to the window and looked out as a grey wolf emerged from the shadows and began to circle the tree. Its amber eyes glowed in the moonlight. She stood, transfixed, waiting to see what it would do. 'Agatha!' William squeaked, his eyes filling with tears. She snapped out of her trance and reached for the door handle. But, before she had a chance to grasp it, she heard a sharp whining sound. She looked out of the window again. The wolf had sunk low to the ground, whimpering like a pup. She flung the door open. Enola looked at her, eyes as wild as the beast's, and the wolf bolted.

Agatha never used that method of punishment again.

*

William caught Enola by the wrist and dragged her down to the ground. He prized the Rash Ivy from her fingers and stood over her, wielding it like a knife. Enola rolled onto her back, her white dress blackened with mud. Her eyes darted from side to side, searching for an escape. He stood there, poised to strike, hands shaking with anger. And then he threw down the plant. Enola pushed herself to her feet. He stared at her for a moment before he turned and walked back along the path towards Agatha.

'I won't do it anymore!' he said.

Agatha inspected the rash on his neck and tutted. 'I have an ointment for that. Let's go inside. Leave that nasty girl to think about what she's done.'

'She won't, though, Agatha. You know she won't,' he said, pulling away from her as she tried to lead him towards the house. 'I'm leaving.'

'Don't be ridiculous,' she said. Enola began to laugh. 'Quiet!' Agatha hissed.

William stormed back into the house and up the stairs. He pulled his hunting bag out from under the bed and began tossing his things into it. He took the dagger Alexander had helped him make from the wooden cabinet next to the bed; an axe; a thick, black winter cloak; a woollen tunic; breeches; and, lastly, *Tales of Merlin the Terrible*. Agatha had given it to him on his ninth birthday. It was a large volume, heavy. He hesitated before he put it into the bag. Then, he fastened the straps and swung it over his shoulder. The leather brushed his neck and it stung like fire. He winced, and wished he had rubbed the ivy in Enola's face.

He came down the stairs and took an empty flask from the shelf above the fireplace, sliding it under his belt. Agatha was standing by the table, watching him.

'I'm sorry,' he mumbled as he walked past her. He couldn't look at her. He left through the open door and closed it behind him.

As he stepped onto the path, he breathed in the forest air and exhaled heavily. Then he began to walk.

'Goodbye, Enola Reverof!' he called. He had no doubt she was watching.

'I have a question,' came a voice from behind. William circled around. His back stiffened as he found himself nose to nose with her. Her eyes danced as she looked at him, like a cat fixated on a mouse. 'How many days without food would it take for an old woman to finally give up and die?'

'She will have food…You'll provide food,' he said with mounting unease.

'Perhaps,' she said. And then she smiled. 'Perhaps I'll leave her to the wolves.'

Agatha started as William kicked the door open and stomped back into the house. Enola followed him inside.

'What's going on?' Agatha cried, placing a hand on her heart as he passed her and went up the stairs. 'No, don't you go up there, girl. You leave him be! What's happened?' she said, blocking Enola's way with her arm.

'William changed his mind. He's a fickle boy with a weak will.'

William turned and came hurtling back down the stairs, stopped only by Agatha's outstretched arm.

'You are a manipulative little bitch!' he shouted, his face turning scarlet.

'I don't have the patience for this. William, sit down so I can take a look at that rash. And you,' Agatha said, turning to Enola, 'out of my sight!'

*

Enola ate supper in her room on her bed. When she finished, she dusted the crumbs onto the floor to attract the mice. Agatha hated mice. Then, she lay back and pulled the fur throw all the way up to her chin. It had been an exhilarating day. She was tired, but she didn't dare close her eyes.

The strange man had appeared again in her dreams. For three nights now he had stood, watching her, on the edge of the forest path. A storm raged around him but he remained rooted to the spot, steadily holding her gaze, a single tear streaking down his cheek. She had a feeling she knew what the dream meant, though she couldn't explain how. Danger was coming.

The next evening, Enola sat with Agatha slicing vegetables and throwing them into the pot above the fire. It was a tedious task. Bored, she threw a whole carrot into the boiling water.

Agatha shrieked and jumped up. 'Ouch!' she said, wiping her hand angrily. 'Do it properly or go and fetch William.'

Enola took her chopping knife and went outside, slamming the door as Agatha began to speak.

'Bring a lantern,' she heard her call, 'it's getting dark!'

But Enola didn't need a lantern; she could see well enough. She ambled along the path, barefoot. The ground was ice-cold beneath her feet. She ran a hand across the bark of a tree as she walked. But, as she moved her hand away, the bark she had touched crumbled to the ground like dust. She stopped and picked up a handful of the powder. It was grey. In fact, the entire tree looked grey, almost…dead. She placed a hand on the trunk again. The same thing happened. Walking to another tree, she reached out to touch it and see if its bark, too, would crumble, when she heard voices. Soft, girlish giggling and a man's laugh.

She left the path and crept through the undergrowth, following the sound. And then she saw him.

'I'll find a way, I promise! I want to be with you,' said William, sitting back against a tree, running his hands through the fair curls of a pretty girl and staring longingly into her eyes. Enola crouched low, watching. The girl was kneeling in front of him in a dark green dress, smiling playfully. She wrapped her arms around his neck and kissed him.

Enola stood and emerged boldly from the undergrowth. William's eyes widened when he saw her and he pushed the girl's hands away, scrambling to his feet.

'Who is she?' asked the girl, startled, as she, too, got to her feet.

'Enola Reverof,' said Enola, watching William as his face became tight and still. 'Now she knows who I am, William.'

The girl looked between them in confusion. 'Who?' she said.

'If you don't do it, I will,' said Enola, raising her knife. She had spent the morning sharpening it on the stone outside by the Silver Tree.

'No!' William shouted.

The girl began to scream. Enola lunged for her but William threw himself between them, seized her arm and twisted it. Enola cried out and dropped the knife.

'William! You have to!' she spat as the girl fled, growing smaller and smaller in the distance until the darkness swallowed her completely.

'No,' said William, letting go of her. He swiped the knife off the ground before she could snatch it and pointed it at her. 'No,' he said again.

'Then I'll tell my father and he'll do it,' she said, turning and running back towards the house, laughing all the way.

'No! Enola!' William shouted, chasing after her.

She burst into the living room. Agatha jumped with fright and the contents of her cup spilled into her lap.

'I have been seen,' Enola announced. 'We must tell my father. I can describe the girl. We should send a bird to him at once!'

Agatha sighed. 'Yes, yes, very well.'

William charged into the house, breathless, his eyes burning with hatred. Enola turned and stepped back when she saw his white knuckles curled over the handle of the knife.

'I hope they find you!' he shouted.

'William!' Agatha said, a warning in her voice.

'I hope they take you!' he said, advancing. 'I hope they kill you!' He pressed the tip of the blade to her throat.

'Boy!' Agatha said, rising from her chair.

'I hope they burn you like your mother! I hope they kill every Mortenstone, every last one of them. I hope the streets run red with their blood and yours!' he cried, his voice cracking as tears began to stream down his face. He threw the knife across the room and walked away to the foot of the stairs, where he slumped down and sobbed into his hands.

'Go and finish the supper,' Agatha said to Enola, stooping to put a hand on William's shoulder. 'And don't boil the veg to death like you did last time.'

Enola stirred the pot over the fire. She added a log to the flames and stoked it with a poker, all the while listening to Agatha as she spoke softly to William.

'Calm yourself, boy. Take a breath.'

'Don't send the raven,' he begged.

'William, it has to be done.'

'But it's my fault. I care for her and now she'll die. Because of me.'

'It's the way it has to be.'

He was silent for a long time after that. Enola didn't look at him. She would tread carefully around him now, she decided. At least until her father came to see her. Then she would leave the problem with him.

As she dished out the food into bowls, William wiped his eyes and traipsed up the stairs to bed.

'Goodnight, boy,' Agatha muttered as the bedroom door closed.

From the corner of her eye, Enola saw Agatha's head turn towards her. And then she approached unsteadily, coming to stand over her by the fire. Enola could not avert her attention any longer. She stared at

Agatha sullenly and was not surprised to see a look of contempt on the old woman's face.

'You are a wretched girl,' Agatha said. 'I have tried to love you. William has tried. But no amount of trying will change you or what you are. Time and love will not thaw your heart. I have given you a home, given you food, kept you safe, and never once asked for anything in return. Well now I am telling you. Behave, pretend, as if you have an ounce of goodness in you. I will send a raven to your father. But you are not to speak or even so much as look at William again. Do you hear me, girl?'

Enola had stopped listening. She felt strange. Something was wrong. Her head was swimming, the room was becoming a shapeless blur. Her chest felt tight. She couldn't breathe. She stood and staggered forwards. And then there was a sharp, stabbing pain in her chest; she gasped, gripping the pot handle over the fire to steady herself. The scorching hot metal burned into her skin and she recoiled, pulling the entire pot and its boiling contents to the ground with a hiss and a clang.

'Oh, why?' Agatha grumbled, raising her arms above her head. 'You've spoiled it! Wretched girl!'

Enola pushed past her and ran for the door.

Out in the forest, she stood, breathing shallow breaths. Her burnt hand throbbed. Suddenly, the feeling went away. But the faint murmur in her chest remained, a threatening, ghostly pain. She pressed a hand to her heart, pushing it away.

The birds squawked up in their nests, unsettled. As she looked around, the Silver Tree caught her eye. It seemed different, somehow. The silver bark that once glimmered in the moonlight was dull and grey, like the other trees along the path. Something was wrong. She could feel it.

The wind picked up. It gushed down the path, plucking leaves from the trees and swirling her hair about her face, exposing the brilliant-white streak, which shone ever brighter in the darkening forest.

18. A DEADLY DISCOVERY

In the morning, Enola was the first to wake. She walked downstairs and sat in Agatha's chair, blinking at the ashes in the hearth. Her sleep had been restless. The wind had howled so fiercely in the night, it was as if the house were surrounded by a pack of wolves. She awoke twice, startled at the thought, her heart thumping, the dull pain in her chest rising and falling with every breath.

The ashes stirred in the breeze that funnelled down the chimney. As she watched them, she thought back to her eighth birthday. The wind had raced down the chimney on that day too, buffeting the flames so that they flickered and thrashed. She had stared at them, transfixed, for hours, while Agatha fretted over William, who had been gone all morning.

When he returned later that afternoon, he went straight to Enola with his hands behind his back, almost giddy with excitement. 'Happy birthday, Enola,' he had said, kneeling before her. 'I know it's not as good as a real one but I hope you like it.' And he pulled the gift out from behind his back and placed it on Enola's lap. He had made her a Latheerian horse out of whittled sticks bound together with tree sap and string. He had even painted two blue eyes onto the model.

It was an ugly thing. It looked nothing like a real horse.

'Oh, isn't that lovely, Enola!' Agatha exclaimed.

'What do you say?' Alexander said, leaning forward in his armchair to examine the horse. 'This is good!' he said to William.

'Enola,' Agatha prompted.

'Thank you,' she said, pushing the horse from her lap onto the seat and dusting her dress.

When Agatha brought the cake out and put it down on the table, William and Alexander went to admire it. Thick, fresh cream oozed from between the fat layers of sponge. Agatha set a jug of hot custard down beside it and slapped Alexander's hand as he reached out to dip his finger into it.

'No. The birthday girl must have the first try,' she said, turning back to the hearth – and gasping.

Enola ignored her and snapped the last leg off the horse and threw all the pieces onto the fire.

Agatha strode across the room and grabbed her roughly by the wrists. 'Why did you do that? He spent a long time making that for you! Wretched little —'

Alexander stepped in and put a hand on Agatha's shoulder. 'She's only a child. She didn't know,' he said. And then he turned to William, whose eyes were glazed with tears. 'You can make another one. For me. I liked it!'

William nodded and his tears spilled onto his cheeks. Agatha went to comfort him.

Enola smiled. And she turned her back on them all to watch the mutilated horse blacken and burn.

The memory faded like a dream. Enola looked up from the ashes as Agatha lumbered down the stairs in her nightgown.

'You should use your stick,' she said.

'I'm fine. Don't tell me what to do,' Agatha snapped, holding on to the handrail for support.

'You're getting old.'

'I've always been old.'

'You'll die soon, probably.'

'You think so?'

'Yes.'

'Well, we shall see.'

Two knocks sounded upon the door. They froze, each turning towards it. After a pause, a third knock came and Agatha sighed with relief.

'Let him in, then,' she said, hobbling down the last two steps.

Enola went to the door, drew back the bolt and pulled it open. Alexander stood on the threshold. His forehead was faintly lined, his beard dark and full, his green eyes somewhat duller than they used to be.

'Can we help you, stranger? Are you lost?' Agatha said, scowling at his beard as she limped across the room towards him. 'I don't like it. You don't look like you.'

Alexander laughed and stepped inside, pulling Enola into an embrace, which she endured with rigid discomfort. When he let her go, she moved back and stared at him expectantly.

'Is it done?' she asked. 'Did you get her?'

Alexander's smile turned to a grimace. He looked almost annoyed by her question. 'I got her,' he said, taking off his cloak. 'You should be more careful.' He moved past her into the room, throwing his cloak onto the table.

'How are things?' said Agatha, offering her cheek for him to kiss.

'Vrax has had another daughter,' he said, smirking.

Agatha walked to her chair and sat down. Alexander followed and sat in the armchair opposite.

'Another daughter! How many is that now?' she said, waving a hand at Enola and pointing to the hearth. Glaring, Enola went to it and knelt to prepare a fire.

'Four,' said Alexander.

'I gather your father isn't pleased.'

'No.'

'Mmm,' Agatha mused, rubbing her chin. 'And Risella? Is she with child?'

'Why do you always ask about *her*?' Alexander said with disdain.

'Because she's your wife.'

'She's barren, I'm certain of it.'

Enola listened as she swept the ash away and lay fresh logs in the hearth. She was glad her father's wife was unable to give him children. If he had another child, he might forget to bring her things, or forget her altogether. And then who would keep Fabian away from these parts of the forest? Who would kill the people who had seen her? William wouldn't. William was always too scared to do it.

As she reached down to pick up the kindling, a blue spark shot out of her finger. She jumped back in surprise. The kindling began to smoke and shrivel inwards. A small flame flickered to life. And, soon, every log was ablaze. Agatha and Alexander continued to talk, oblivious to what had happened, while Enola stared at her hand, screwing it into a fist and then opening it again, inspecting it closely.

'Here he is. Good morning, William,' Agatha said as William walked down the stairs.

Enola twisted around to look at him. He kept his eyes low, but the lids were swollen, his lips downturned. He mumbled something and traipsed over to the table to sit by himself.

Agatha watched him for a moment and then said quietly to Alexander, 'It was his…lady friend... who saw Enola.'

Alexander nodded, looking uncomfortable, and glanced quickly at William.

'Nasty work but it has to be done,' Agatha said. 'Now where was I? Ah yes, I —'

'How, exactly, did you kill her?' asked Enola, watching William. He didn't look up, but she saw his hand ball into a fist on the table.

'Enola!' Agatha said firmly.

'He's getting angry again,' Enola said. 'He was angry last night. He had a lot to say then. You should have heard the terrible things he said to me, father. If Agatha hadn't been there, he would have slit my throat, too. He came right up to my face with a knife and said he hopes Fabian Mordark finds me and burns me like uncle Lucian burned my mother.'

The colour drained from Alexander's face. He turned his head slowly towards William, who was gazing back at him, still as a deer before a hunter. And then Alexander was across the room, dragging William from his chair.

'No, Alexander!' Agatha cried.

William kicked out, upturning the table, as Alexander threw him to the floor and pummelled his face.

'Stop!' Agatha shouted. 'Stop it, now!' Alexander shook her off, knocking her to the floor, when she tried to pull him back. Then he fastened both hands around William's neck and began to throttle him.

The blood rushed to William's face and the veins in his forehead swelled. He choked and spluttered, trying to prize Alexander's fingers away. His eyes bulged.

'Alexander!' Agatha pleaded in despair.

The stabbing pain in Enola's chest returned with breath-taking force. She gasped and doubled over, but she didn't look away. All night she had thought of this moment. Her father was taking care of the problem, like he always did. It was what she wanted. But... no. She shook her head. No. He was killing him. She straightened up. William couldn't, mustn't, die. Darkness was coming and, when it did, she would need him. She knew it. She knew it as if she had seen it all play out a thousand times before in her mind, as if it had already happened. As the realisation hit her, she looked at the window; beyond it, standing on the forest path, was the old man from her dreams. His face was full of sorrow. As he stared at her, the pain in her chest intensified, snatching the breath from her lungs. She clutched the back of the armchair. When she looked again, the man was gone.

'Stop,' she whispered, her throat closing up, smothering the word. Alexander didn't listen; he continued to strangle William, his teeth bared like a beast's, while Agatha watched on hopelessly. 'Stop,' Enola said again, as William's eyes closed wearily and his legs stopped flailing.

The door burst open and slammed against a cupboard, and a torrent of leaves blew into the house, swirling around the room and extinguishing the fire. Alexander removed his hands from William's neck to shield his eyes. William crawled away from him, coughing and retching.

The howling wind quietened. The leaves fell to the floor. Enola looked at Agatha and, for an instant, thought she saw fear in the old woman's eyes – eyes that darted to the open door when there came a low groan from outside, followed by a creaking, splintering sound. Enola held her breath.

Silence.

Another mournful groan rumbled through the air. Then, there was an almighty *crash*. The ground shuddered. The house shook. Enola dropped to her knees, covering her head, as jars fell from the mantelpiece and smashed, silver liquid splashing all over the floor and sizzling on the hot ashes in the hearth. Pots and pans fell, clattering, from their hooks. Books flew from the shelves. Agatha shrieked and clamped her hands over her ears. And, suddenly, all was still again.

Nobody moved, except for Alexander, who sprang to his feet and ran to the door. Enola watched from the ground as he stared out, saying nothing, his mouth agape. The quiet became unbearable. She got up and staggered to the door after him, and looked on in disbelief at the colossal tree blocking the eastern path, bark as grey as a wolf's pelt and turning greyer still, crumbling, falling away, dying before her eyes. It loomed over the path like a tower.

Alexander left the house as if in a trance and walked limply along the path towards it.

'Don't go out there!' Agatha shouted after him. She looked truly afraid now.

But Alexander had already passed into the shadow of the fallen tree, drawing ever closer. Enola watched from the doorway with trepidation, when he stopped. He turned abruptly and she saw the whites of his eyes.

Then she heard it. Voices, carried on the wind. Men. Thundering hooves.

'Agatha!' Alexander shouted, running now, back towards the house. 'Run!'

Agatha pushed past Enola and slammed the door shut, drawing the bolt across and pressing herself up against it. 'They've come!' she said. 'William, up, up! It's time.'

William got to his feet, looking dazed as Agatha crossed the room to her chair and dragged it aside.

'Help me with this,' she said, lifting the corner of the rug. William helped her haul it back to expose the rotting floorboards. And a trap door. Agatha motioned for him to open it. After three heaves, the door opened with a groan.

Cold air rushed up from the darkness below, into which a narrow ladder descended. William stepped back.

'This passage will lead you to the edge of the realm,' Agatha said, looking at them both. 'Then you must run. Run through mist and shadow until you pass from the forest to the water's edge. You will come to a boat. It will take you to the Land of the Banished. Do not stop until you get to the boat. Do you hear me? Go now. William will know the way,' she said, meeting his bemused look with one of confidence. 'Follow William,' she said to Enola, 'and only William!'

'*Only* William? What else is down there?' Enola said, paralysed with fear as she stared into the black hole. There were shouts coming from outside now. They would burn her if they caught her. Or worse.

'William!' Agatha said, slapping him across the face. 'Wake up!'

William's eyes came back into focus. The marks around his neck were turning purple.

There was a barrage of banging at the door.

'Go!' Agatha said, pushing them towards the trap door.

'You have two seconds to open this door, old woman!' came a deep voice from outside.

'Hurry now!' Agatha hissed.

William began to climb down the rotting ladder. Enola followed, looking up at Agatha one last time before the old woman threw the trap door shut and they were plunged into darkness.

*

Alexander tried to reason with Vrax. 'What would you have done? Tell me, what would you have done, if it were your daughter?' he shouted. Vrax did not answer him, only went on smashing his fist against the door.

The other men were dismounting their horses. Tobias was amongst them; Alexander's stomach lurched when he saw him. He turned back to Vrax and pulled him away from the door.

'Stop! Listen to me!' he pleaded.

Vrax shoved him hard in the chest. Alexander stumbled backwards and fell to the ground.

'You lied to us. For all these years. Your family!' Vrax spat.

'She's my daughter!' said Alexander, scrambling to his feet again.

'She's a Reverof bitch!' Vrax said, moving slowly towards him. 'I was dangled over a Worgrim pit like meat and whipped to the bone. I had my flesh washed with their poison until my skin burned away - because of you! But don't fret, brother, there is a potion for that. There is a potion, so I could endure it all over again!' He brandished his scorched wrists. The skin was marbled with scars. He laughed manically. 'Twelve years, I have been treated like an outcast by our father - for a mistake I never made!' He looked at Alexander stonily as his men surrounded the house. 'Now you can answer to him,' he said, turning back to the door. Then he drew his knee to his chest and kicked.

Alexander leapt forwards as Vrax stormed into the house, but Tobias had him by the throat in a chokehold in an instant.

'Where is she?' came Vrax's impatient shout from inside. And then Agatha screamed, and Vrax was dragging her from the house by her hair. Her thin legs churned up the dirt as she struggled and screeched. Vrax threw her to the ground at Alexander's feet and took out a knife. Alexander gave a choked cry and writhed in Tobias's grasp. 'Shut up!' Vrax shouted, crouching low to position the tip of the blade over Agatha's heart. 'Where. Is. She?' he said to her, prodding her chest with the knife as he uttered each word.

Hot tears welled in Alexander's eyes as he fought to break free, but Tobias's grip only tightened. His head began to feel light and strange. There was a distant ringing in his ears.

Agatha looked at him and shook her head sadly. 'It's time, boy,' she said.

When Vrax plunged the knife into her chest, she didn't make a sound.

Tobias released Alexander and he fell to his knees as another tree began to groan nearby. He bit his fist, shaking, unable to contain his grief, and watched despairingly as Agatha's eyes stared blankly up at the treetops they could no longer see.

Vrax pushed himself to his feet and wiped his hands.

'Don't look so glum. Anyone would think you had a heart,' he said. Then he turned and called to his men, who emerged from Agatha's house laden with potions, coins and other trinkets. 'Spread out. Head south. They won't have gotten far,' he said to them, before he bent down and wrenched the knife from Agatha's chest. 'Tobias! Come! We're leaving!' he called as he walked back to his white horse.

*

Tobias finished leafing through the last of Agatha's books and walked around the living room once more. The table had been overturned, the chairs scattered, the fire snuffed out. It certainly *appeared* to have been a hasty escape.

He went back upstairs and began ripping into the mattresses and pulling wardrobes and cupboards away from the walls, searching for secret hiding holes. As he dragged a cupboard across the floor in the smallest bedroom, a piece of old, musty parchment floated out from behind it and landed by his feet. He picked it up and examined it. The young man in the picture was kneeling over a grave in the woods. His face was streaked with tears. In his hands he held a smooth, round stone. When Tobias looked closer, he saw that, in the left corner, barely distinguishable from the lines of the trees, was the shoulder and arm of a cloaked woman. In the right corner read the letters E.R. He placed the picture face down on the remnants of the bed and walked back down the stairs.

As he crossed the living room to the door, he became gradually aware of a sharp clanking sound coming from outside. He hesitated and then left the house. Outside, he saw Alexander on his feet with a shovel in hand. He was digging relentlessly, directing all of his aggression at the grave, grunting as he thrust the shovel into the earth. He took no notice of Tobias.

'It'll be dark soon. You won't finish in time,' Tobias said, feeling a hint of pity for his older brother.

Alexander stopped digging. His brow was wet with sweat. Tobias nodded to the rocks that lined the path outside Agatha's house.

Alexander began collecting armfuls of rocks and carrying them to Agatha's body; he stacked them around and over her.

Tobias watched silently. And then his eyes drifted to the old grave. The mound of dirt was crumbling back into the hollow in the wind. It was as if he'd been struck by his father's stinging whip. The idea came into his head so suddenly, he had to stop himself from gasping. He went back into the house discreetly, though he suspected Alexander wouldn't have noticed if he'd set the whole place alight in front of him, and began his final search.

19. MERLIN'S OLD MAGIC

Fabian scraped his fingernails along his jaw. It was late, he was tired, and he loathed being kept waiting. What was taking so long? He rose from his chair and began to pace up and down restlessly.

'Where is he?' he hissed at the nervous servant girl in the corner of the bedchamber. 'Useless. You're all useless,' he said, striding past her to the door and flinging it open.

'Alexander!' he shouted, his voice echoing down the corridor. A cluster of servants at the other end scattered and hid themselves away.

The boy he had sent in search of his son rounded the corner then. He was alone, approaching cautiously with his hands knotted together.

'He's not in the castle, my Lord,' the boy said when he reached him. 'A farmhand saw him enter the Dark Forest this morning.'

Fabian slapped the boy. 'Go,' he said, his hand smarting.

'What's the matter?' came a sultry voice, as the boy scurried away. Fabian turned to see Risella emerging from her chamber, her long, silk robe trailing on the floor. She was a beautiful woman, in a strange, intriguing way. Her eyes, black as night, danced devilishly as she stared at him. Looking into her eyes was like staring into two endless pits, plunging into a terrible darkness filled with untold horrors. But, though he should have felt afraid, it always excited him. She was a dangerous enchantress. As she moved slowly towards him, her hair, black and sleek, rippled like water over her shoulders down to her breasts, which were barely concealed by the nightgown.

'What do you want?' he said impatiently.

Risella drew back, feigning offence, and then smiled darkly. 'I came to see what was the matter. You seem…tense,' she said, stroking his arm affectionately. 'Can I be of service?' she whispered, leaning in, her breath hot in his ear.

'You should keep better track of your husband,' Fabian said, shrugging her off. 'I wish to speak with him and he is nowhere to be found. Probably rooting some wench in the forest!'

'Don't be vulgar. What could be so urgent at this hour? Come to bed,' she said, pulling him by the hand towards her chamber.

Fabian resisted. 'No.'

He needed to speak with his son. He had been feeling strange all afternoon. Something was bothering him, but he didn't know what it was. Alexander would know. He could trust Alexander.

Age had not been kind to Fabian. His mind was failing him. He forgot orders he had given, expenditures he had approved, the names of his generals. He had even begun to wonder if he had not already spoken to Alexander about whatever it was that troubled him. As his memory deteriorated, he grew more insular and suspicious. They were all testing him, trying to catch him out - Belfor, Vrax, Tobias, his men, the servants – waiting for any sign of weakness. His army was ready, the men as healthy as they would ever be. This was the perfect time, now all the hard work had been done, for someone to strike him down and take the glory.

And then there was the question of the girl. She kept him awake at night. He could not rest until he knew for certain what had become of her. He hoped that, somewhere out there, her bones were rotting in a ditch. Or, if she lived, that no one yet realised who she was, and that he would find her in time to slit her throat himself.

'My Lord! My Lord! Come quickly. There's something you must see! Down by the forest!'

Fabian turned in surprise to see a young servant running towards him, arms flailing, the whites of his eyes whiter than his milky skin. Before Fabian had a chance to blink, the boy was running back the way he had come.

'Stay here,' he said to Risella, pushing her into the doorway of her chamber.

Outside, a crowd had formed down by the border.

'What's happening?' Fabian shouted, but no one stopped to answer him as they swarmed towards the forest. He lifted the folds of his cloak and began to run down the hill with them.

Belfor saw him coming and parted the crowd. When Fabian reached him at the forest's edge, he gripped his fat cousin's shoulder tightly. 'What?' he said. 'What is it?'

Belfor turned and signalled to one of his soldiers, who was standing in the forest. The man raised his hand and an ice-blue orb materialised and floated above his palm.

Fabian had to grip Belfor even tighter to stop his legs from buckling. He looked at the orb with tears in his eyes. The crowd watched in awestruck silence. Fabian sucked in his breath and stood up straight, shaking his greasy mane from his shoulders. Then he looked at Belfor and nodded.

'Assemble the army!' Belfor shouted.

*

Lucian collapsed into bed, his back aching. It had been a long day overseeing the construction of the permanent army settlement in the lands beyond Merlin's Way. He resented helping with the effort, being stuck outside in the cold, battered by the fierce winds, associating with builders and stonemasons. But the admiration his presence evoked from townsfolk and soldiers alike did bolster his spirits somewhat.

Master Hagworth would be eating his words. He had proved the schoolmaster wrong. He was leading from the front, was he not? The people loved him, did they not? Even when the fool Mirthworth had dropped a stone slab from the top of a tower and damaged the new stable roof, he had stayed his hand, smiled, told him it was no matter, despite the fact it had set the entire effort back days, perhaps weeks. How he had wanted to punish Mirthworth for his incompetence, to push him from the tower. He had exercised restraint, as he had done every day for twelve excruciating years. But, as each day crept by, it took a little more of his patience with it.

He listened to the fire as it crackled in the hearth and began to fall softly to sleep. Suddenly, the bed jolted and the chest on the far wall shook. Lucian sat up and looked around blearily. Everything was still, everything in its place. Perhaps he had dreamt it, he thought, as he let his head sink back onto his pillow. As he closed his eyes, the castle bells began to ring. He sat bolt upright. The chamber door flew open and Thomas burst into the room.

'The spell is broken!' he cried, breathless and wild-eyed. 'The Dark Forest... The spell is broken!'

Lucian jumped out of bed. The stone floor felt ice-cold underfoot as he rushed across his chamber to dress. His hands were shaking.

'Get down there. Tell the men we march now!'

20. THE PASSAGE

'Can you see anything?' asked Enola, as she and William stepped tentatively through the darkness. They had been silent for so long, she had forgotten the sound of her own voice. It seemed foreign to her now.

'Shh!'

The tunnel was wide and cavernous and seemed to go on forever. Enola had only a vague impression of her hand as she ran it along the rough wall; hardened by the ages and the unnatural cold, it felt more like stone than earth. She could just pick out William in the darkness, though he was becoming less clear as he trudged on ahead over the uneven ground and began to wade through another filthy pool of water that filled a deep crater. Enola followed and drips splashed onto her head from above as she crossed the pool. She shivered and clamped a hand onto her head, which was becoming numb with cold, as she clambered out.

'Do you know where you're going?' she pressed.

'SHH!'

'Say that to me again and—'

'What?' William said, turning abruptly. 'What will you do?'

Enola stopped in her tracks, trying desperately to think of something terrible with which to threaten him.

But, with a stab of regret, she realised that, in their rush to escape, she hadn't brought her knife.

'If you don't shut up,' William continued, 'I'll take you back there and hand you over to them.'

Enola pursed her lips. If she'd had her knife, she'd have put it through his eye for speaking to her like that. She almost smiled as she imagined it.

'They'll kill you as well,' she said when William began to walk on. He stopped again and turned. But, just as he opened his mouth to speak, the distant sound of sloshing water echoed through the tunnel. Enola's skin prickled and the cold feeling on the top of her head seeped down through her body. 'They're coming.' She breathed the words, her heart racing, and saw her own cold fear reflected in William's eyes. William grabbed her hand and, with a forceful tug, they were running. The distant splashing became frantic.

They ran and ran, deeper into the tunnel. But, no matter how fast they went, the footsteps grew louder, echoing all around them. Enola's lungs burned. Behind her, she could hear the ragged breaths of their pursuers. They were close.

A hand shot out and pulled at the back of her dress. She stumbled, falling to the cold, wet ground. But William didn't stop; he dragged her along like a hunter with a dead animal, until the skin on her legs began to scrape away and she shrieked, twisting out of his grasp.

The moment he let go, two hands seized her.

'No!' she shouted, as a man hauled her to her feet, wrapped his arms around her waist in a crushing grasp and began to move back down the tunnel towards Agatha's house. Arms trapped against her sides, Enola kicked and thrashed and screamed. The sound reverberated deafeningly against the walls. 'I'll gut you!' she cried in a wild, rasping voice. 'I'll gut you, I will!'

The man started to laugh. But when William spoke, his laughter died.

'Who are you?' William said, his form taking shape in the gloom as he came closer. The man stopped and his grip on Enola tightened. There was no one else with him. He was alone. 'What did you do to her? To Agatha?' William said, his voice quavering.

'Move on, boy, if you want to live,' said Tobias.

'What did you do!' William shouted.

Enola stopped struggling and stared at William as he began to breathe rapidly, his chest heaving.

'The old hag feeds the crows,' said Tobias.

William roared with fury and ran at him. Tobias let go of Enola and drew his dagger. Enola spun around as the blade sliced through the air towards William's throat. She lunged for it, arms outstretched, eyes fixed on the flashing silver, and a blinding light burst from her hands. Tobias cried out and there was a dull thud as he dropped to the ground. Blood gushed from his nose and ears and, as Enola stood over him, she could see that his eyes had rolled to the back of his head. She stared at the white slits and kicked his foot. He didn't stir.

'He's dead,' she said, crouching low and feeling around for his knife in the gloom.

William sat back against the tunnel wall with his head in his hands. 'They killed her.'

'I know,' said Enola, and she found that she wasn't as glad about Agatha's death as she thought she would be. She could never go back there now. Everything she owned was now lost, ripe for someone else's taking – and the blue stone with it.

She sat across from William in silence, listening to the drips as they fell from the tunnel roof and splashed into the puddles. Agatha had told them not to stop until they reached a boat. And, for the first time in her life,

Enola felt a strong desire to heed the old woman's advice.

'We should go. There could be more of them,' she said, getting to her feet.

William wiped his eyes and stood. He put an arm in front of Enola as she made to move off. 'Knife,' he said wearily.

Enola tightened her grasp on the handle. 'No,' she said.

He wrenched it from her hand so quickly she barely knew it was happening. Then he walked on.

'Give it back!' she shouted, running after him half-heartedly, for she knew he never would.

'How did you do that, back there?' William asked, when Tobias was long behind them.

'Give me the knife and I'll tell you,' said Enola. Her hands were still tingling and she felt strange, weaker somehow, unsettled. She hadn't intended to do it, she didn't know how she had done it; but she wouldn't tell him that.

There had been a time when she had used magic freely. She remembered it well. She was good at it. She enjoyed it; loosening torches from their brackets on the castle walls; setting fire to the bedsheets; destroying ugly mushrooms without even having to touch them. But that had come to an end in the Dark Forest. All the power she ever had, snuffed out like a candle. Until now. She thought again of the fire in Agatha's hearth, sparked to life by her hand alone, thought of the grey, crumbling bark on the trees in the forest, and of the tree that had fallen across the path, quite dead. And she began to wonder…

'Why did you do it?' William asked.

'What?' she said distractedly.

'Why did you tell her your name?' He was talking about the girl. The girl she had seen him kissing. Dead now.

'She saw me,' Enola said.

'Because you wanted her to see you! Why couldn't you just leave us alone? Who were we harming?' William snapped. When she didn't answer, he strode on at a quicker pace. But Enola stopped still. She had been so lost in her thoughts, she had followed him straight past the tunnel that branched off to the left of the main path, walking as if in a dream.

'Wait!' she hissed. 'Wait!'

'Shh!'

'Stop! How do you know we're going the right way?' she said, retracing her steps until she was standing by the entrance to the second passage.

William stopped. 'What?'

'How do you know we should be taking this path instead of that one?' she said, pointing to the left. 'Why do you know and I don't? What did Agatha tell you?'

Agatha had always left her out. She would mutter things to William and Alexander and then fall silent when Enola came into the room. It was as if the old crone wanted her to know she was being excluded from something. It was infuriating. The memory made Enola feel suddenly glad that she was dead.

'What are you talking about?' William said.

'How do you know if we're going the right way?'

'What do you mean?'

'How do—'

'This is the only way!' he snapped, looking around wildly. 'Is this another game?'

'No, look here! Come!' she said, beckoning him. He didn't move.

'Enola, whatever you're doing, we don't have time for it.'

'Look!' she exclaimed. 'Can't you see? Don't you have eyes?'

'I see you pointing at the wall,' he said.

Enola's stomach knotted up. She glanced at the left passage and then looked again at William with mounting unease. And, as she did, she saw a flickering movement in the corner of her eye. She turned her head and then backed away quickly, pressing herself against the tunnel wall. Drifting through the darkness, silvery white and translucent, was the form of a woman.

'There's someone here.'

'Stop it, Enola,' William said, marching towards her furiously and looking where she looked.

'It's not a game,' she said, frozen with terror as the spectre came closer, closer, closer. 'It's coming!'

'Shut up! Do you want to die?'

Enola screamed as the figure emerged from the passage onto their path. William jumped with fright and backed right through it.

'What?' he said angrily.

The figure floated towards Enola, who sank to the ground, heart pounding, unable to move, as it stopped and stretched out a hand to her. Its fingers were wispy and insubstantial. But its face… She stared long and hard. She knew the face well, the eyes - no longer blue.

'Mother?' she said.

'Enola, look at me,' William said, kneeling beside her. 'She isn't here. There's no one here. Just us. We need to go.'

Enola shook her head. 'She's here.'

'She's not here. She's dead.'

'I know she's dead,' Enola said. She wasn't a fool. And yet she couldn't deny what she was seeing, couldn't deny the face she had looked at every day until she was four years old - her mother's face, ugly in death, as in life. 'She is here. And she's not alone. There's a man next to you. And a woman. And a boy,' she said, peering at the silvery shapes bent over William, who shuddered violently and scrambled away from the wall.

'This is a sick game!' he hissed. And he turned and stormed off, crashing through the puddles, disappearing into darkness.

'William!' she called. Her own voice echoed back in reply.

The figures drifted away into the passage, merging together like smoke, except for Iris; she lingered and stretched out her hand again. Enola hesitated, looking in the direction William had gone. When she turned back to her mother, she was surprised to see that she had moved to the tunnel opening. For some unknown reason, Enola had a strong feeling that she should follow her, that Iris Mortenstone's path was true. She felt drawn to her, like they were being pulled together by powerful magic. She took one step towards her. Iris moved deeper into the passage. Another step. Iris's hand remained outstretched. Her lips moved but didn't make a sound. Her fingers began to clutch for Enola, dancing in the darkness like silver smoke. Enola took another step and reached out for her. As she touched her mother's hand, it became solid and a wave of heat hit her with such force, she was almost knocked off her feet. The fire was eating into her skin, melting it away; she could taste the smoke, see the crowd below, nameless faces, watching, silent. She wanted to scream but her mouth was filled with dark, thick smoke.

William's fingers curled around her arm. She jumped at his cold touch. The fiery pain ceased, the faces disappeared. She was in the tunnel again. And the figures were all drifting further and further away. She could no longer tell which was her mother. She took several long, deep breaths, running her fingers over her face and finding it whole, the skin undamaged. Sweat trickled down her forehead as the wind rushed past her through the tunnel. She remembered the day her mother died; she remembered the screaming as she hid behind the curtain in that strange bedchamber; she remembered the foul smell as her father carried her out of the castle into the square. Remembering was one thing, but feeling it… Her hands shook uncontrollably. That's what they would do to her if they found her, the Mordarks. They would burn her. There was no worse a death than death by fire.

'Come this way,' William said. He looked afraid. Enola let him guide her along the path. And, as they walked, she noticed him staring at her.

'I wasn't making it up,' she said.

'No,' said William. 'No, I don't think you were.' After a long silence, he spoke again, 'Didn't you ever wonder how I ended up with Agatha?'

'Yes,' she said. 'But no one ever told me.'

'Your grandfather banished my family from The Light when I was an infant. He stripped us of magic. My mother and father made it to Agatha's house and then died of a fever, along with my brother. That's Agatha's version of things. But you know how it is. They were probably robbed or attacked. Probably by your father,' he said.

'Probably,' she concurred. William looked at her crossly.

Suddenly, a sharp pain bit deep into her chest. Gasping, she put a hand to her heart and her legs gave out from under her. As her head hit the ground, an image of Master Hagworth came into her mind as he looked from the dead fairies to her with dawning realisation. Then Agatha was before her, sitting across the room in her chair, staring at her with contempt. And Agatha turned suddenly into Josephine Mortenstone, who hissed that the cursed child should be killed in her sleep. The memories flashed before her. She couldn't breathe, couldn't shut her eyes.

'Enola!' William shouted.

In front of her now was a Silver Tree, standing alone, its branches bare. Inside the tree, trapped within its bark, was a withered old man with long white hair and a white beard. The man from her dreams. He looked at her gravely and then closed his eyes and let out a slow breath. He did not take another.

Enola felt a plummeting feeling in her stomach. The man vanished. Her mouth flew open and black tendrils of smoke spiralled out, rising from the depths of her body, escaping, dissipating into the icy air.

Lying there in the darkness, she felt weightless, free, as the curse left her.

21. THE MEETING OF TWO LORDS

Lucian staggered down the stairs to the entrance hall, snatching breaths through the pain that swelled in his chest. He mopped the blood that streamed from the gash in his head with the sleeve of his tunic. He had fallen outside his bedchamber, hit his head. A bad omen; the first blood spilt had been his own.

The entrance hall was in total chaos. Servants and cooks were fleeing from the lower floors, laden with silverware, dashing for the doors as hunting hounds bounded in from the courtyard, yelping and howling, the chains that secured them to their posts in the kennels trailing on the floor behind them. Guards were shouting incoherent orders in their vain attempts to bring order.

Still winded, Lucian pushed his way through the throng to the castle doors, where he collided with Gregory Vandemere, who looked relieved to see him.

'My Lord, we must hurry. The attack has begun. What is your command?'

'Push them back! Don't let them break our lines!' Lucian said. Gregory nodded, threw his arms into the air and vanished.

Lucian looked around the hall and spotted Langlot, head of the Mortenstone guards, emerging from a darkened corridor.

'I want one hundred men to stay behind and protect the castle!' he shouted.

Langlot looked at him, banged his fist against his armour and then bellowed the order in a gruff, commanding voice that drew guards into the hall from every direction. As they gathered, Lucian turned to leave the castle. But he stopped suddenly and looked back. Eve was standing at the top of the great staircase. She looked like a lost child, shoulders hunched, eyes wide with fear. And, in that moment, he felt a dreadful, heavy feeling in his heart. Crossing the hall again, he climbed the steps and went to her. She looked startled as he placed a hand on her arm, and the gesture felt so unnatural to Lucian that he withdrew it gladly.

'Hide, Eve. Go somewhere far away. Take a horse. Ride now!' he said.

Eve looked at him. Her sunken eyes seemed too large for her drawn, hollow face. 'I want Thomas to come,' she said in a small voice.

'I need Thomas here. Go. I'll send guards with you. You'll be safe.'

She regarded him mistrustfully. Lucian could hear the shouts from the courtyard growing more urgent. He didn't have time for gentle words anymore.

'Go!' he shouted. Eve flinched and shrank into herself. Lucian looked to the three guards waiting at the bottom of the staircase and nodded.

As they escorted Eve down the stairs and out into the courtyard, he followed. And he saw his sister half turn to look back at him before thinking better of it.

Lucian almost passed his mother by as he strode across the courtyard, but something made him glance at the dungeon doorway. Josephine was standing in the shadows, watching men flood from the armoury with shields and swords and leave through the open gates. When Lucian saw her pale, gaunt face, he at first thought her expression was wrought with fear. But, as he approached, he saw that her eyes were wild with nervous excitement. She looked truly mad.

'Go with Eve. I've sent her away,' he said. Josephine started in surprise. She had not seen him. She stared at him for a moment without recognition. 'Mother?' he said, unnerved by her reaction. 'Go with Eve. And don't come back until I send for you. It's not safe here.'

'No,' she said, her eyes fixed on the gates.

'But mother—'

'This is my home. This is where I will wait,' she said, gathering her shawl about her.

'The spells are dead; the old magic is gone!' he snapped. 'If we can't hold them back, they will come here and they will kill you!'

'If you cannot hold them back then I am lost no matter where I run,' she said finally.

Lucian gave up. Sighing exasperatedly, he turned and ran towards the gates.

'Lucian!' Josephine called suddenly. He stopped and looked over his shoulder. For a fleeting instant, her eyes were filled with regret and sorrow, but then a stony calm passed over her face. She closed her mouth, and whatever she was about to say remained unsaid.

Lucian hurried on. He used to make a point of looking at the scorch marks in the square where Iris had been burned, but now, as he passed them, he averted his eyes. Looking down the sloping lane towards the Grassland, his mouth fell open. The Dark Forest was burning as brightly as the pyre his sister had perished upon, great flames and plumes of smoke rising from the treetops, surging up to meet the black sky. His heart turned over in his chest. He began to run. Behind him, with a steady rumble, soldiers and Mortenstone guards came charging from the castle courtyard and Merlin's Way, bound for Stone Lane. They formed a tight circle around him as they ran. Lucian saw the sigils on their shields and breastplates: Mortenstone, Vandemere, Doldon, Stonedge, Le Fay.

All along Stone Lane, townspeople were emerging from their houses and screaming when they saw the forest ablaze in the distance. Mothers wrapped their arms around their children and vanished into the night, escaping while they still could, abandoning Lambelee, abandoning him, their Lord.

'I want every man and boy down at the forest!' Lucian shouted. Four Vandemere soldiers peeled off from the pack and began kicking down doors in the lane, searching for recruits.

The deep crackling of the fire grew louder as Lucian and his men crossed the Grassland and stormed through the deserted camp towards the forest.

'With me!' Lucian shouted, breaking out in front, drawing his sword and leading them into blackness.

He crashed through the forest, blind, and ran head-on into a tree. Roaring with pain, his head spinning, he cried, 'Stop!' Behind him, the sound of thudding boots ceased.

'Lights!' shouted Brinston Tarolock, a seasoned soldier in the Mortenstone Army. The old man's face was illuminated suddenly as he flicked a ball of light to life above his palm and tossed it in front of them. The ball lit the surroundings as it flew through the gloom. There was a sharp, collective intake of breath as the men bore witness to the impossible – magic, in the Dark Forest. Tarolock himself looked stunned. One by one, the men conjured balls of light in their hands.

'No!' Lucian shouted. 'Save your strength.' The men extinguished their lights.

They continued on through the forest, following Tarolock's orb as it glided through the darkness, throwing light across the greying trees, which creaked and groaned so loudly it sent a shiver down Lucian's spine.

When the smoke reached them, passing by silently like a cloud of poison, he tightened his grip on the handle of his sword, his heart thrumming in his ears. They were close. An unnatural orange haze backlit the trees ahead, swallowing Tarolock's orb. Lucian pushed on faster. He could hear the distant din of battle now. Faster, faster he went. And then, through the trees, in a vast clearing, he saw them. Hundreds of men; a frenzy of thrashing limbs and swords. The trees on the other side of the clearing were on fire, ferocious flames roaring and climbing and showering down over the figures below.

Lucian gasped for breath as he ran, the smoke thick in his lungs. The screams were shrill in the air now. And he could see, as he drew nearer, that the lines had dissolved; his men had lost all order. He opened his mouth to shout, to announce his presence, let them know that help was here at last, when a wall of heat hit him. He flew backwards, dropping his sword, and landed hard on the ground. The silver ring on his finger turned hot, burning into his skin. He cried out, trying to pull it off, but it was stuck fast. Sitting up, eyes watering with pain, he abandoned his efforts and seized his sword. Then he got to his feet, looking around wildly, trying to form a plan. For the first time in years, he thought of his father. What would he have done? How would Matthew Mortenstone have brought order to his men, re-formed the broken lines? How would he have saved them?

Suddenly, a green bolt of light shot past his cheek, exploding against a tree behind him. With a groan, the tree buckled, and the men around him scattered. Lucian jumped out of the way and rolled across the ground, feeling the earth tremble beneath him as the tree fell. Lurching to his feet again with a guttural roar, he charged forwards, his face dripping with blood, his right cheek scorched and peeling. Tarolock was at his side now; he took down the first man who ran at Lucian and quickly pulled his sword from the man's belly to hack off another man's head.

Lucian staggered on without him, looking for black armour to stick his sword into. But, all around him, men were silhouetted by the intense light, indistinguishable.

He heard a terrible screeching sound and whirled around to see a man running from the battle towards him, his entire body engulfed in flames. Lucian leapt aside and the man tore past him, his screams turning to gurgling rattles as the flames licked at his throat. Lucian watched him fall and felt his own throat constrict. He was suddenly aware of the dirty smoke that filled his nostrils, the stinging pain in his eyes, the ferocious roaring of the fire, the ringing of swords and shields deflecting spells. And, in that moment, as the battle unfolded around him, he felt an overwhelming sense of his own mortality. He, Lucian, descendent of Merlin the Good, whose blood possessed more power than the whole of Lambelee and the Low Lands combined, could die tonight just as easily as any of them.

A great beast of a man emerged from the orange haze and stomped towards him then, baring his teeth, an axe raised above his head. Lucian threw out his left hand instinctively, spreading his fingers. A ball of blinding light burst from his palm and careered through the air, smashing through the man's armour. He flew onto his back without a sound, eyes cast up to the heavens, as the white-hot fire ate through his heart.

Breathless, Lucian stumbled onwards. He felt weak. Ahead, he could see a man in black thrusting a sword into a Mortenstone guard repeatedly, until the guard's pulverised innards spilled out over his silver armour. Lucian ran at him, brimming with rage, and plunged his sword into the man's side, deep enough to kill him, but slowly. The man screamed and dropped his weapon. As Lucian withdrew his sword, he looked up to see a figure silhouetted against the fiery mist, long black feathers adorning the collar of his cloak, which hung still despite the wind. He had heard the tales. Every child had heard the tales. The Lord of the Dark Lands; his cloak of feathers plucked from creatures of darkness. A chill ran through him. This was the man who haunted his dreams. The man he had pictured a thousand times in his mind. The man he had grown so used to imagining that seeing him now made him feel as if he had stepped into another nightmare. He felt himself shaking. All those night terrors. All those years, plagued by the figure who now stood before him.

The battle cries were swallowed by black silence as Lucian stared into the eyes of Fabian Mordark.

22. THE SPECTRE

Alexander opened his eyes and blinked up at the orange mist that hung in the air. It was dark now. He was in the forest. The dirt was cold beneath his head but the air was hot, stiflingly hot. His lungs stung as he took a breath. He sat up and looked at the mound of rocks beside him. And, as if a thick fog had cleared, he remembered. Agatha. He pushed himself to his feet and looked down at the grave in despair. Agatha was dead.

Distant shrieks punctured the silence; bloodcurdling, tortured cries. Alexander's head snapped up. He stared around, alert. Who was that? What was happening?

Suddenly, the ground shook. A thunderous explosion knocked him down onto his back and a blinding light blistered through the air above. He screwed his eyes shut. A hot wind rushed over him. He could feel the blood trickling from his head into the dirt. Disorientated, ears throbbing, he rolled onto his stomach and dragged himself across the ground towards Agatha's house. When he reached it, he groped for the door but found that it was open, hanging precariously on one hinge, the wood around the frame splintered. He got unsteadily to his feet and stumbled inside.

The strange light from the forest seeped dreamily through the doorway into the living room. As Alexander looked around at the upturned chairs and shredded books, the day's horrors stung him afresh. Agatha's whole world was now nothing but debris on a soiled floor.

And then his heart stilled. Over by the hearth, the trap door lay open. The rug had been hastily pulled aside, so that a part of it sank over the opening.

Enola.

In his own selfish grief, he had forgotten all about his daughter.

He hastened towards the trap door and climbed down onto the first rung of the ladder. Cursing himself, he clambered back up again and began to look for the weapons he had placed by the fireside that morning. As he reached beneath the upturned armchair, his hand brushed over something smooth and cold. He knew it at once and quickly pocketed the blue stone before continuing his search. But he could not find his weapons.

As he jumped from the last rung of the ladder into a freezing pool of water, his boots filled and he shuddered.

'Enola!' he called. 'William!' His voice was swallowed by a deep, cold, empty darkness. He staggered forwards a few steps, the water spilling out of his boots. Everything was black. The smell of death permeated the air. Heart pounding, he began to walk, brushing his hands against the pocked walls for guidance. There came a rumbling boom from high above. Dirt crumbled from the tunnel roof a foot above his head, powdering his hair, slipping down the back of his tunic. Startled, he quickly shook it away and wiped his eyes with his forearm. What was happening out there?

He had awoken that morning next to Risella and turned away from her when she tried to run her hand over his naked chest. He didn't know why, but even his wife's mere touch filled him with revulsion. When she had asked him to accompany her to the Worgrim pits to watch them feed, he immediately resolved to visit Agatha and Enola. And William. He hadn't planned to, but anything to avoid spending the morning with his wife, whose lust for blood surpassed even his father's. He had not eaten breakfast – Agatha would make him something hearty, he knew. And off he had set, to see Agatha for the last time.

How had Vrax known? Had he led him to her? Had someone else seen Enola? Informed on her? And why now? Why, after all these years, was his father still pursuing her? What could he possibly want from a Reverof girl?

Alexander was so absorbed in his own thoughts, his heart almost stopped when he stumbled over something hard on the ground. He staggered forwards, regained his footing, then turned back around. Bending low, he reached out and felt… a hand. It was a body. A man. He had been dead for some hours now; his skin was stone cold. Alexander ran his fingers over the man's face. When he realised who it was, the shock snatched the air from his lungs. Despite the darkness, he turned his head away, not wanting to see.

Of both his brothers, Tobias was the one he loved most. Alexander had always protected him, even when he knew his younger brother was wrong, even though his loyalty was not always reciprocated. But, this time, Tobias had gone too far. If Alexander had been here when it had happened, he would not have helped him.

A memory came to him then. Tobias could have been no more than five. His eyes were red and swollen from crying as he sat at the table, refusing to eat his cabbage. No matter how many threats Minder Poxworth made, Tobias would not swallow the wilted greens. Eventually, Poxworth threw his arms into the air and announced he was going to call for their father to come and punish him. As he marched off, Alexander turned to his brother and told him to eat the cabbage. Tobias shook his head.

'It can't be worse than what father will do,' Alexander reminded him. But Tobias was stubborn, too stubborn for his own good. Both boys jumped as they heard their father's flinty voice in the corridor outside. 'Eat the cabbage!' Alexander urged. Tobias pursed his lips. No. Alexander reached over, scooped the cabbage onto his spoon and quickly stuffed it into his own mouth as the door burst open and Fabian entered the hall. Alexander chewed the rubbery food as fast as he could. Fabian walked up to the table and stared down at Tobias's empty plate. Then, he turned back to Poxworth, a question on his raised brows, and Alexander swallowed his mouthful.

'It's empty,' Fabian said.

'It…I…It wasn't. Not when I left. He wouldn't…he wouldn't eat it,' Poxworth stammered, panic in his voice.

Fabian turned quickly to his sons. 'Is this true?' he asked. Both boys shook their heads.

'No, father,' Alexander said. 'He's lying. He said he wanted to get Tobias into trouble. He wanted to see you beat him. It excites him.'

Poxworth's mouth fell open. 'Liar!' he shouted, advancing towards Alexander. Fabian held up his hand. Poxworth stopped in his tracks.

'Let us walk,' Fabian said to him. Alexander and Tobias exchanged a devious look. They never did see Poxworth again.

Alexander closed Tobias's eyes and blinked away the stinging ache in his own. His brother had paid a high price for his disloyalty. And only now did he realise that he and Tobias were more alike than he could have imagined.

He walked on numbly, his sadness tinged with relief – relief that it had not been Enola he had found dead on the ground.

Further along the passage, the left-hand wall he had been running his fingers over took a sharp turn. He stopped and went across to the other side of the tunnel, where the wall continued along a straight path. There were two passages. But which way? Some instinct was telling him to take the left path. And, as he stumbled blindly towards the opening, he saw a silvery white light flicker to life in the distance. He froze.

'Who's there?' he said, trying to keep his voice steady. The silver light was growing larger, floating towards him, and starting to take shape. A trick. But no… A figure. 'Stay back!' he said as it came closer, closer. And then his mouth fell open. The figure flickered again and vanished. Alexander felt as if his stomach had dropped from under him. It was her, he was sure of it.

Iris.

He staggered back, taking fast breaths. Suddenly, the ground shook. More dirt crumbled down onto the path from the roof of the tunnel. In the distance, he heard a panicked voice. It was a man's voice. But he didn't get up.

He had betrayed her. And she had died screaming. The guilt was too much to bear. He buried his face in his hands.

She was wary when she first met him. Smart girl. Why hadn't he just let her go on her way? Why had it been so important to change her opinion of him? He slammed his head against the tunnel wall again and again in anger. It wasn't his father. He hadn't done it for his father, to glean information; he knew that now. It had never been about that. He had seen the way she looked at him that day and he didn't want her to think he was a monster. He didn't want her to see him for what he truly was. Because, if she had, she could never have loved him.

'I'm sorry,' he said through his tears, looking up and staring into the blackness, waiting, hoping that Iris would return – if she had ever really been there at all.

23. WAR AND WORGRIMS

Fabian stood completely still in the clearing, watching Lucian. He was taller than he had imagined - and lean, like Vrax. He looked lost on the battlefield, lost even as he buried his blade in a Mordark soldier's side; a child with a sword. And when he stopped and looked up and Fabian stared into his eyes, he saw exactly what he had expected to see: fear.

Fabian's lips curled back over grey, decaying teeth as he opened his mouth and released a guttural cry. He felt his power rushing through him as he screamed into the night. Lucian Mortenstone would die on his feet. Fabian threw out his arms, locked them straight, fingers splayed, palms facing his enemy. A surge of green light burst from his hands. But Lucian reacted at once; before the green fiery light touched him, he raised his arms and white light shot from his palms.

Fabian felt a jolt as the bolts clashed with a thunderous *crack* and began to snap and spark, climbing through the air to overcome one another, switching and jumping like lightning. He pushed harder, forcing more and more power from his body, willing the Mortenstone rat dead with every fibre of his being. But, suddenly, he started to feel strange. His arms grew heavy. His cries ran dry. And, with pain so excruciating it brought tears to his eyes, his long fingernails split in half, the cracks riding to his very nailbeds. Without a second thought, he directed his green bolt at the ground between him and Lucian. It ignited in an instant, vicious flames leaping up high, creating a barrier between them. He saw Lucian's arms drop to his sides before the fire hid him completely from sight.

'Fall back!' Fabian shouted, running from the battle, running from the fire. 'Back! Back!'

He staggered through the forest, away from the screaming and the slaughter, into darkness.

When he could run no further, he stopped and leant against a tree to catch his breath. Floods of men overtook him, fleeing the battle, taking no notice of him as he vomited blood all over his boots.

'Water,' he said, his voice faint and raspy.

A Mordark soldier, who was bent double panting beside a nearby tree, his face covered in blood, stood and approached unsteadily. He took out his flask, held it to Fabian's lips and placed a hand on his back. Fabian shook him off savagely. 'I don't need your help!' he said, snatching the flask from him. A searing pain shot up his fingers and into his spine; his cracked nails oozed with blood. He dropped the flask and gasped. 'Get me something for this!'

The man quickly produced a small bottle of dark liquid from beneath his sleeve. 'This will heal them,' he said, pulling out the cork to drizzle the thick potion over Fabian's fingers. The deep cracks in his nails sealed in an instant and the pain subsided. Fabian sighed with relief and stooped to pick up the flask of water.

'My Lord, my Lord!' came a panicked shout. Fabian wheeled around as a soldier bounded towards him, eyes wild with terror. 'My Lord, they're dousing the fires! They're preparing to advance!'

A cold sweat broke out on Fabian's brow. 'Hold them back!' he ordered.

'My Lord!' came another cry. Belfor was running towards them. Fabian almost didn't recognise his cousin; his face was smoke-blackened, his hair all but completely burned away. 'The Worgrims!' Belfor shouted. 'They're attacking our men!'

Fabian's heart stilled. He blinked at his cousin. Then, flinging the flask of water against a tree, he roared with fury. 'Shoot them down!'

Belfor nodded and ran back the way he had come, calling men to him.

Fabian tried to follow but his legs wobbled and his head swam. He sank down against the tree and started to laugh. He was just a boy, Lucian Mortenstone, just a boy. No match for him. His laughter grew manic. The soldier who had handed him the flask watched on in alarm. Fabian threw his head back, laughing and laughing until he choked on his own blood. Defeated by a child – wouldn't that make a wonderful song! Only, Lucian Mortenstone was no longer a boy. And Fabian remembered now, as he looked down at his withered hands, that he was an old man.

24. JOSEPHINE MORTENSTONE

Lucian hung back as his men advanced after the retreating Dark Families. His chest throbbed and every breath brought a fresh stabbing pain with it.

Bodies lay scattered, disfigured, in the clearing, flesh melting from bones. Lucian did not know whether it had been the fire or the deadly Worgrim venom that had done such atrocious things to the bodies, and he never would. The beasts had swooped down upon them so suddenly, their great black wings fanning the red flames, their scaly talons outstretched as they plucked men from battle and carried them away. Some stayed to feast upon the men, whose screams were shrill and chilling, for they were still alive when the beasts began to eat them. Lucian had taken cover beneath the trees, away from the clearing. But he watched. Watched as the Worgrims finished and flew up over the treetops to join their kin, shadows flitting across the white moon, bound for The Light.

'Lucian?' Thomas said, emerging from a haze of smoke and coming to stand in front of him. His face was covered in dark, dried blood. Lucian stared at him, his vision moving in and out of focus. Thomas looked at him gravely. 'Lucian!' he shouted suddenly, catching him in his arms as Lucian's legs gave way.

'I'm alright,' Lucian said weakly, clutching his chest. Guards rushed to him but Lucian shook his head. 'I'm alright,' he said again.

Thomas pulled him to his feet but, when Lucian swayed once more, he carefully lowered him down to sit against a tree.

Lucian wiped the sweat from his brow. It took a great effort simply to lift his arm. And, as he sat there, staring at the devastation around him - the ash, the dead, the grey shells of fire-eaten trees, the swathes of smoke hanging over it all like a shroud - his nose began to bleed.

'Lucian, you must rest,' Thomas said. Then he turned to the guards around him. 'Pull the men back. Regroup. We attack again at first light!'

'But, my Lord, we have them on the run!' a guard protested.

'Pull back!' Thomas said. 'That's an order.'

*

Belfor approached Fabian slowly, looking fatigued, and fell to one knee. 'Shot two down. Lost about forty men,' he said dejectedly.

Fabian rubbed his hands together and held them up to the small fire that had been lit for him. But he didn't feel the fire's warmth. And his strength, even after a bowl of meaty broth, had not returned.

'Lucian Mortenstone has pulled his men back. Gives us time to breathe, rest up,' Belfor continued. Fabian's head turned at the news. 'They're scared, my Lord. The lot of 'em. They don't know what they're fighting for. And that rat doesn't know what he's doing. We'll take the castle by morning.'

'We fled the battle. He didn't,' Fabian said.

'Yes, we fled. But I saw the fear in their eyes when the beasts came down,' said Belfor. 'Swooped in as our men were retreating. Attacked us. Plucked and tore at us, tossed the mangled bodies to the ground when they were done. We lost good men. But not in vain. When I returned to shoot the beasts down, I saw the boy Mortenstone; horror-stricken he was. The creatures may be out of our control, but they have done all that we intended. The Mortenstones are weakened. They doubt. They *fear*.'

Fabian thought on his cousin's words for a long time. Perhaps he was right. Perhaps there was still a chance. His body may have failed him, but his men would not - not with Belfor leading them. It wasn't over yet. He looked deep into his cousin's eyes. 'No one harms her,' he said.

Belfor looked at him knowingly. 'No one harms her.'

*

The sky swarmed with creatures of darkness. The Worgrims squawked and screeched as they circled above Mortenstone Castle, searching for flesh. Archers shot flaming arrows at them but they were too far out of reach.

And then it began. The beasts swooped down and plucked guards from the towers and parapet, taking arrows to the breast like scratches from a thorn.

Josephine shrank back into the dungeon doorway. She clutched the pendant around her neck and kissed it as screaming soldiers were carried off into the black night. Her knuckles turned white and her heart thundered so fast in her chest, it almost drowned out the sound of the creatures above. She had never felt so alive. Slowly, she turned the pendant over in her hand

and smoothed her thumb over it. The glinting green eye of the serpent flashed in the light. She remembered when he gave it to her. She remembered it all, as if it were a dream from which she had just awoken. It felt more real to her than any part of her life before or since.

Her father was a strict man and she had grown tired of his controlling ways. She often joked that she could not even visit the privy without him knowing about it. And she was probably right. She was fourteen years old, and at an age where she was ready to test every boundary he had set.

To defy him, as so many children in The Light defied their fathers, she crossed the border into the Dark Forest. She had done it before with her friends when she was younger. But this time was different. This time, she went alone, with purpose, walking far, far away from him and his control to make her point. And, for once, she felt free. Before she was even aware that she had walked into a trap, it was all too late. A sack came down over her head and a heavy hand pressed against her mouth so she couldn't scream. Deft hands bound her arms and legs. Her captors spoke in hushed whispers to each other about how pleased their lord would be, for she looked wealthy, perhaps noble.

She made it no easy task for them. She fought and struggled the entire way. The men dropped her several times and cursed her. But they did not hurt her.

They arrived at Castle Mordark in the dead of night. She heard a terse conversation between her captors and a guard and the screeching sound of a gate opening to permit them. Horses scuffed their hooves against stable doors. A rotten smell hung in the damp air. Her captors carried her into the castle, their footsteps hollow against the cold stone floor, and set her down on her side before they ripped off the sack.

She remembered the fear she felt as she stared at the strange faces peering down at her. A middle-aged man bent to touch the collar of her purple gown.

'It looks like our fortunes have changed,' he said with the faintest of smiles. His eyes were green – as green as the tales told. He looked weary and older than his years. 'Don't worry, little girl, we shan't harm you.' He turned to look over his shoulder. 'Fabian, take the girl to the dungeon. Ensure she is properly fed and watered,' he said. A young man stepped forward and nodded dutifully.

The moment she saw him, she knew her fate would be entwined with his. He was tall. Strong. His eyes, as green and piercing as his father's, excited her, filled her with longing. He untied her and led her down to a dungeon cell, while the rest of them negotiated a price for her captors' efforts and a price for her ransom. She was terrified, but Fabian's presence calmed her. He asked her name and sat with her in the dark until she gave in to exhaustion. He came for her himself the next morning when his father wanted her for questioning. He brought her delicious food from his father's table, not the stale muck they threw the other prisoners in the dungeon. He made sure the guards treated her well, gave her a bed to sleep on - it was made of straw and laced with lice, but it was better than the ground.

As the years passed, Fabian's father, Edrell Mordark, granted her more freedoms. She was given a comfortable room in the main part of the castle and her very own servant to order about. Edrell profited greatly from her imprisonment; he increased her ransom every time her family sent the money he had previously demanded. And she was not the slightest bit troubled by it.

The Dark Lands were every bit as grim as she imagined they would be. The land was slowly drowning in bogs and the people looked half-dead; they went about their days in a dreamlike state, never pausing to rest or look up from the tasks they were carrying out. And, to save their strength for the relentless toil on the sodden farmlands, they hardly said a word.

The sun never shone upon the cursed lands and she soon forgot what it was like to feel its warmth against her skin. But it didn't matter to her, really. Because she had Fabian. By the time she was seventeen and he twenty-four, they had formed a bond stronger than any she had ever known. He promised her that he would love no other. He gave her his pendant to signify the promise and his love for her. He visited her bedchamber most nights and there they would lie, entangled in one another, and plan their future together. They dreamt that, one day, they would take The Light, unite the realm once more and rule together in Avalon. They would put an end to the ancient dispute. They would find a way to break the forest's enchantment so Fabian could cross the border. Those were the days of endless dreams.

But, on the eve of her eighteenth birthday, when she was down by the forest's edge, the unthinkable happened. Her family, accompanied by fifty strong men clad in armour, took her back. There was no battle, no bloodshed. They simply plucked her off her feet and carried her away, just as the Worgrims had picked men from the towers.

They brought her back to The Light and thrust her straight into a union with her cousin, Matthew Mortenstone, whom she loathed. He had been an arrogant, brash sort of boy and those qualities had not waned in manhood. The deed was done so fast she had no time to grieve the life they had stolen from her. Suddenly, she was Matthew's wife, and pregnant. She could not go back to the forest; her father had her under his control once more. He had men following her, day and night. Her life was no longer her own. And it struck her that she had never truly been free at all. But was it so terrible to favour one kind of imprisonment over another?

It was all she could do not to throw herself from the highest tower. The one thing driving her to stay alive was the hope that, one day, she would see Fabian again. She would be able to look him in the eye and tell him she had no part in any of it. She had not escaped - she would never have left him of her own free will. She supposed that somewhere deep down he knew that. She just had to help him remember.

But, as the years wore on, her mind became plagued with doubt. Her father was long dead. She had had countless opportunities to slip away back to the Dark Lands. Why hadn't she? She knew why. Fabian was an impulsive man - it was one of the things she loved most about him. But what if his rage was such that he acted before he heard her side of the tale? She was afraid. It was easier to stand back and dream of what might have been than face him as he was now, after a lifetime apart.

She thought of Iris, terror-stricken upon the pyre, and felt a stab of remorse. She had been dealt with too harshly. Everyone knew it. Lucian's motives were his own but Josephine was ashamed of her reasons. Iris had dared to do what she no longer had the stomach for; she had ventured into the Dark Forest. In many ways, she had been jealous of her daughter. Iris had the ignorance of youth to protect her. For a time, at least. Iris had the courage Josephine yearned for. But her courage had taken her to an early grave, Josephine reminded herself. Her own caution had spared her... for a time. But when Fabian's son killed Matthew, she knew it was a message. He wanted her to know of his fury, she was sure of it. He was coming for her, to wreak vengeance. She was terrified. And she was elated.

*

Lucian woke as the last of the fires were extinguished and acrid smoke billowed across the makeshift camp. As he pushed himself up from the ground, his arms trembled under his own weight, so fragile that, for an instant, he thought his bones would snap.

'Are you strong enough?' Thomas's question was tinged with doubt. Lucian nodded, but he could tell from Thomas's expression that they both knew he was lying. Thomas glanced around helplessly. 'I could lead them,' he offered.

Lucian barely had the energy to shake his head. The men could not fight with heart if he stayed behind and watched them charge to their deaths. It had to be him. The darkness suddenly felt thick and suffocating without the great fires. And cold, terribly cold. Lucian began to shiver.

He had been a stern ruler, he knew - at times, senselessly harsh. But he had been a leader they believed in, one they trusted to guide them. When men looked at him, they saw strength. But now, as they regarded him, he could see the disillusion in their eyes. Had it all been a clever guise? Had Lucian Mortenstone ever been worthy?

The men stood around him, huddled together, countless faces, names he would never know. Hundreds of men, staring at him, looking for hope in the cloying darkness. And then something strange happened. A haunting voice broke the long, brooding silence. Thomas had begun to sing.

'*In the Land of Light, Where good men reign, We will stand tall, Through toil and pain…*'

Every eye turned to Thomas and, as he drew breath, another man, several rows back, continued the Song of the Realm.

'*Great Merlin's Light, Cast down on all, Our land of peace, Will never fall…*' His voice was deep and strong.

The men around him stirred. And then, together, they all started to sing.

'When evil gazes on us,
And we hear the castle bells,
We shall look back without fear,
And we will remember well,

'Those Mordark eyes of emerald green,
The eyes of cunning, traitorous fiends,
The men who shunned good Merlin's love,
And fell from grace from high above.

'We will not walk behind those men,
We bow before our master's throne,
Our hearts and souls, all that we own,
Are yours Lord Mortenstone.'

The oppressive darkness seemed to lift as they sang the old words. Lucian's throat tightened with emotion. He looked up at the sky. A million stars glinted brilliantly in the cloudless sky. The light gently bathed his face. It was beautiful. A beautiful night. A beautiful end.

'Light conquers darkness,' he said faintly. All heard him.

*

When the dying words of the song faded, an uncomfortable silence settled over Fabian's ranks. Fabian himself felt his gut clench. Those were not the sentiments of a weakened side. He looked around for Belfor but the pig was nowhere to be seen. Of course he was out of sight, he thought with contempt. Belfor was no fool.

Fabian caught sight of a boy clad in black armour that was much too large for him. He extended his finger and beckoned him. The boy looked terrified and, with a nudge from the man behind him, reluctantly came forward.

'How old are you?' Fabian asked.

'Ten,' the boy said.

Fabian felt a twinge in his gut again. He exhaled heavily. 'Ten,' he said, looking away. He shook his head slowly before turning to stare at the boy again. 'When my boys were ten, they were as weak as chickens. You seem like a brave ten-year-old. Am I right?' The boy turned back to the man behind him and then gave Fabian a small nod. 'Of course you are. Bravest man here, I bet,' Fabian continued. 'Your sword, do you have a sword?' The boy shook his head and looked at the ground. It was a foolish question, Fabian realised. The boy hadn't the strength to wield a sword, nor to pierce a man's armour. He was just fodder. Fabian wondered why they had even bothered to suit him in armour. He ruffled the boy's hair; his touch seemed to startle him. He gave a low, gruff laugh. The boy looked up to meet his eye and Fabian could see, in that wide stare, that the boy was afraid; he knew his fate. 'They will write songs about your courage,' Fabian whispered, knowing that his words would mean nothing to the boy but saying them all the same. He looked at the boy once more before he turned and limped away.

He would never forget his face.

25. BETRAYAL

William had begun to wonder if Enola would ever awaken. She lay there, lifeless on the ground, for what seemed like hours. He had shaken her, sprinkled water on her face, even tried to carry her the rest of the way, but it was no use. Giving up, he sat beside her in complete darkness, holding a hand over her mouth often, to check that she was still breathing.

He let his eyes drift closed for a moment, and only then did he realise how exhausted he was. He hadn't eaten in a day; he was famished and weak. His head started to loll to one side. Sleep was pulling at him. When he could fight it no longer, he slumped forwards and surrendered. But the second he did, there was a sharp, sudden gasp. The sound shot through him, filled the tunnel. He jumped with fright.

'Enola?' he said, putting a hand on her shoulder as she sat up and heaved fast, heavy breaths. Her hair was sticky with blood.

'They wanted me to draw a picture,' she said. Her voice was deep and croaky and, for a moment, she sounded just like Agatha.

'What? Who wanted you to draw a picture?' William said. 'Enola?' He couldn't see her in the darkness. He shook her shoulder gently.

'In the valley!' she said. Her words echoed all around them. 'Mother was afraid of me. Master Hagworth, he was afraid.'

'Enola?' said William, alarmed now. 'I don't understand what you're saying.'

'Who is the old man in the tree?' she asked.

'Enola—'

'In the castle... there are secret passages... They called me the cursed one. They whispered...I heard them...'

William edged away from her. She was rambling like a mad woman. The fall had done something strange to her head.

'I... can you walk?' He stood and groped in the darkness for her hand, helping her to her feet.

'Why did—?'

'Shut up!' he snapped. He didn't want to hear any more. She was frightening him. He held her hand tightly and began to walk. Enola stumbled, disorientated. He steadied her and then put his arm around her waist to support her. He was so focused on keeping her upright as she staggered along the tunnel, he did not see what was ahead until they had stopped to rest.

Leaning back against the wall, breathless and dripping with both sweat and the water that leaked from the tunnel roof, he saw it. In the distance, a weak, milky light pricked a hole in the darkness. He felt a huge wave of nervous relief. They were close. He could see the end of the tunnel.

Suddenly, the sound of boots splashing through water echoed through the tunnel. A shiver ran up his spine. Tobias flashed into his mind. But it couldn't be him. Surely, it could not. Tobias was dead. He had seen the blood himself.

He looked back into the blackness.

'Come on!' he said, pulling Enola forwards, towards the light.

As they approached the mouth of the tunnel, William's heart began to pound furiously. This was it. Low branches concealed the opening. Morning light seeped through the thin leaves. No wind stirred them. No birds sang. The thudding boots in the distance sent ripples through the black puddles on the ground. William stopped and stepped out in front of Enola, blocking her path. He could see her now, her pale face, her blood-soaked scalp, her large, staring eyes. He pressed a finger to his lips and signalled for her to stay where she was. Then he ducked beneath a branch and left the tunnel.

*

Enola waited, listening. Outside, a twig cracked. Then, silence. Her head throbbed. She felt sick. All she wanted to do was lie down and sleep.

'All clear,' called William.

Enola pushed a branch aside and staggered out of the tunnel.

The trees were sparse in this part of the Dark Forest. They seemed even more monstrous, somehow, standing alone and unobstructed. They towered over her, trunks grey and twisted, with branches bursting from them like thousands of rotting arms. William was standing beside the nearest tree, a little way in front, his head bowed. Enola stared at him for a moment and then cast her eyes up. Dusky fingers of light filtered through the large gaps in the canopy high above.

'Thank you, William!' came a low voice. Enola froze as a hand slapped against the side of her neck and pulled her in like a hook. Her throat was forced up against the crook of a man's arm and he held her there so tightly she choked with every breath. Over his arm, she could see William watching. He did not seem surprised. 'Do you know who I am?' said the voice. There was a smile hidden in it, somewhere.

'Vrax,' she choked, forcing the word up as if it were poison.

'Very good,' he said. 'Clever little witch.' He released her suddenly and smashed his fist into the back of her head. She flew to the ground, stunned, and the world turned onto its side. The trees, the ground, the light and the shadows began to merge into one another. She felt oddly light, as if she had become detached from her body. 'Are you going to be a good witch?' Vrax said, grabbing a fistful of her hair and tugging her head up off the ground.

Enola could feel her hand tingling, a dull and distant sensation, like a gentle tapping at a faraway door. But the feeling was growing. And her hand was pulsing. She raised it slowly into the air.

'She has powers here, my Lord! You should bind her hands!' William said.

Quick as a cat, Vrax let go of her hair and pulled her arms behind her back, forcing them into an impossible position. Enola felt a sharp, searing pain shoot up and down her arms.

'You'll break my arms. You'll break my arms!' she shrieked.

'Help me!' Vrax shouted to William, who walked towards them and crouched beside Enola. 'Hold her arms here. Tighter,' said Vrax, and he bound her wrists together as William held them in place. When Vrax had finished, he stood and looked at William uncertainly. 'Perhaps I should cut them off,' he said.

'She'll bleed to death before you get her back to your father,' William said.

Vrax grunted. 'Blindfold her,' he said, reaching into a sack and pulling out a rag, which he tossed to William.

Enola stared at William venomously as he knelt over her with the rag. He was a coward, a traitor. She hated him. More than Agatha. More than anyone. She had never felt such fury. He didn't look at her but kept his eyes on the strip of cloth as he brought it to her face. Everything went black as he fastened it over her eyes.

'Good lad,' said Vrax. 'You can go now.'

Enola heard a jangling sound as a coin pouch was tossed from one man to the other, and then footsteps. William was walking away.

She screamed with anger and frustration as she lay there, unable to move. The pulsing feeling in her hand had gone. She felt tired, frail. Her throat dried up. Her head was splitting with pain. And then she heard something… Something to her left. Rustling. The sound stopped suddenly. Then, a rush of footsteps. A shout. A struggle. A thud.

Enola's blindfold was pulled off hastily and she found herself staring up at her father. He was breathing heavily and he looked pale. His eyes were red and ringed with deep shadows. He looked almost unrecognisable. He looked old.

'It's alright. You're alright,' he said. Vrax was lying unconscious on the ground behind him.

Enola winced as Alexander frantically pulled and twisted the rope that bound her wrists and cursed under his breath. The rope was coming loose. She could feel the stinging pain in her wrists receding. She closed her eyes, giving in to the heavy weight of her eyelids and the queasy feeling that turned her stomach.

Suddenly, she heard her father gasp. It was a sound that seemed to suck in all the air around them, plunging the forest into a terrible silence. Enola opened her eyes and looked up to see the tip of a blade protruding from her father's chest. Behind him, eyes glittering with malice, stood Vrax, who withdrew the sword and then thrust it into Alexander's back a second time.

'No!' Enola breathed.

Alexander stared at the tip of the sword with indifference before Vrax pulled it out again. Then he looked up at the forest and his eyes rested on something in the distance. 'Is that it?' he said, a faint smile flickering to his lips before he dropped to the ground beside Enola. His eyes drifted shut, as if he had fallen into a deep sleep.

'No. Get up!' Enola said through gritted teeth. 'Get up!'

Vrax staggered towards her and hauled her to her feet by her hair. She screamed with pain. She hoped William could hear her. She hoped her screams haunted him forever.

'Come, little witch,' said Vrax. He gripped the back of her head and dug his fingers into her scalp. 'Eyes forward!' he said, forcing her to walk, leaving Alexander behind on the ground.

One thought whirled around Enola's mind as she went. If only she had her knife. If only she had her knife. The things she would do if only she had her knife.

*

William stood staring at the shimmering veil of mist. It hung in the air, spreading across the forest like a white wall. He had come to the edge of the realm. He could step through it, he knew, continue to the boat. *And never return*. But he didn't move any closer. He thought, instead, about the promise he had made to Agatha. He said he would look after Enola, deliver her safely to the Land of the Banished. He had not kept his word. Could he live with himself, knowing that he had betrayed

Agatha's dying wish? Perhaps he could… After all, he had never really been given a choice. It was expected of him, but no one ever *ask*ed him. He squeezed the pouch of coins uneasily. Regardless of whatever promise he had made or been forced to make, he had accepted payment from the man who had killed Agatha. Could he live with that?

He had not expected to cross paths with Vrax Mordark when he left Agatha's house the previous night. He was distraught, furious, unable to think of anything but his beloved Bette, whom Enola had sentenced to death. He knew she had revealed herself to Bette on purpose, knowing what would inevitably happen. He walked for a long time, hating her, wishing she had never been born.

The screaming gale had masked Vrax's approach. When, suddenly, William found himself before him, he could not resist the desire to tell him everything.

'I have some information. About the girl you seek,' he had said. Vrax's eyes lit with interest.

They crouched together in the hollow of a tree as the wind roared all around them.

'She's a vicious girl. A savage. She won't go easily. She's like a wild animal. And, one more thing, you must come quietly! If they hear or suspect you, they'll send us to the Land of the Banished. There's a passage. I don't know where it is but they'll take us to it. It leads to the edge of the Dark Forest. That's all I know.' His words spilled out faster than he had time to think.

Vrax craned his neck to listen, before the wind took the secrets. 'I know of The Passage,' he said with a nod. 'I've seen where it ends. I can find it again, if I must. But it won't come to that, will it? They won't know I'm coming, unless someone is going to give me away? Are you?'

William shook his head vehemently. 'No, my Lord. I want her dead as much as you do.'

'Do you?' Vrax said, regarding him suspiciously. 'Why is she still alive then? Don't want to get your hands dirty, is that it?'

William shrugged. 'I just want to live in peace.'

Vrax rolled his eyes. 'Hah! Well you won't find peace here. Go to the Land of the Banished. Now, listen. This goes no further. Do not tell a soul.' His eyes flashed and his finger shook as he pointed at William. 'Or I'll come for you and I'll gut you! It must be me. I must make the discovery! Tell me how to get to this house.'

'I would ask a favour first,' said William. 'Please, please don't harm Agatha - the old woman. She only keeps Enola there because your brother told her to.'

Vrax nodded impatiently and stood to leave the tree hollow. 'Yes, boy, you have my word. I won't harm her.'

William regretted what he had done the instant Vrax departed. He clawed at the skin on his face in anguish. How could he have placed Agatha's life in the hands of Vrax Mordark? He bit his nails down to the quick as he thought about the irreversible thing he had done. His life would not be the same after this night. Agatha's would not be the same. And Enola... well, she would lose her life come morning time. What had he done? Did he truly expect Vrax to let him live at the end of all this? He, who had helped conceal Enola Reverof from him for all these years? No. He had doomed them all.

In the morning, when he awoke to the sound of Agatha grumbling about something unimportant downstairs, he convinced himself it had all been a dream. Perhaps it would be easier to go on pretending that it was.

He rattled the pouch of coins Vrax had given him. It was heavy, bulging with gold and silver. Enough for a lifetime. He let it fall from his hand and felt instantly lighter.

*

Enola cried out as Vrax sank his nails into her arm.

'Quiet! You'll frighten my horse,' he said, removing his hand. His nails left deep red marks in her skin, which stung enough to bring tears to her eyes.

As they rounded a dense briar thicket, Enola saw a white horse with piercing blue eyes in the distance. It was an enormous creature, larger than any normal horse. It stared at her warily as she came closer.

'Hurry up,' Vrax said, shoving her hard in the back. Enola stumbled and fell to the ground, her chin smacking the cold dirt with a soft thud. 'No, no, no!' she heard Vrax shout over the thunder of hooves. The ground shuddered as the horse galloped away. Vrax ran after it, cursing furiously.

As soon as his back was turned, Enola seized her chance. She pulled her arms free of her loosened bindings, pushed herself to her feet and ran.

She saw Vrax in the corner of her eye, abandoning his chase, coming for her now, cutting across the forest to intercept her. She ran faster, faster, her legs burning. She could not slow. She would die if she did.

'Bitch!' Vrax shouted. He was behind her. She could feel his rage. She ran, blind with terror, weaving left and right around the trees like a hunted animal, trying to shake him off. But he was closing the distance between them, crashing over dead branches, which shattered beneath his weight. Crows squawked and hissed in their nests above. Enola gasped for breath but the air that filled her lungs didn't seem enough. Her chest ached. He was going to catch her.

Her heart skipped a beat when her foot caught on a tree root. She plummeted to the ground, her ankle twisting sharply, and landed hard. The wind was knocked from her. Wheezing, she dragged herself forwards, clawing at the dirt, until she could go no further. She rolled onto her back, too tired to go on, and looked up at Vrax. He was standing over her, eyes alive with hunger. But as he reached down to grab her, there was a flash of movement. Something large collided with him and knocked him off his feet. Enola sat up and stared in disbelief as William fell down on top of him. Next moment, they were fighting, rolling on the ground, trying to overpower one another.

Enola scrambled to her feet without a second thought and ran. The trees passed by in a blur. And when the ferocious shouts were long behind her, she dared to hope that she would escape with her life after all.

The pain in her injured ankle grew steadily worse as she raced through the forest. She pushed on as far as she could, until it became unbearable. Then she stopped and tucked herself behind a tree to catch her breath and gather her senses. That was when she saw it.

The white horse spooked as she staggered towards it, grunting and kicking its front hoof out as if to ward her off. Its mane shone purest white and almost appeared to glow as it tossed its head in distress, trying to free itself from the branch around which its reins were tangled. Enola approached the creature. It shifted about uneasily, as if it sensed what she would do next. Reaching up, she untangled the reins from the branch. As soon as they were free, the horse began to back up, but Enola didn't let go. She pulled the horse towards her. It came reluctantly, rearing its head and stamping at the dirt, its flanks rippling with muscle.

Latheerian horses moved faster than the east winds. This horse would save her life. Heart pounding, she looped the reins back over its head, put her foot in the stirrup and hoisted herself up onto its back. The horse screeched and reared up on its hind legs. Then, it leapt into a gallop. Enola clung on, willing it to slow down, but if it understood her thoughts, it did not heed them. She saw the ground rushing by. The reins hung slack around the horse's long neck as it charged deeper into the forest, back the way they had come. Enola felt a cold flood of panic. She could not go back. Her father was dead. Agatha was dead. William had betrayed her. She had nothing to return to. Only death. She sat up in the saddle, grasped the reins and pulled them taut. The horse slowed momentarily, before straining against the reins and continuing on at a gallop. Enola slipped from side to side in the saddle. *Stop*, she willed it. *Stop*. She could not go back there. The Land of the Banished was her only hope now. She had to turn around.

'Stop!' she screamed.

*

William choked as Vrax pinned him to the ground by his throat. He spat blood in Vrax's face in desperation and, as Vrax recoiled, smashed his fist into his jaw. The skin on his knuckles split open. Vrax fell backwards. William lunged after him but, as he did, Vrax drew a dagger from his belt and thrust it upwards towards him. William grabbed his arm to stop him. Beads of sweat broke out on his brow as they struggled and the dagger inched closer and closer to his chest. William's hands began to shake as he pushed back against Vrax with all his strength. This was for Agatha, he thought with mounting rage. He would avenge her if it was the last thing he did. He gritted his teeth and pushed harder. And, slowly, Vrax began to weaken; his arm bent inwards and the dagger turned to point now at his heart. Vrax's eyes burned with determination as he forced the knife back towards William. They fought on, silently, the cold blade twisting and turning. And then, at last, it sank deep into its target.

William's eyes bulged as he looked down at the dagger. Blood spurted out over his hands. He began to tremble. An empty silence drowned out the sound of his ragged breaths.

He felt cold.

26. THE WHITE WITCH

It was a dark morning. Lucian led his men in silence through the forest in a steady line. Thomas walked beside him, a comforting presence. And it struck Lucian then that he had never thanked his brother for his years of loyal service. Thomas could have deserted him after Iris's death - it was clear that he wanted to - but he had stayed by Lucian's side and done his duty. He had married who he was told to marry, when he was told to marry. He had counselled Lucian and endured endless torment.

Lucian wanted to say something to Thomas now, as they walked, but found he could not. Instead, he glanced at him, caught his eye and nodded - a swift gesture of his gratitude. Thomas nodded back.

The Worgrims had begun to circle again, waiting to swoop down and enjoy a fresh feast. There would be no avoiding them; the fires had burned away great parts of the Dark Forest, leaving Lucian's army exposed as they advanced. But there was no point fretting over this. It was just one of many ways to die. And most would die today. Of that he was certain.

*

Fabian put a hand up to stop his men as they came to an abandoned house on the edge of the eastern path. The men fell still almost at once and looked on as Fabian stooped down beside a mound of rocks and picked up a silver ring. It was cold. When he turned it over and saw the serpent engraving, his stomach dropped. It was Alexander's ring. Beside a makeshift grave.

'Move these rocks!' he ordered. 'Now!' His heart began to race. He had not heard from Alexander in two moons. Part of him did not want to see what was buried beneath the rocks, for fear it would be him. It then occurred to Fabian that Vrax and Tobias were not there, either. None of his sons had accompanied him into battle. 'Where are my sons?' he said, as five weary men came forward and began to remove the rocks from the heap. 'Send for them. I want them brought here, now!' He staggered towards Belfor, away from the grave.

'My Lord, a word of caution,' said Belfor, clutching his arm and looking around anxiously. 'We must not give away our position. If they hear us, our plan will fail.'

Fabian scowled at him. No one could tell him what to do, especially not his fat cousin. But when he spoke next, it was in a hushed voice. 'Find my boys.'

'We cannot afford to spare even one man. Do not forget, my Lord, what it is you have worked so hard to gain.'

Belfor's boldness stunned Fabian. And every one of the three hundred men they had selected for this undertaking had witnessed it. Fabian did not know how to respond. He could not stand there idly and allow Belfor to speak to him that way. But nor could he harm his cousin. He did not have a strategic mind like Belfor; without him, the mission was doomed.

271

It had been a hurried plan, devised as the first of the grey morning light bled into the dark sky. They had had little time to move these men to the eastern path, away from the battleground. And they would have even less time, once the battle had begun, to circle in and surround Lucian Mortenstone's army. It was a plan filled with risks and uncertainties. But, in Fabian's weakened state, it was the only hope he had.

'My Lord?' The voice broke the stony silence. Fabian let his eyes linger on Belfor before he looked to the man who had spoken. It was a young soldier; he was standing beside the mound of rocks, the top of which had been removed. The soldier stared down into the cavity and then shrugged at Fabian. 'Just an old woman, my Lord.'

Fabian walked over to the grave and looked at the body. He felt an enormous rush of relief as he set eyes on the old woman. He stood up straight and breathed a deep sigh. Alexander was not dead. But he had been here. He was in the forest.

'Would you have us cover it back up, my Lord?' asked the young soldier. Fabian shook his head and glanced at the body again with indifference.

'Leave it,' he said. 'Save your strength.'

He turned and walked slowly back to Belfor, wondering what he should do with him, when, suddenly, he heard a low rumbling noise. He stopped dead. Belfor looked at him, eyes widening. The sound grew and grew. Fabian felt the ground tremble beneath his feet. As he listened, there came a distant and almighty roar, which gathered momentum like a wave, until the very air was vibrating.

It had started.

*

Lucian's heart thundered in his chest as he charged. With his men around him, he felt strong. He filled his lungs and shrieked, tears streaming from his eyes as the cold wind rushed past.

The Dark Families emerged from the gloom like shadows, surging through the forest towards them, the rattle of their black armour and shields drowning beneath their murderous cries. Above, the Worgrims' screeches were shrill. But Lucian felt no fear. He fixed his eyes on a soldier with a steel, horned mask, moving through the trees at the front of the Mordark army. Everything else seemed to melt into the darkness around him. Lucian ran faster, faster. He could see the man's cold breath steaming through the slits in the mask. As he closed the distance between them, he raised his sword into the air; it sang as he brought it down to strike, but the man blocked his blow with his own blade and, pushing back with the force of a beast, sent Lucian staggering backwards. The man advanced without pause. Lucian choked up a clot of blood and quickly spat it to the ground. Then, letting his sword arm fall limp at his side, he focused intently on the two black eye holes in his opponent's mask. The man was mere inches from him now, lifting his sword, preparing to deliver the killer blow… when he froze. His arms began to jerk and spasm, but he didn't let go of his weapon. Lucian felt a throbbing pressure behind his own eyes; the man was resisting him. Lucian squeezed every muscle in his body, straining, clenching, until he heard a loud popping sound. The pressure eased. Blood spurted from the holes in the mask. Then, with such suddenness Lucian could only gawp, a Worgrim dived down, plucked the man off his feet and launched back up into the air with him dangling lifelessly in its beak. The sword dropped from his hand, landing in the dirt before Lucian, who doubled over and put his hand out to steady himself against a tree. His vision blurred for a moment and then returned.

Screams rang out all around him as men clung desperately to life. And he felt it, beneath his skin. Death was here, in the forest, waiting for them all. He would die today, without any heirs. He knew it, as he knew day followed night.

Oh, how he had tried to do what was expected of him. Five stillborn children. A wife who had paid the ultimate price for it. And, after all the pain and anguish, he, Lucian, marked the end of his line. He had failed to secure for The Light what it needed most. If he could just achieve the one thing he desired before his time was up, he knew his rule would not have been a complete, hopeless waste. If he could kill Fabian Mordark, his rule would have meant something.

'Where is he?' he demanded as Tarolock fell back against the tree to pull an arrow from his left arm. Tarolock held his breath as he snapped the arrow and tossed it to the ground. He turned to Lucian.

'He isn't here!' he shouted.

'What do you mean he isn't here?' Lucian said, looking around wildly. Was this merely the first wave? Did Fabian Mordark have more men in reserve?

The battle raged around him; men fell, Worgrims swooped, fires blazed once more, and Fabian Mordark was nowhere to be seen. Lucian watched with mounting despair; his battle strategy was failing yet again. The lines had broken. The men seemed to have forgotten their training, using magic to kill where a swing of the sword would have sufficed. They were growing weaker by the minute.

'Get the men back into line!' Lucian barked at Tarolock. 'Tell them no magic! They're losing strength!'

Lucian stayed by the tree as Tarolock ran back into battle screaming the order. And he turned his attention to the men of Draxvar as they cut their way through the Mordark forces. They did not need to be told what to do, these fierce men of the north. They relished the hunter's kill, slicing through flesh and bone. They moved as if in a dance; figures in black with masks of purest silver, which bore the faces of dragons, sweeping through the enemy as fast as the east winds.

Lucian watched them, transfixed. And then he broke out of his trance and his fear came rushing back. Where was the Lord of the Dark Lands? Why was he hiding?

*

Josephine began to shake as she stood in the castle entrance hall, surrounded by whimpering maids and servant girls, who huddled together and prayed to the White Witch, as if it would make a difference. All of the guards were dead. The castle stood defenceless.

Josephine could hear the screams coming all the way from the Dark Forest. It chilled her to the core. She was afraid. And yet some instinct was telling her to leave the castle and go there, to the heart of the battle. She looked around at the women waiting to die. They remained at the castle not out of loyalty but fear. Fear to act. If they were wise, they would be miles away from danger by now, heading for Latheera or fleeing through Mortenstone Valley towards Draxvar. They were weak. She was not like them. She was not weak. She gathered up her skirts and passed through the doorway into the courtyard. She heard them all calling for her to come back and crying hysterically when she continued towards the gates.

Saskian the elf emerged from the stables and limped after her. He was decrepit now, his eyes milky-white and unseeing, but he reached her quickly.

275

'No, my lady! Please, come back inside!' he said, pulling at her arm.

Josephine turned. He was a pitiful sight. She remembered a time when had stood tall and proud beside her husband. But those days were long gone.

'Saskian,' she said gently, steadying him. 'You have done your duty. Save yourself.' And then she walked on, out through the gates, across the square, towards the Dark Forest. He didn't pursue her. And even if he had, she would not have listened to him. She had to do something. They could all live if she stopped them and told them the truth. She only hoped she was not too late.

*

Five Mortenstone guards formed a barrier around Lucian, blocking every blade and enchantment directed at him as he hastened towards Thomas, who had fallen back against a tree, gasping for breath.

'Where is he? Have you seen Fabian Mordark?' Lucian shouted, crashing into the tree beside his brother. Thomas shook his head and grimaced, clutching his leg. He was wounded.

'We need to retreat,' Thomas said. 'It's a trap!' As he uttered the words, a Mortenstone guard lunged forwards and thrust his shield out to protect Lucian's head. Lucian wheeled around as a bright spark bounced off the steel. When the guard lowered the shield, his eyes widened with horror.

A vast horde surged through the forest towards him. Hundreds of men, roaring triumphantly as they came. Fabian was at the front of the charge, his eyes wild with hunger, his long cloak billowing behind him as he closed in to surround Lucian's army.

The Mortenstone guards looked to Lucian for instruction. Their eyes burned with fear. They were shouting. Thomas was shouting, shaking his shoulder, signalling frantically for men to form a shield wall, some form of resistance. But Lucian could not hear them; it was as if he had been plunged into a deep, dense silence, in which his shallow breaths were all that filled the void. He saw their lips moving, saw eyes looking at him while he looked out. And he felt that familiar pulsing sensation in his gut. The feeling was growing, rising through his tired body. This was the end.

He felt quite calm as he pushed past the guards, away from their protection, and began to run. Towards Fabian. Towards his fate. He threw down his sword, running faster now, a growl in his throat. And, as he drew near, he saw a word form on Fabian's pale lips, a word Lucian had never spoken, a word from a time… before. *Avalon.*

Lucian stopped and threw out his arms. Power rushed up through him with blistering force. And, shrieking like a man on fire, he let it burst free. A blinding bolt of light shot from his palms. Fabian stopped and raised his hands. Lucian felt a burning, stinging swell of pain in every part of him as Fabian's bolt of light clashed against his.

The winds howled and the trees thrashed. All around them, men were falling, flying backwards, dropping their weapons, shielding their eyes from the bright light. The Worgrims abandoned their hunt and scattered, disappearing into the clouds. Lucian staggered towards Fabian. The hot, white light stung his eyes as he closed the space between them. His legs felt like stone. He could feel his heart fading, feel the life leaving his body. But he wanted to stand before him, this monster who walked his nightmares and darkened his dreams. He wanted to look into Fabian Mordark's eyes as he killed him. With one final push, Lucian unleashed everything he had left in him. He roared as the light from his hands intensified and surged through Fabian's green bolt, swallowing it, moving towards his chest.

Fabian stared at him in stunned surprise, his mouth falling open.

Lucian moved closer, closer and, as the light illuminated his face, his eyes flashed emerald green.

*

A clap of thunder crashed overhead as Josephine crossed the Grassland. The ground shook. A fierce wind blasted from the Dark Forest, hitting her so forcefully she was knocked off her feet.

She looked up at the sky as she lay there, stunned; dark clouds were swirling above, splitting open as lightning coursed through them. Another clap of thunder rumbled through the air. Josephine rolled onto her front and crawled the rest of the way to the forest. When she reached it, she slowly pushed herself to her feet, gasping for breath, her chest heaving as she began to sob. In her heart, she knew it was over.

She ran through the darkness, forcing herself onwards, deeper into the forest, crying so furiously she could not see.

Gone were the screams, the war cries, the ringing screech of swords that, from the castle, had seemed too much to bear. Now, there was only silence. Only her. For a moment, she was a girl again, running through the Dark Forest, away from her father. Running home.

Her breath caught in her throat when she came to him, sprawled on the ground among the dead. The living watched on, enemies alike, their swords lowered. Every eye in the forest followed her as she walked to Fabian and sank to her knees beside him. It was over.

But, as she put a hand to her mouth to stifle her grief, Fabian's eyes opened wearily. She stared at him in shock. The web of lines around his eyes deepened as he smiled weakly up at her. He looked so very different now, and yet exactly the same.

'Is this a dream?' he whispered. Josephine shook her head, tears spilling from her eyes. Fabian gazed at her longingly. 'Would that it were... an eternal dream.'

Josephine stroked his cheek softly and smiled. Then she lifted his hand and curled his fingers around the pendent that hung from her neck. 'I never left you,' she said.

Blood leaked from Fabian's mouth as he tried to speak.

'Shh,' Josephine said softly. She reached out to wipe the blood away when there was a high-pitched screech. She turned quickly towards the sound. In the distance, she could see a white horse. It was glowing in the darkness, galloping towards them over the burnt earth. As it came closer, Josephine saw the figure upon its back. She knew that face - from a time long ago.

Fabian laughed feebly as he stared at the white horse. Then he turned back to look at Josephine. 'I took too long, my love,' he said, his fingers slipping away from the pendant. 'We are old now.' A single tear rolled down his cheek as he closed his eyes. They did not open again.

'In our dreams we shall meet. We shall have endless adventures,' Josephine whispered, clasping his hand in hers.

'Mother?' came a gentle voice. Josephine looked up. Thomas was kneeling on the ground across from her, a perplexed expression on his face. He was cushioning a man's head with his hands. Josephine drew a sharp breath. It was Lucian.

'My boy!' she said, letting go of Fabian. She began to crawl towards Lucian, her vision blurring with tears, her skirts dragging along the ground, sweeping earth and twigs along with them. She cupped her hands around Lucian's face and kissed his forehead. His eyes were open and vacant. He was dead.

*

Enola's knuckles turned white over the reins as the horse hurtled through the forest towards a clearing. All around, faces were appearing out of the darkness, turning to look at her. A scattering of weak fires burned on the ground and across the charred trunks of fallen trees. The Mordark serpent blazed emerald green on discarded shields in the firelight. The ground was littered with bodies. There had been a battle here. Enola's heart pounded faster and faster as she swept by. Fabian Mordark had hunted her for years and now she had come to him. And, with cold dread, she felt the horse begin to slow. She kicked it and jerked the reins desperately but, in spite of her efforts, the horse fell into a walk.

The men parted as the horse moved into their midst. They stared up at Enola curiously as she passed but made no move to seize her. There were more men ahead, standing in the dull blue light of the clearing. And bodies, piles of bodies - more than Enola could have counted - strewn across the ground. She looked around wildly, searching for an escape, as the horse crossed into the clearing. If she could jump down, could she outrun them? Weave a path they could not follow? Perhaps - if she did it now, darted straight to the other side of the clearing and slipped into shadow…

The horse stopped abruptly as it neared the edge of the clearing. This was her chance. Enola stared at the ground and prepared to jump. She moved to swing her leg over the saddle when the horse started to back up and toss its head in distress. Enola froze. There was something out there, moving through the darkness towards them. She could hear rustling. It grew louder. It was coming closer. The men turned their heads towards the sound. The horse was grunting now, twitching nervously. Enola's breath curled into white smoke as a chill crept into the air. She looked deep into the darkness, not daring to blink. Suddenly, the horse reared up. Enola clung to its neck and closed her eyes as a blinding light engulfed them, spreading outwards like shards of white fire. An icy wind rushed through the trees, whistling, howling. Leaves and ash flew through the forest, whipping past Enola's face. The wind was screaming now, shrill in her ears. And then it stopped, as suddenly as it had begun. The light faded. The shadows returned. The horse crashed down onto its front hooves. And the forest fell back into silence.

Enola blinked away the dazzling light that lingered behind her eyelids. Around her, the men began to murmur. She stared at them as, one by one, they dropped to their knees and laid down their swords. She heard a man whisper, 'She has come' and followed his gaze to the shadows beyond the clearing.

When the figure emerged, her heart stilled.

The old woman was pale-skinned and her white hair hung in thin wisps over her shoulders. She looked at Enola knowingly as she walked towards her, feet bare and blue with veins, a dark bloodstain on her nightgown. She no longer limped, as she once had, nor did she use a stick for balance. She moved calmly and swiftly. She looked younger somehow, the lines in her face less distinct, her back straight, eyes twinkling.

Agatha.

Enola stared at her blankly as she came to stand beside the horse. What dark magic was this? She shook her head in disbelief. Agatha was dead. They had killed her - Tobias Mordark had told them so in the tunnel. "*The old hag feeds the crows*" he had said. And yet… here she was. Had Tobias lied?

'You're not dead, then,' said Enola.

'No,' said Agatha. 'Why are you here, girl? I sent you away.' She cast her eyes around the clearing searchingly. 'Where is William? And your father?'

When Enola did not answer, all trace of Agatha's smile disappeared; her eyes became cold, her thin lips even thinner. She turned her head and walked on without another glance at Enola, who felt strangely ill-at-ease. There was something odd about Agatha, something unfamiliar. A presence, or perhaps an absence, of something. Whatever it was, Enola did not think Tobias had lied.

Agatha approached Thomas and Josephine Mortenstone in her bloodied dress. Thomas stared up at her in astonishment while his mother glared at the men around them, whose heads were bowed low before Agatha, their faces almost touching the dirt. Lucian's body lay between them. Agatha stopped in front of the new Lord Mortenstone but looked at the men instead, gazing down at them thoughtfully before she spoke.

'Look around you at the *waste*,' she said, gesturing the bodies, her nose wrinkling with disgust. Slowly, the men raised their heads. 'Ask yourselves why. Why did it happen? Who is to blame for *this*?' she said, stabbing a long finger towards a headless body propped against a tree. 'Your brothers, your fathers, your sons. Gone. Lost. You will never get them back. Who killed them? I will tell you who. The ones who built the barrier. The ones who banished their kin to a world of darkness. Their cruelty, their greed, did *this*,' she said, signalling the headless body once more. 'When you die, they *thrive*. They feed on your misery. I will not allow it. The time of Mortenstone has come to an end. I have come to end it.' She raised her arms. The cold wind began to blow. The men looked at her with fear in their eyes as the wind thrashed and roared through the forest. When Agatha lowered her arms, the wind calmed.

Josephine stood suddenly and spat at the ground before her feet. Thomas, too, began to rise, shaking his head in bewilderment.

'Forgive me,' he said, 'but I have done you no harm. You cannot—'

'You may have my forgiveness, Thomas Mortenstone,' said Agatha. 'But you'll pay for it with your life.'

Thomas moved for his sword but Agatha was too fast. She waved her hand and he flew back against a tree. And there he struggled, unable to move, as a thick tree root began to slither towards him and coil around his body, lashing him to the tree.

Agatha looked at Josephine next, then nodded to the men kneeling around her, whose armour bore the bold green Mordark serpent.

'Her, too,' she said.

Josephine shrieked as the men seized her and dragged her to the tree. The roots snaked over her feet and around her legs, binding her to the trunk next to Thomas.

'We have Jacobi Vandemere, son of Iris Mortenstone!' came a shout. There was a disturbance as a young boy, no older than fifteen, was hauled to his feet and pushed through the crowd towards Agatha by two Mortenstone guards. They looked at her expectantly, awaiting an order.

'Yes, him as well,' she said after a moment's pause. Her brow furrowed slightly as they led the boy to the tree. 'Disloyal,' she muttered. She raised her chin and, instantly, the two guards were thrown back against the tree with him. They shouted and writhed, but the tree roots only coiled tighter around them all.

Enola watched in stunned silence. She remembered Jacobi. He was her brother. He looked around wildly, tears streaking his dirty face. His silver breastplate had a deep crack down the middle and his fair hair was red with blood.

'Agatha, what are you doing?' Enola said. Agatha had always been hateful, but she had also been fair. This woman standing before her now was nothing like the Agatha she once knew. Even her voice had a strange edge.

Agatha turned to look at her. 'Your father loved you, girl. And I made him a promise. So, I will show you mercy,' she said.

Suddenly, there was a bloodcurdling cry.

'Run!'

Agatha whirled back around as Jacobi and Josephine vanished. The tree roots drooped, falling slack where the two had stood. The remaining guards began to shriek, fighting desperately to free themselves, while Thomas continued to shout at the top of his lungs, 'Run! Run!' He was pale. He heaved the words as if it pained him to do so. And then Jacobi appeared again, mere metres from the tree, gasping as he staggered away. He was weak. His body flickered into nothingness again and then reappeared. He fell to the ground.

'Run, Jacobi!' Thomas shouted. The boy pushed himself to his feet and began to run.

Agatha stared after him until he disappeared into the gloom. Then she turned to the men with serpents on their breastplates and said, 'I think it's time for a hunt. Bring them to me alive.' The men sprang to their feet at once and went after Jacobi.

Agatha drew a deep breath and, as she did, a great stillness fell upon the forest. Every sound, every movement ceased.

'Avalon shall be restored. We will build it together,' she said. 'But there is no place in the new world for traitors.' She looked at Thomas Mortenstone and spat at the ground. Thomas, however, was not looking at Agatha. He was staring upwards. The treetops high above had begun to stir, shaking and rustling as if alive with a thousand birds. Agatha smiled darkly and held her palms up towards the sky. She tilted her head back and opened her mouth, snatching, gathering the air. Her throat made a rattling sound.

Enola's horse began to shift about restlessly. The men near her took the horse's distress as an ominous sign, stood and began to back away.

Agatha closed her mouth and slowly lowered her head. Then, with a suddenness that sent Enola's horse rearing up with alarm, she flung her arms out in front of her and released a monstrous cry. From her mouth blew a ferocious wind, which hit the first line of men and sent them flying backwards.

Enola's horse bolted, hurtling out of the clearing towards The Light, spurred on by the wind that rushed behind it. The gale was gaining momentum, tearing through the forest, ripping branches from trees. The horse cut around them as they fell, impaling the ground like spears, and galloped on faster as a deep, creaking noise sliced through the wind. Enola looked back. The men were running for their lives; behind them, a tree was rocking, straining against its roots. And, suddenly, there was a loud s*nap* as the roots broke. Enola kicked the horse on; as it raced across another clearing, a great shadow slipped over them. With a mournful groan, the tree began to plummet towards the men, towards her. Enola squeezed her eyes shut and held fast to the reins. There was an almighty crash as the tree smashed into another trunk high above her head. The horse screeched and continued on, unscathed, as the other tree began to sway. Soon the ground, the very air, was quaking with crashes and screams.

The horse burst from the forest and stormed through an abandoned camp, knocking aside pots and cauldrons, leaping over upturned chairs and mounds of firewood, racing all the way to the other side of the Grassland, where it slowed and finally stopped beneath a small, solitary tree. The castle loomed up ahead on the hill.

Enola slumped forwards, breathing heavily, dripping with cold sweat. The ground shook again so violently she was almost thrown from the saddle. She grabbed a tuft of the horse's mane to steady herself and looked over her shoulder. Men were pouring out of the forest like ants fleeing a burning nest; the trees followed, crashing onto the Grassland, crushing them in the final moments of their escape. Others - the strong and able - appeared out of nowhere, safe from the reach of the falling trees, and collapsed as the effect of the transportation took its toll.

When Agatha materialised, she did not drop to her knees, overcome with exhaustion, like the men. She stood calmly in the middle of the Grassland, as chaos raged behind her. She remained this way for a long while, her back to the forest, eyes fixed on Mortenstone Castle, until there was a deep, ground-trembling *boom*.

Enola sat up. Her jaw dropped as she stared unblinkingly at a sight too astonishing to comprehend. The Dark Forest had fallen.

In the hours that followed, the Grassland slowly filled with survivors, who clambered from the ruins sickeningly maimed, some half-dead already. But Agatha was not there to see it, to offer help or comfort, for she had gone to the castle, escorted by a host of Mordark soldiers. They followed her without hesitation, while others watched on silently. Enola thought that perhaps Agatha had seen her as she passed on her way towards Stone Lane but, if she had, she made no outward sign of acknowledgement.

Enola got down from the horse and sat beneath the tree, wondering what to do, where to go, how it had all come to pass. Of all the people destined for greatness, Agatha seemed the unlikeliest of them. She was a mean old hag who had spent most of her life hidden away in the woods. She had never given Enola reason to think she was anything more than she appeared.

As the horse grazed and Enola peeled strips of bark off a stick, she noticed a middle-aged man staring at her. He was sitting with a group of men on the ground nearby. The men were muttering to one another soberly as they tended their wounds - but not this man. He was watching her curiously, his bushy brows pulling together as he frowned. Enola looked away; her heart was beating quickly now. What if the Mordarks were still hunting her? What if this man knew who she was? When she turned back a moment later, the man was still watching. And then he rose to his feet and began to walk towards her. Enola stood with the stick in her hand, brandishing it like a knife. And then the horse's head snapped up. To Enola's surprise, it grunted excitedly, tossing its head up and down, its white tail swishing, and trotted over to the man, who stopped, his weathered skin crinkling as he broke into a smile. He threw his arms about the horse's neck and his eyes filled with tears.

'Oh! It *is* you! My old friend, you've come back to us!' The man pressed his cheek to the horse's fur and sobbed.

'Who are you?' Enola said, approaching him. The man looked at her and straightened up, wiping his tears.

'I am Robert Swampton, miss. This horse belonged to my family. Or at least he did… We had to sell him, years ago, when we fell on hard times. I never thought I'd see him again,' he said, stroking the horse's nose affectionately. 'Forgive me. He is yours now?'

Enola shook her head. 'Take him,' she said. 'I have no need for him now.'

'Truly?' he said, unable to disguise his glee.

'Truly.'

'Oh, I cannot thank you enough. You must have something in return. You must!' he said excitedly. 'Gerald! Bring Nimowae!' he called, waving to a young man with red hair and a smoke-blackened face. 'My son's young filly,' he said to Enola. 'She is strong and capable. A Latheerian! No one has yet ridden her. We used her to pull the carts to battle. She is waiting to form a bond.'

'I can't ride. The horse would be wasted on me,' Enola protested.

'She will make a valuable companion,' he said, as his son led a skittish black horse towards them. Its brilliant blue eyes were darting cautiously in every direction. 'Poor thing. Her nerves are frayed, but she will heal in time and she will serve you well.'

When his son reached them, he handed the reins over to Enola, who took them reluctantly. Robert Swampton smiled with satisfaction and then gave a start as the bells of Mortenstone Castle began to ring. All across the Grassland, people were turning to look at the castle. Some stared in awe, others in fear.

'It feels strange to live it, to see it, don't you think? Merlin's Great Prophecy at last realised,' said Robert. He paused for a while, staring at the castle, and then looked at Enola and smiled. 'A new age, indeed. Good luck to you, Miss,' he said. And he and his son walked back to their small group with the white Latheerian horse, leaving Enola with Nimowae, who flinched when she raised a hand to stroke her.

The bells rang until dusk. Most people remained on the Grassland, huddled together around fires for warmth. And there they sang and drank and talked into the night, unaware of the darkening atmosphere in the streets around the castle, which were teeming with people, all waiting for Agatha to re-emerge, shoving and pushing each other to get closer to the gates.

The Dark Families had already begun to raid the empty houses and shops on Stone Lane. Enola sat beneath the tree, cold and sodden, watching as they carried paintings and purple Mortenstone banners across the Grassland to burn on the fires. Among them were the men who had escorted Agatha to the castle; they cheered as it all went up in flames and returned to Stone Lane in search of more Mortenstone relics to feed the fire. Enola felt a hot rush of anger. She was half Mortenstone, after all. And she had a strong sense that those were her belongings, and the wicked things they were doing to them, they were also doing to her.

The darker the mood became, the more restless Nimowae grew. Enola had let go of her that afternoon, hoping she would trot off in search of Robert Swampton, who had long since departed. But Nimowae did not leave her. All day, she kept her eye on Enola, checking that she was still there as she grazed. Now, Enola found herself keeping a watchful eye as Nimowae skittered about, frightened by the crazed men around her.

'There, there,' said a soothing voice. 'They won't hurt you.' Enola looked up as an old man came around the side of the horse and ran a shaky hand along her curved neck. He seemed preoccupied with calming Nimowae, but when he spoke next, it was to Enola. 'They always want the stallions with the strong backs. But it's the mares that will truly surprise you. A mare knows when to think and use her intuition, and when to listen. And she's loyal,' he said, finally turning to look at Enola. His face was tired and the skin sagged around his jaw. But it was a kind face. 'I am Master Hagworth,' he said. 'And you are Enola Reverof. Oh yes, I know those eyes.'

Enola sat up straight. She remembered him. Schoolmaster Hagworth of Mortenstone Castle.

'Did Agatha send you?' she said.

Master Hagworth pushed his frayed bag strap off his shoulder and the bag fell to the ground with a soft thud.

'Mortenstone Castle is no longer my home,' he said. Then, with some effort, he crouched down and began to rummage through the bag. 'Ah,' he said, retrieving a hunk of bread wrapped in a cloth. 'For you.' He offered it to her. Enola took the bread, perplexed. 'My journey will be long, but yours will be longer still,' he said, closing the bag and lowering himself down to sit on it. 'Before I begin my journey, I would like to confess something. I taught your mother, as you know. She was a sweet girl. Spirited, but sweet. She knew right from wrong, and always strove to do the right thing. I am ashamed to say I used this to my advantage, to try and convince her not to have you,' he said, lowering his gaze in shame. 'I did all I could to stop her, for I knew what you would become. The life of a Reverof follows the same pattern. It is a dreadful curse. A curse we all feared. When you were born, when you walked your first steps, when you cast your first spell, I felt only despair. Where your mother was kind, you were cruel and cunning – everything I had expected you to be. But that was before I truly opened my eyes. Do you remember that day in Mortenstone Valley? You did terrible magic, unforgivable. Magic you were too young to know. But, without it, perhaps I would not have seen what I saw. Do you know what I saw that day?' Enola shook her head. Master Hagworth leaned in, his eyes glinting. 'Something greater yet to come. Greater than this,' he said, waving a hand at everything around them. 'When I looked at you, before that day, I saw only a curse. I did not see the girl trapped within. I did not see the girl you would one day become. You will do great things, Enola Reverof.'

Just then, a shriek pierced the air and was quickly silenced by a hard *thwack*. They both turned to see two Mordark soldiers dragging an unconscious man off towards Stone Lane. 'Mortenstone sympathiser!' they shouted for all to hear as they passed.

Master Hagworth did nothing to hide his horror.

'I awoke this morning to a new world,' he whispered. The raging fires were reflected in his spectacles. 'The old magic is dead, my young pupils held captive in their own home. The future of the Mortenstone line teeters on the brink of destruction.' He looked down at his hands, long and thin and spotted with age. 'I am an old man. I do not have many years left. It would be easier to give up, to pledge my allegiance to this woman. But I cannot do that, because I know in my heart it is wrong. And you must always pay attention to what your heart is telling you. It might not lead you to the safest path, indeed it might take you to the most perilous path of all, but it will always lead you to the path that is true.'

'Wise words,' Enola said. Master Hagworth laughed softly. 'Where will you go?' she asked.

'It would be wise not to tell you,' he said. 'But I will. I shall return to Latheera, where I grew up. It is incredibly peaceful there, though, I admit, I have not been back in a great many years.'

'Would you like my horse? You'll get there faster with her.'

'No, no, dear girl. You will be needing the horse.'

'I won't. I can't even ride,' she said.

'You will learn.'

'But I've nowhere to take her. I don't have a home anymore.'

'No? And there is nowhere else you might go? No journey you wish to complete?' he said, peering over the spectacles on his crooked nose.

'The Land of the Banished?' said Enola, wondering how he knew. 'I can't go there.'

'Can't you? Why ever not?'

'The path is blocked under all that,' she said, pointing at the great, mountainous shadow of fallen trees, silhouetted in the moonlight.

'There are other ways to the Land of the Banished, Enola. The Dark Forest marked only one.'

'How do you know that?'

Master Hagworth chuckled and rubbed his chin. 'Because I am wise!'

'Show me, then. Tell me how to get there.'

'Sadly, I do not know. While there is magic in my blood, that realm cannot call to me, but there are others to whom it can. Others who know the way.'

'Who? Tell me!'

'Patience, patience. You will get there, Enola.'

'You don't know that.'

'But I do. The story is already written,' he said. And, with that, he pushed himself to his feet, sighing heavily. Then, as if in afterthought, he added, 'When you get there, you will need an ally. You will find him in a place called Camelot. His name is Mordred.'

Bewildered, Enola picked up Master Hagworth's bag and handed it to him. He smiled at her knowingly.

'Long live the White Witch,' he said. Then he bowed his head, turned and shuffled away.

As Enola watched him go, she wondered whether he would complete his journey. She hoped he would, though she believed he wouldn't.

When he had stumbled out of sight into darkness, Enola turned around and met a cold, white face, inches from her own. She almost screamed. Standing in front of her, swathed in a dark cloak, wisps of white hair creeping out from beneath her hood, was Agatha.

'Who is he?'

'No one. An old man,' said Enola.

'Is that so? Making friends?' Agatha said, staring over Enola's shoulder with deepening interest. Enola scowled at her. 'What are you sulking about, girl?'

'I'm not sulking.'

'Yes you are. You're always sulking about something. But you've no reason to now. The last of old Merlin's magic is dead. Your curse is lifted. Smile, for once in your life. Carry on the way you are and I'll—'

'Did you find them?' Enola interrupted.

Agatha's eyes flashed before her expression quickly turned blank. 'Who?'

'You know who,' said Enola. As calm as Agatha was pretending to be, Enola knew that, inside, she was furious that Jacobi Vandemere and Josephine Mortenstone had escaped.

'I will find them,' Agatha said in a clipped tone. Enola smiled darkly as Agatha's lips pursed with suppressed anger. 'You can wipe that smile away, girl. I will find them. I will kill them. All Mortenstones!'

'I'm a Mortenstone,' said Enola.

'You are a Mordark!' Agatha snapped. 'And you'd do well to remember it. Blood is important. Your blood saved you today. You'd be dead if your father wasn't your father.'

Enola stared long and hard at Agatha. And it was only then that she noticed how green the old woman's eyes were. And, suddenly, it occurred to her, the reason for Agatha's loathing of all Mortenstones.

'They banished you,' Enola said.

Agatha closed her eyes. 'Don't push me, girl.'

'But why? Whatever did you do?' Enola continued. 'Something terrible?'

'I'm warning you…'

'Or perhaps you didn't do anything. Perhaps you didn't deserve to be banished. Perhaps *your* blood couldn't save you, Agatha Mordark.'

'Say one more word and you'll burn for it,' Agatha said in a low voice. She looked rattled, vulnerable somehow, as though the truth shamed her. But she did not deny it.

'You can't threaten me, old hag. You are the White Witch. You are here to protect me,' Enola said mockingly.

'Protect you?' Agatha said with a sneer. And she leaned in, fixing her flinty eyes on Enola. 'I am here to *rule* you.' She looked towards Stone Lane, where the crowds were jostling to get closer to the castle. 'Look at them,' she hissed. 'How long have their old masters been dead? Just this morning, they would have died for them. People are all the same. They follow power. They care not who wields it. They want to be led. They want to be told. And they'll bend anything I do to make it fit their old words. They'll make it fair,' she said. 'Come to the castle. I want to show you something.' She took hold of Enola's arm roughly.

'No,' Enola said, pulling away.

'Stubborn little wretch. Would you really abandon me now? After all I've done for you? Have you no gratitude?' Agatha said, shaking her head with a look of disgust. 'You remind me of *him*. Merlin the Terrible.' She spat at the ground. 'Mortenstone filth! You even look like him. Same smug face. Same eyes. He would have despised you,' she said, moving closer, until Enola could feel the old woman's stale breath on her face. 'He would have murdered you while you were still in your mother's belly. Your father's head would have been impaled on a spike outside the castle walls. Remember whose spell it was, Enola Reverof. Think of all the wicked things he would have done, had I not put an end to his evil,' Agatha said. Enola stared at her blankly. Agatha nodded slowly and her thin lips curled into a secretive smile. 'I ended him. *Wonderful* Merlin the Good. Do you know where I did it?' She pointed towards the fallen forest. 'It was a trap. I waited a long time, but I got him eventually. I've always been good at hunting. He'd grown weak, weaker than his old magic. So, I used it against him.' She laughed then. 'Brought down by his own spell. One would think the Great Prophet would have foreseen what I was about to do,' she said, smiling manically. 'And you, his own blood, didn't feel him, hadn't the slightest inkling that he was just outside the door the whole time. You took from him, you drained life from him every time you drank from the Silver Tree. I wonder if he screamed in there. I'm sure he felt it. I'm sure it was excruciating. I'm sure he regretted his spells every moment of every day of his miserable life.'

A cold feeling trickled down Enola's spine. The Silver Tree that creaked and groaned outside Agatha's house... The man from her dreams who stood on the forest path beside it, tears streaking his face... Merlin.

But it couldn't be true. It had been more than a thousand years since his time.

'You're lying. No one can live that long,' Enola said.

Agatha smiled again. 'Magic is a curious thing. His magic sustained him while he was trapped within it. But now, as you see, the spell is dead. And Merlin along with it,' she said, eyes twinkling with pleasure.

'And you? When will you die?' Enola said.

Agatha began to laugh. It was a cold, harsh sound. 'I am the White Witch,' she said. 'I will live forever.'

27. A NEW AGE

Moments after Agatha vanished, the frenzy began. Shouts and screams spread through the crowds along Merlin's Way, Brim Street and Stone Lane. Something was happening up at the castle.

Across the Grassland, people were deserting their fires, running towards the commotion. Enola followed them, pulling Nimowae behind her until she reached a wall of people at the end of the lane. And then she saw the cause of the disturbance. In the distance, standing on the ledges of the castle windows, were four children. They were in their nightgowns, and they had nooses around their necks. Behind each child was a man in black. Enola's heart began to race. Her sister, Rose, was standing in one of the middle windows, hugging her arms around herself. The younger children were frozen with terror.

'Mortenstone scum!' the crowd jeered, waving their fists in the air. And then they began to chant, 'Off! Off! Off! Off! Off!'

When the men shoved the children from the windows, the crowd exploded with bloodthirsty cheers. Enola watched as if in a dream, as the bodies writhed and twitched. The shouts grew faint and hollow around her, the sea of heads blurred. But she could see the children still, clear as day, swaying at the ends of the ropes, limp now.

Enola turned and led Nimowae along the side of the last building on Stone Lane, where she slid down against the wall and stared into darkness.

Despite her efforts to stay awake in the cold night, she opened her eyes to a bright morning, as if only moments had passed. Her bruised legs ached from the cobbles and her back was stiff from sitting against the stone wall. She rubbed her hands together to bring back the feeling in her fingers and squinted up at the sun. Suddenly, a dark shape eclipsed it. Enola blinked in surprise. Standing over her, his hands and clothes covered in dried blood, with dark shadows beneath his eyes, was William. Quite alive. Quite unharmed. She stared at him in stunned silence for a moment, and then her lips curled into a snarl.

'Traitor!' she spat.

'I'm sorry,' he said, staring down at her guiltily. 'I came back for you, though. That has to count for something.'

'It counts for nothing,' said Enola, turning away from him to face the wall, where she watched his shadow against the stone. Waiting. Waiting. But he didn't leave, no matter how hard she willed it.

'Are you William?' came a deep voice then. Startled, Enola turned quickly to see a man standing before William, wearing a cloak as black as his beard. He had a sword sheathed in his scabbard.

'Yes,' William said, though he sounded uncertain.

'The White Witch requests your presence,' said the man.

'Who?' William asked.

'The White Witch requests your presence at the castle.'

William looked uneasy. 'The castle?' he said, taking a step backwards and glancing at Enola mistrustfully. 'I went back for her,' he said to the man, who looked confused. 'I didn't hurt her. Whatever she's told you, it isn't true. I went back for her. I didn't let him take her!' He took another step away. The man moved his hand to the hilt of his sword.

'The White Witch requests your—'

William turned to run, but the man was already lunging after him. He grasped his shoulder and William stumbled and fell.

'No!' he shouted, thrashing madly as several other men rushed to restrain him. 'I came back for you, Enola! Tell him! Tell him!'

Enola could only stare, bewildered. Did he think she could stop them? That this was one of her traps? That these men were following her orders? No. They were here at Agatha's bidding.

A crowd had begun to gather. William was shouting still, as his arms were pulled behind his back. The man in the black cloak was bent over him, speaking urgently. 'Stop struggling! Listen to me!' But William paid him no heed; he continued to writhe on the ground, until another two men piled on top of him. They knelt on his back and forced his head against the cobbles. Unable to move, his face turning purple, William gave a final roar of frustration and fell silent.

Suddenly, people in the crowd began to gasp. The men, hearing this, looked over their shoulders and, eyes widening, released William at once.

William pushed himself to his knees, breathing heavily. When he turned and looked up at the old woman standing over him, his mouth fell open.

'Agatha?' he said.

Agatha wore a black cloak, like that of the guard, who shuffled backwards now, his head bowed. Her eyes filled with tears as she stared at William.

'It *is* you,' she said. Her mouth twisted unpleasantly with emotion. 'I thought you were dead.'

'I thought you were,' said William.

'Come with me, boy,' Agatha said, holding out a trembling hand. William took it and got to his feet.

'What's happening, Agatha?' he said in a low voice. 'Who are these people?'

'Come to the castle, boy. We can talk. I will tell you everything.'

William stared at her for a moment and then looked around at the many eyes fixed on him.

'Come,' Agatha said again, and she took his hand and led him on.

*

William stopped before they had gone far, remembering Enola. He looked back and saw her peering around the corner of the building at the end of the lane. She was as filthy as a beggar, and as thin.

Agatha followed his gaze. 'Leave her. Don't waste your time,' she said, and she gave his hand a gentle tug.

William continued on without protest. But, as he looked up at the castle and saw the dead children swinging in the wind, he noticed how cold Agatha's hand felt against his skin.

She held on to him tightly all the way up the lane and through the square, which was filled with people reaching out to touch her, to receive blessings.

The crowds did not pursue them once they had walked through the giant iron gates into a large courtyard. And all the sounds from the square died away.

The courtyard looked exactly like the drawings in one of William's books, only those images depicted a place teeming with life; tired stable boys preparing horses for mount, flustered servants ferrying pitchers of milk, blacksmiths beating swords into shape, long-eared elves playing instruments on the castle steps under the watchful eyes of castle guards. Now, the courtyard was empty and quiet, save for the ropes, which creaked above them. William couldn't bring himself to look up at the children again.

A sick feeling brewed in his stomach as he climbed the stone steps behind Agatha, who stopped when she reached the top and turned to look at him. William resisted a shudder as he came to the top step; he was standing directly beneath the bodies. He wanted to keep walking, to get away from them, to pass through the castle doors into the darkened hall within. But Agatha did not move.

'This is our home now,' she said, smiling up at him. Above them, the ropes creaked again. Agatha's eyes drifted upwards and settled on the dead children. 'My men have been scrubbing their excrement off the steps all morning. Terrible nuisance. But what else can you expect from a Mortenstone?'

William's skin prickled as she spoke. Everything about Agatha seemed...different, cold.

'I should have saved one for you,' Agatha continued. 'Then you would finally have had your revenge for what Matthew Mortenstone did to your family. A pity.' She hesitated then, looking out towards Stone Lane, her forehead wrinkling as she raised her eyebrows in consideration. 'Perhaps there is another...' She met his eye and it was as if someone had kicked him in the gut. She couldn't mean it? He choked as he tried to speak, coughing and spluttering. Agatha placed a hand on his shoulder. 'Are you unwell, boy?' she said, looking concerned.

'Just tired,' he said. 'But... I don't understand. You told Alexander you'd look after her.'

'And I did,' she said. 'I put a roof over her head, I raised her, I protected her - for twelve years! And do you know how she repaid me?' William shook his head. Agatha mimicked him, shaking her head with a look of contempt. 'She told me you were dead – to hurt me, no doubt. The curse is gone and she is still rotten to the core. Alexander should have left her here for Lucian Mortenstone to deal with all those years ago. But no, the kind soul that he was, he rescued her, and he died for her, and she couldn't give a damn.' Her rage made her voice tremble and William found himself suddenly fearful for Enola. He knew Agatha had never really cared for her - she pretended, to make Alexander happy. And now there was no one to pretend for anymore.

'Here's what we'll do,' she said, squeezing his hand between hers. 'We'll get you up to bed for some rest. Tomorrow, we'll fetch the wretched girl and keep her in the dungeon until you've decided what you want to do with her. There's no rush. She's at your mercy now.' And, with a dark smile, Agatha stepped through the doorway into Mortenstone Castle.

∗

The next morning, Enola awoke to the incessant growling of her own stomach. She had half expected Agatha to send her something for supper. But no food parcel had come. Instead, she devoured the last of Master Hagworth's bread. It was a pitiful meal, made more pitiful by the fact she had had to fight for what remained of it when a drunkard tried to take it from her.

It was during this meagre supper that a man had emerged from the castle bearing a roll of parchment, which he held at arm's length to read from.

'The White Witch,' he announced in a deep, booming voice that carried all the way down to the end of Stone Lane, 'today declares that Dark Families may occupy empty homes and the homes of traitors in Lambelee. The Low Lands and Draxvar are free to all for the taking. Any Vandemeres or Doldons still living are to be handed over to The White Witch in the name of justice. Those who attempt to help conceal them will meet the same fate as the traitors.'

It had rained furiously after the man nailed the declaration to a post in the middle of the square. But word spread far and wide regardless. Hordes of people left in the night, driven by the prospect of new homes and land of their own. By morning, the Grassland had emptied by more than half. Enola stared at it now in the bright light of day, and the mountainous ruin that loomed over it. The ones who had stayed were working together to search for bodies in the wreckage. They stood, twenty to a tree, moving their arms up with a concentrated effort. The trees crept forwards marginally, or rolled a fraction to the side, crumbling, covering the people below in a thick coat of ash. It was slow, laborious work. Enola wondered if they would ever recover all of the dead. And how long would it be before they cleared a path through to the Dark Lands, to the families who had been left behind?

'The White Witch offers you this cloak with compliments,' said a voice behind her. Enola turned, drawn from her thoughts, to see William, dressed in fine new clothes, accompanied by two men in black. William held the thick cloak out for her. Enola stared at it longingly. She wanted to snatch it from him and wrap herself up warm and sink into a deep sleep. But she couldn't accept it, not with Agatha's taint all over it. She shook her head reluctantly.

William's eyes widened suddenly, as if he was trying to convey a message she did not understand. 'The White Witch insists,' he said, stepping forwards. As the men prepared to follow him, he raised a hand and they stopped at once.

William walked to Enola and wrapped the dark cloak around her shoulders. 'Be ready to leave at midday,' he whispered.

Enola's heart began to race. She looked over his shoulder at the guards, who watched them suspiciously.

William fastened the serpent brooch on the front of the cloak and stepped back to look at it. Its emerald green eye gleamed in the light.

'The White Witch will be pleased to know you are warm. She requests your presence this afternoon at the castle. I will come for you when it is time and accompany you there.' His eyes flashed again. 'Is your horse fit and strong?'

Enola nodded, understanding the hidden meaning in his words.

William gave a tight smile. 'Good. This afternoon, then.' He bowed his head and then turned and walked away with the guards, both of whom looked back at her as they went.

When they had disappeared from view, Enola grasped Nimowae's reins and led her to the lone tree on the Grassland. There, she stared at the young filly, preparing herself for what she was about to do. If they were to make their escape that afternoon, she would need to ride her first, to form the special 'bond' Robert Swampton had spoken of. Placing her hands on Nimowae's sleek back, Enola pushed off from the ground hard and swung herself onto the horse. Nimowae jumped nervously, then stopped and became deathly still. Enola sat, waiting for something to happen. For a moment, she wondered if Robert Swampton had been mistaken. What if this was just an ordinary horse? But, suddenly, she felt a wave of airy lightness wash through her, as though her mind and body had been swept clean. She smelled the grass, the smoke in the air, felt the cool wind blowing her hair. And, oddly, she felt afraid, on edge, vulnerable.

Her sense of the activity by the edge of the fallen forest seemed to sharpen. She heard hacking and grunting as men sank their axes into trees. She looked up at them and, for a fleeting instant, the trees were ablaze again, black smoke thick in the air. The men were screaming as swords sliced through their flesh and giant creatures swooped down from above. Enola blinked and the vision faded. She stared, astonished, at the remains of the forest, her heart pounding. These were not her memories. These memories belonged to Nimowae. She leant forward and patted the horse's neck gently.

'It's over now,' she said. And, almost at once, the tense knot of fear in her stomach ebbed away.

It was the strangest feeling Enola had ever known. They were one now. Bonded forever. Nimowae's thoughts and fears had become hers, just as hers would become Nimowae's. She had never shared anything with anyone before. But she was glad to have Nimowae, glad to have a friend.

Enola remembered a day, long ago, when her entire family had ridden off to the Wild Wood for a hunt. They all had Latheerian horses; her mother, her uncles and aunt, her grandfather and grandmother, even Edward Vandemere had been given one. She had watched from a window as they raced out of the castle courtyard atop their steeds, without bridle or saddle, completely in tune with the creatures. It had looked spectacularly majestic. She had envied every single one of them. But now there was no need to feel that way; she had a Latheerian horse of her very own and nobody could take that bond away from her. Even if they became separated, she knew Nimowae would spend the rest of her life trying to get back to her, just as the white stallion had returned home to Robert Swampton.

Enola had never looked after anything before; she killed any animal she came across in the Dark Forest. But this would be different. She would take care of Nimowae. Always.

When William emerged, alone, from the castle gates that afternoon and came down the lane, Enola was watching. She made sure he had seen her before she slid off Nimowae's back and led her to a cluster of tents, where pots of broth bubbled over small fires and women skinned rabbits, while children sang songs about the great White Witch. Enola pulled Nimowae behind a tent, out of sight from the castle, and waited.

The moment William rounded the corner, she leapt forwards and slapped him across the face. He staggered back in surprise, clamping a hand to his cheek.

'What was that for?' he snapped.

'Never betray me again,' she said, her fingers stinging. She had been looking forward to doing that ever since their encounter that morning. William glowered at her but nodded all the same and, when Enola climbed back onto the horse, he followed clumsily. The instant he sat down, Nimowae flinched and began to skip around in jittery circles.

'Woah! Woah!' he said, wrapping his arms tightly around Enola's waist. He seemed nervous, perhaps more so than Nimowae.

Eventually, Nimowae adjusted to the weight she was now carrying and calmed. Enola patted her neck soothingly and urged her on without uttering a word.

Nimowae started to walk, taking slow, tentative steps. As they emerged from behind the tents, Enola stared up at the castle.

'Agatha won't like it - losing you,' she said.

'That's not Agatha,' said William. 'Not anymore.'

Nimowae's ears pricked up and, grunting, she broke into a canter, carrying them away along the edge of the fallen forest. Enola clung to the reins as William clung to her and glanced at the remains of their old life, now an impassable mound of ash and bark and dead magic. It had been a dark and dangerous place. Enola ·had resented living there, unable to venture beyond its borders, unable to venture anywhere at all, unable to use her powers, or glimpse more than a handful of stars at night. But, now that it was gone, she felt the heaviness of its absence. After all, it was her home. Soon the trees would be gone, chopped up and burned in hearths at night, and it would be as if the Dark Forest had never existed at all.

Suddenly, the castle bells began to ring. Enola turned her head, drawn from her thoughts, and gasped. Eight black horses were charging across the Grassland, ploughing through the women and children in their path. Their riders were cloaked in black, wearing horned masks that concealed their faces.

'William!' Enola cried.

William looked around and his eyes grew wide. 'Go!' he shouted. 'Go!'

Nimowae broke into a gallop, but she was not as fast as the white Latheerian had been. The riders were gaining on them, so close Enola could see the foam frothing in the corners of the horses' mouths. The rider at the front lifted his arm and spread his fingers. In a moment, he would be near enough to cast his spell. Enola stared desperately at a fallen tree, willing it to move. The tree tremored and then, suddenly, lifted from the ground with a loud groan and slammed into all eight riders. The horses shrieked as they fell and were quickly silenced as the tree crashed down on top of them.

People were running now, away from Enola and William, towards the castle. But, amongst the chaos, figures in black began to materialise. One figure, two figures, five, ten, pursuing on foot behind Nimowae.

And then, ahead of them, taking shape as if from smoke, Agatha appeared. Her hair flailed about her head in the wind like snakes. Her eyes were full of fury. Nimowae jerked to a halt and reared up in terror. Enola clung to the reins for dear life and looked back as the black figures moved towards them. When Nimowae's hooves crashed back down onto the earth, Enola kicked hard. She could feel the horse straining to push through Agatha's spell. But, no matter how hard Nimowae tried, she could not go one step further.

Enola felt a tightening feeling around her neck then. She looked at Agatha, who smiled as she squeezed her pale hands slowly into fists. Enola choked, clutching at her throat as it began to close up.

'Agatha, no!' William shouted, taking the reins from Enola and yanking them violently to one side to steer the horse from the old woman's path. But Nimowae could not turn, could not escape the spell that entrapped her. William abandoned his efforts as a man in a black mask grabbed his foot and tried to drag him down off the horse. William kicked out and struck him hard in the chest, sending him reeling. Then, with trembling fingers, he drew a silver knife from his belt. When the man lunged forward again to seize him, he plunged the knife through the mask into his eye.

Enola's insides were ready to explode. The blood was rushing in her ears, her head, roaring through the veins that bulged in her neck. She was starting to feel dangerously light, weightless. And then she heard the man's screams behind her as he slipped off William's blade to the ground, blood spurting from his mangled eye. And those screams seemed to coax her back. Louder and louder they grew, until she could no longer feel the excruciating pain in her skull. Suddenly, a deafening burst of noise filled her ears. The castle bells, loud and shrill, Nimowae's frightened whinnies, William's shouts, Agatha's cold laughter. Enola looked up and stared into the old witch's eyes as more men arrived to surround Nimowae. And, as she did, she felt a powerful pulsing feeling in the pit of her stomach. Her hands began to shake. A boiling, fiery heat burned through her body, gathering strength, rising from the depths, surging to the surface… Enola's vision cleared in an instant. The strangling grip around her throat loosened, then disappeared altogether. She gasped as her lungs filled with air. And, all the while, the feeling was rising, rising. With a guttural cry, Enola flung her arms wide and felt the power shoot from her like a bolt of lightning. Agatha was snatched off her feet and thrown backwards through the air, landing with a bone-shattering *crack* and a scream of pain. Her white hair covered her face in a tangled mess; she pushed it out of the way and looked up at Enola, her mouth hanging open, eyes wide with disbelief, and shook her head again and again. She wasn't laughing anymore.

Enola looked around at the men, all staring at Agatha in astonishment as she sank her long nails into the soil and dragged her crumpled body across the ground towards them. While they watched her, Enola slowly picked up the reins and squeezed William's hand. It was the smallest of signals, but she felt his grip around her waist tighten.

'Go,' she breathed. Nimowae's head snapped up. And, suddenly, the ground was rushing beneath them as she barged through the men, knocking them down, and galloped past Agatha, who reached out a feeble hand as they went.

'William!' she cried. 'William!!!!' It was a tortured sound.

They didn't look back.

The War of Light and Dark draws near,

And with it all that we have feared.

But when the time does come to pass,

Fire, blood and spells all cast,

Evil will be surely gone,

From all of wondrous Avalon.

The days of sorrow, toil and plight,

Will end with she who fights our fight.

She'll rule nigh on one hundred years,

And sail the river of our tears,

When death does claim her for its own,

And another sits upon her throne.

But they shall be of equal heart,

Chosen by the matriarch,

To continue on her quest for peace,

From western shores to swamplands east.

Forever more we shall be rich,

All hail our saviour, The White Witch.

ACKNOWLEDGEMENTS

I would like to thank my mum, who sacrificed many hours of her time reading and editing this book, and who supported me throughout the writing process - give that woman a medal! And a big thank you to Louise Dyer for designing such a beautiful cover.

ABOUT THE AUTHOR

J. J. Morrison was born in Colchester, Essex and grew up in a 17th century manor house, which laid the foundations for her love of all things old and mysterious. She began writing The White Witch in her final year at King's College London, where she read English Literature, but created the central character for a school project when she was twelve years old.

To find out more about the author, visit her on Instagram: @jjmorrison_author

97914872R00191

Made in the USA
Middletown, DE
07 November 2018